PENGUIN BOOKS

GOOD AT GEOGRAPHY

Good at Geography is Jane Westaway's first adult novel. *Reliable Friendly Girls* won Best First Book at the 1997 NZ Post Children's Book Awards, and a young adult novel *Love & Other Excuses* appeared in 1999 (both from Longacre Press). Jane is a reviewer and a journalist, and has also been a social worker and a ministerial speech writer. She was born in England, and came to New Zealand in 1964. She has two adult children and lives in Wellington with Norman Bilbrough.

Acknowledgements

Written with the assistance of a *Reader's Digest*–New Zealand Society of Authors–Stout Research Centre Fellowship, and a Creative New Zealand project grant. Thanks also to Chris Else of Total Fiction Services for helpful comments on early drafts.

An early draft of Chapter 1 appeared in *New Writing 3* edited by Andrew Motion and Candice Rodd (Minerva in association with The British Council, 1994).

GOODATGEOGRAPHY

Jane Westaway

PENGUIN BOOKS

PENGUIN BOOKS

Penguin Books (NZ) Ltd, cnr Airborne and Rosedale Roads, Albany,
Auckland 1310, New Zealand
Penguin Books Ltd, 27 Wrights Lane, London W8 5TZ, England
Penguin Putnam Inc, 375 Hudson Street, New York, NY 10014, United States
Penguin Books Australia Ltd, 487 Maroondah Highway, Ringwood, Australia 3134
Penguin Books Canada Ltd, 10 Alcorn Avenue, Toronto, Ontario, Canada M4V 3B2
Penguin Books (South Africa) Pty Ltd, 5 Watkins Street, Denver Ext 4, 2094,
South Africa
Penguin Books India (P) Ltd, 11, Community Centre, Panchsheel Park,
New Delhi 110 017, India

Penguin Books Ltd, Registered Offices: Harmondsworth, Middlesex, England

First published by Penguin Books (NZ) Ltd, 2000

1 3 5 7 9 10 8 6 4 2

The assistance of Creative New Zealand towards the publication of this book
is gratefully acknowledged by the publisher.

Editorial services by Michael Gifkins & Associates
Designed and typeset by Egan-Reid Ltd
Printed in Australia by Australian Print Group, Maryborough

Thanks to Raewyn Dalziel for permission to use a sentence from *A History of
New Zealand* (page 213) by Keith Sinclair, Penguin Books, 1991, on page 59.

CONTENTS

For Norman, with love

You're only young once, they say,
but doesn't it go on for a long time?
More years than you can bear.

An Experiment in Love
(Penguin Books, 1996)

PROLOGUE

ENGLAND 1985

ANOTHER RED ARROW SHIMMERED OVERHEAD. THE TIDE OF dazed passengers wheeled and trudged on, and Isobel leaned hard on her trolley. The walkway was so interminable she was beginning to believe they had covered most of the distance between Auckland and Heathrow on foot. She felt detached, safe; travelling was the only natural state now, arrival unthinkable. Then, up ahead, she sensed trouble. She faltered, but too late. She glimpsed a barrier and a seething horizon, then a profile ancient and daunting as a cliff-face. She gave a squawk of alarm and released the trolley. It bounced off the barrier, spilling its baggage, and nearly bowling a woman in a sari. She lunged after it only because the crush put a dash for freedom in the opposite direction out of the question.

She was swamped by prehistoric shapes and smells. There was a flurry of near-miss hugs and not-quite kisses, no one apparently knowing how else to cope with the shock of each other's presence. Her mother had fierce arms that let go abruptly. Her sisters were ten and twelve, yet someone masquerading as Gillian's husband offered a limp English hand. Her mother clasped her own hands under her chin and uttered little gasps. Isobel rubbed her eyes but her vision refused to clear – every member of her family was split by a glittering fault line, their features shimmering dangerously. A full twenty years since her last migraine, she thought she had outgrown them. But already she was doubting her ability to outgrow anything.

'This is Holly,' she said, a hand on the child's shoulder, reluctant to hand her over.

'Hello, Granny,' said Holly. Oh God, thought Isobel, she expects to be loved.

'*Grenny*! Oh the darling,' cried Isobel's mother.

'*Dahling*,' grinned Holly.

'And this is Piers and Katrina,' announced Gillian. They were pale and incurious, and to Isobel's astonishment, each offered Holly a hand. 'You can kiss her,' suggested Gillian. 'She's your cousin.' All three drew the line at this.

Isobel stared through the chaos of Arrivals at a lanky Australian she had identified back in Bangkok as a drug dealer. He was enveloping a tiny old lady in his arms. Even drug dealers had mothers.

'Right,' boomed Gillian's husband, who clearly considered enough unstructured time had elapsed, 'this is the plan. All Cartwrights in the Cartwright family vehicle – that's you, Gillian, and Piers and Katrina, and me of course. Giltrap luggage in our commodious boot. Giltraps and Midwinters – that's you, Irene, and Cynthia and Isobel and Holly – in the Midwinter vehicle, Irene at the helm. We'll regroup at the Midwinter residence at' – he consulted his watch in exaggerated fashion – 'oh-eight-thirty hours, give or take, depending on traffic flow and chosen route. Right, follow me.'

Irene, thought Isobel, that's a good idea, I'll call her Irene. She relinquished her trolley to Gillian's husband with a murmured thank you and a mental scramble for his name. The party shuffled raggedly after him as he forged through the press, deploying Isobel's trolley like a battering ram and leaving a trail of infuriated victims.

The parking building was grim after the artificial summer of the terminal and Isobel inhaled a wintry soup of exhaust fumes and kerosene. The sliver of sky beyond was as unrelenting as the concrete ceiling. On command, Gillian's husband's platoon marched to a far corner. Isobel's mother fumbled for keys then frowned into the turmoil of cars, people and baggage. 'Oh dear, it's dreadfully busy, isn't it?'

'Told you I'd drive if you were nervous,' said Cynthia. Isobel's youngest sister flourished diphthongs and vowels which Isobel knew would be a cause of as much distress to their mother as Gillian's BBC tones were a source of pride. Already the sound of her own speech struck her as outlandish. How could one small woman have produced three daughters who spoke in such markedly different accents?

'I'm not nervous, darling,' said her mother, stiffening her shoulders. *It's a long time, you'll be shocked by how much she's aged*, Isobel's friends had warned. And she had tried to imagine it – not the age, but the shock, implying care and affection. Yet the old-lady tremor in her mother's voice startled her. 'Now where did we park exactly?'

Not on that floor, as it turned out. They searched the floors on either side. 'Fuckin' hell, Mum,' grumbled Cynthia.

Language, Isobel! 'Cynthia, I wish you wouldn't.' It was so mild, it scarcely constituted a reproach. 'Now if you'd driven in with me . . .'

'I came by tube,' explained Cynthia. 'She wanted to leave in the small hours.'

'*She?*' echoed their mother through pursed lips. 'The cat's mother?'

'A cat?' bounced Holly. 'Ooh good. Ours got run over and Teddy put it in the compost to grow silver beet which I hate.'

'Fancy you ending up with Teddy,' murmured Cynthia.

'What sort of car?' inquired Isobel briskly. 'Holly's good on cars.'

Radiating scepticism, her mother parted with minimal details, and minutes later, Holly led them towards a shiny compact. 'There,' announced Isobel's mother, as if it were her own achievement.

'In the back with me, Hol,' said Cynthia.

'Nice car,' said Isobel, clicking the seatbelt. What she meant was, different car; as if she had expected her mother to show up in the vehicle she had driven on the other side of the world twenty years earlier.

Her mother was preparing herself for movement by gripping the wheel and glaring at the wall ahead. 'Daddy bought me such awful old cars. I don't think he liked me to be independent, you know.' She wrenched the gear-stick and the car hiccuped to within centimetres of the wall. 'After he . . . afterwards, I took the old one to the little man down the road and he said, "Mrs Midwinter"' – the car sprang backwards and a gleaming Jag braked violently – '"Mrs Midwinter, that husband of yours needs a boot up the you-know-what."'

'Bum,' supplied Holly.

'I had to tell him about Daddy, poor man, he was most upset. "Salt of the earth, that man," he said. "Salt of the earth."' Restraining the urge to point out that her mother had just contradicted herself made Isobel's teeth hurt.

They jerked to a halt at the exit barrier and her mother waggled a ten pound note out of the window. A man in a greasy peaked cap strained to reach it, then gave up and came out of his booth. 'Dear me,' he remarked acidly. Isobel rubbed her head to hide her face.

'Everybody loved Daddy, they were all at his funeral.' The man returned with change and tipped his hat sarcastically as they lurched away.

'Isobel's got a headache,' said Holly.

'Oh, darling, you should have said,' cried her mother, doing sixty in third. A truck driver shook his fist. 'You still get migraines, do you?' Her tone contained equal parts concern and moral judgment.

'Repressed rage,' remarked Cynthia helpfully from the back seat. 'Look, Hol, Windsor Castle.' Isobel turned to catch Holly's expression and was overwhelmed by nausea and the pounding in her head.

Holly frowned as Windsor Castle juddered past. 'Why's it that boring grey?'

'Oh,' cried Isobel's mother, momentarily letting go of the wheel, 'she's used to all those funny little painted New Zealand houses, isn't she, like Wendy houses, I always thought. Goodness, do you remember the first holiday we had there? Hundreds of earthquakes in a couple of weeks.'

'Surely not,' said Isobel, as mildly as she could. How did her mother manage to make a swarm of massive geological events sound like childish misbehaviour? Grinding her teeth was making the headache worse. Spots of half-hearted drizzle specked the windscreen as they hurtled down a deserted high street. Sketchley Drycleaners. Marks and Spencer. Sainsbury's. Isobel felt a little shock as each name fitted a spot deep inside her like a long-lost jigsaw piece. 'It's summer at home now,' she said, trying to believe it.

'We had a wonderful summer,' declared her mother. 'The hottest on record.'

Isobel smiled politely. 'Lovely. Would you pull over? I'm going to throw up.'

'At last, Midwinters and Giltraps,' boomed Gillian's husband from the front door. 'We were beginning to think you'd gone via Basingstoke.'

Irene's party trooped up the crazy paving path past a moronically happy gnome with a chipped hat, and stepped onto a mat that bid them an abrasive welcome. Isobel felt vaguely betrayed – her mother had once been famous for her taste, had instilled it in her oldest daughter.

'Actually,' said Isobel, squeezing past Blah with her cabin bag, 'we're not Giltraps. I haven't been a Giltrap for ten years and Holly never was one. We're Midwinters.'

Blah shot her a startled look that rapidly metamorphosed into a patronising smile. 'Uh-oh, whoopsadaisy. On the alert, Gill, women's libbers on board.'

'Isobel threw up in the gutter,' reported Holly.

Piers and Katrina eyed Isobel. She tried a friendly grin but they shrank back. She wondered what Gillian had told them, or rather, how much. Cynthia helped lug the cases upstairs. 'Is this . . . you know, normal?' Isobel inquired.

'Yep,' said Cynthia, and disappeared.

Isobel gazed out at the miniature garden. It was monotone and lifeless. By contrast the bedroom was experiencing a flush of spring growth. There were rosebuds on the curtains, on the valance around each bed and on the wastepaper bin, and the wallpaper was sprigged with wildflowers. She sagged onto one of the beds. Facing her was a photograph of herself aged six or seven and looking far more alert, self-possessed and resourceful than she felt now. She frowned at it through a haze of pain and exhaustion. It had spent her childhood in a drawer regularly raked through during frantic searches for scissors or glue. When had it been salvaged, framed in gilt and elevated to this mysterious new status? She gazed around the room for the other photo, the one that had hung in both houses on both sides of the world like an icon, and a reproach. *Daddy and I on our wedding day when you couldn't wear White because of the War.* Instead of White, her mother wore an elaborate bonnet tipped over her brow, and an ungainly corsage. Isobel's father was in uniform, sitting side on to display an array of badges on his upper arm. She had always been disinclined to believe either of these glamorous young people were her parents. They looked like film stars, they looked as if the War suited them. Her mother's proud unruffled smile filled the black frame and there was no room in it for children.

'Right, now what would we all like to do?' Her mother's voice rang up the stairs and Isobel realised she had momentarily blacked out. 'Isobel, darling? We're trying to decide what we all want to do.'

'What *do* people do at this ungodly hour on a Sunday morning?' Cynthia was grumbling as Isobel wobbled downstairs. Gillian was on the couch, knees together, hands clasped in a pleated lap; her husband leaned on leather elbows behind her. Cynthia's dungaree-clad legs were draped over the arm of a chair, and Piers and Katrina, arms at their side, were staring frankly at Isobel from the hearthrug. *Here we all are because of you,* they seemed to be saying, *so what are you going to do about it?*

Only Isobel's mother appeared to have other things on her mind. 'I thought we'd have lunch at one-thirty.'

'Do we have to eat an enormous meal in the middle of the day?' muttered Cynthia.

'Please, Cyn,' said Gillian. 'That'd be lovely, Mother. Save me cooking supper when we get home.'

Mother, thought Isobel, maybe I could call her *mother*.

'The meat will have to go in at, say, eleven, the potatoes at twelve. I thought we might have sprouts and carrots. And a can of fruit to follow, if you don't mind, I can't cope with desserts these days.' She was genuinely apologetic.

'Sounds lovely, Mother,' said Gillian. 'Doesn't it, Jeffrey?'

'Super.' Jeffrey rubbed Jeffrey's hands.

'So we can all have a nice talk for an hour,' said Isobel's mother, arranging herself on the couch next to Gillian. 'It's so lovely to have you all together again.'

''Cept Dylan,' said Holly solemnly. Except Daddy, thought Isobel, although any minute he would surely amble in.

'Just like Christmas, having you all together,' Isobel's mother went on. Then, with a pained smile, 'We had such lovely Christmases, didn't we, when you were all young. Oh dear.'

There's the smell of mandarins, cigar smoke and stuffing, and the feeling of too many sweets before dinner. Isobel squints, grits her teeth and carefully waggles the region she has very recently identified as her hips, and the new red hula hoop goes one, two, wobble, three. She is going to get to a thousand before dinner. She hula-hoops to her pile of presents in the corner of the lounge where her new compass gleams importantly. *Eight, nine, ten* . . . Father Christmas usually gets his instructions from her mother, but the compass, she is sure, was Daddy's idea. Daddy reads maps the way other grown-ups read books, pointing out natural features, tracing contours and rivers, A roads and footpaths with his big nicotine-golden finger. *Fifteen, sixteen, seventeen* . . .

Andy charges into the lounge with a blood-curdling yell. 'Let me, let me.' The sheer quantity of wrapping paper seems to have gone to his head. His older brother Danny, on the other hand, has not budged from the settee, refuses to even look at his new soccer ball. Isobel can't be sure what Danny is sneering at, but suspects it's the whole idea of Christmas. She makes a strenuous effort, around him, to disguise her own delight. Especially since last night.

Getting out of the bath, Andy looked up at Isobel's mother with sharp little eyes and said, 'You're not my real mum, are you?'

She's not mine either, Isobel longed to say. She rolled the word round her mouth. *Mum* was what Rita called Mrs Coop; it was obviously unsuitable for Isobel's mother. When Isobel was too old for *mummy* – when she had passed the eleven-plus probably – she'd invent something new. Something dignified but clever, which would not leave her open to accusations of cheek.

'I'm going to call you mum,' Andy decided, lifting his arms to let Isobel's mother dry him.

At that point Danny came thundering down the landing and clobbered his brother over the head. 'She's not your bloody mother so shut up! Our mother's gone. She went when I was six,' he informed them with grim emphasis. 'You're Mrs Midwinter and that's what he's got to bloody call you.'

'What do you mean, your mother went?' Isobel inquired cautiously when her mother had whisked Andy away to write to Father Christmas. 'Where did she go?'

Danny glowered. ''F anyone knew that, we wouldn't be at the Home.'

'So are you an orphan?' She thought of pink rock, the sticky shards in your mouth and Debworth Cove written right through to the end. Written right through her to the end was Isobel Irene Midwinter. But what if you were an orphan?

Danny's glower intensified. 'What if I am?'

She was deeply envious. Orphans had all the luck. They never had to say *thank you* and *can I*, they could just go off and seek their fortunes. Although she couldn't understand why Danny and Andy were seeking theirs, here in the Midwinter house. She had asked but her mother had only said the girls had no idea how lucky they were and ought to count their blessings. She made it sound as if they had cheated at something.

'Shut up staring,' snapped Danny, narrowing his eyes dangerously. 'And shut up asking questions, nosy parker.' Which brought her investigations to a standstill.

Sixteen, seventeen . . . 'Let me, let me,' bellows Andy again, and rushes at Isobel, knocking the hoop to the floor. Her mother appears briefly in the doorway, camouflaging an inquiring frown with a festive smile, so Isobel steps out of the hoop and hands it over. She kneels and gives Andy's shiny new dump truck an idle shove.

'Mine!' He lunges, still inside the hoop, and topples a festive log from the coffee table. He grabs the truck and takes off with another whoop, leaving Isobel to reassemble the log. She frowns fiercely but it's no good, she lacks her mother's artistry. Glitter sticks to her fingers, the holly draws a Christmassy bauble of blood. Then, just as she gets the candle to stand upright, the puppy staggers in, all bounce and lick, and knocks it down again. Isobel fondles his ruffled chest. Her father brought him in from the garage this morning, grinning broadly. 'Oh, David, a corgi,' her mother breathed. But she was too busy hugging Isobel's father to appreciate how adorable it was, and Isobel secretly vowed to make him love her the best.

Her father is shovelling coal on the fire. Isobel hula-hoops towards him – *twenty-one, twenty-two* – in the hope of sensible conversation. 'Like your presents, do you, girlie?' he says. Then, before she can formulate a reply, 'Mmm?', and he disappears into the kitchen, a miniature glass of sherry in each hand.

'Out of the way, stupid.' Gillian scrambles from Isobel's vengeful kick, clutching a doll to her chest. She is wearing a pathetic nurse's uniform and the doll's head is poorly bandaged. *Twenty-four, twenty-five* . . . No one would ever give Gillian a compass.

'You haven't got telly,' Danny accuses from the settee.

'Bad for us,' pants Isobel inside the hoop.

'They're snobs, your mum and dad.'

'Thirty-one, thirty-two, are not,' declares Isobel hotly, although he's right, Rita has said as much too, though less unkindly.

'Bloody are,' says Danny. 'You talk posh and your house is posh and you say mummy and daddy. Bloody snobs.'

'You've got a hula hoop,' says someone from the door. It's a taller version of Teddy, with a new front tooth and its curls an even fierier red.

'Thirty-five, thirty-six,' gasps Isobel, by way of greeting. 'How old are you now?' She lives in hope of one day catching him up.

'Teddy, this is Daniel.' Isobel's mother wipes her hands on her apron. 'You boys could play football together. Outside. That would be nice, wouldn't it.'

They glare at each other. Isobel glares too – Teddy is hers. 'Come and see my presents,' she orders, and bribes him with a coin from a little net bag. She watches him peel off the gold and nibble the chocolate, pretending not to notice that Danny is watching too. 'Look,' she tells Teddy, thrusting the compass under his freckled nose, 'this is so you don't get lost.' The needle quivers and settles. 'East is . . . the front door. Down the garden is west. And Rita's house is north.' She decides not to pass on her father's bewildering explanation of north and true north. She prefers to believe in the truth, and that compasses always tell it.

She is up to fifty-one under Teddy's approving eye when an impressive scream echoes down the hall. She hula-hoops to the foot of the stairs where everyone is gathered expectantly. Isobel's mother is coming down with Cynthia on her hip, one hand locked on Andy's skinny arm. 'He hit her, David!' She is outraged as she displays a red mark on Cynthia's face, and Cynthia's yells redouble for the audience. Andy grins. Aunty Iris puffs on her cigarette holder. Uncle Max, whom Isobel gives a wide berth to deter from ruffling her hair or walloping her bottom, booms, 'Goodwill to all men!'

'Another Bristol Cream, old man?' Daddy offers.

'The goose,' cries her mother, releasing Andy and Cynthia and racing to the kitchen. The puppy squats and piddles, and Isobel hula-hoops back to the lounge.

'He your boyfriend?' sneers Danny, who is still on the settee. Isobel regards Teddy and considers the incident in the tent at Debworth Cove, Teddy's white unsuntanned parts shining in the gloom, that eager look.

'No,' says Teddy with admirable firmness. 'We're just friends. Like brother and sister.'

Danny looks as contemptuously on this as he did on the concept of Father Christmas. 'Bet you bloody are,' he says, as Isobel's mother comes in with a box of crackers.

'Daniel, I've told you before, no swearing. Isobel, I'd like some help with the table. Gillian, wash your hands. Cynthia, you know the rules – presents in the corner, not all over the floor. Come on kiddies, the goose is just about ready and Daddy's going to carve. Oh no, not another puddle.'

'Goose?' says Uncle Max, behind her in the doorway. 'Did someone say goose?'

Isobel's mother yelps and slaps his arm. 'Max Haines,' she laughs, and goes back to the kitchen.

'A homo then,' continues Danny.

'No he's not,' declares Isobel, with more confidence than she feels.

Teddy is staring at Danny, clenching and unclenching his fists. 'Go on then,' sneers Danny. 'Hit me.'

'Sixty-nine, seventy, I think you ought to hit him, Teddy.'

'Isobel, I asked you to help me.' Her mother's face is red and shiny and she smells roasted. 'What's the matter? Not arguing, are you? It's Christmas.'

Danny turns his cool gaze on her. 'And that man out there is *your* boyfriend.'

Isobel's mother struggles for a smile. 'Uncle Max? He's an old family friend, Daniel. We've known him for years, haven't we, Isobel? And Aunty Iris and Teddy.'

Isobel is so surprised she almost loses count – her mother wants her to be on her side.

'He's your boyfriend,' says Danny, not taking his eyes off her. 'Your fancy-man.'

'I beg your pardon?' Isobel's mother stiffens, making it hard for Isobel to wriggle her hips. *Seventy-two, seventy-three . . .*

'I bet you *do* it, you two.'

Isobel's mother utters a cry as if she has been struck. As her hand connects with Danny's shoulder, he grabs the football and with the sort of movement Isobel has seen executed on Rita's television on a Saturday afternoon, drop-kicks it hard down the room. It's more like an explosion than a window breaking. Everyone crowds into the room then freezes in the blast of cold through the jagged hole. Isobel can see people's breath, though not, she is sorry to find, quite what it is that Uncle Max and her mother might do. *Ninety-nine, a hundred . . .*

'They're going back, David, they've got to go back.' Her mother is quivering dangerously. *A hundred and nine, a hundred and ten . . .*

'Come on, it's only a broken window,' says Daddy with great good humour. Danny too is smiling for the first time since he's been in the house.

'It's not just the window. Take them back, David, they can't stay, I won't have it.'

'Calm down, Irene. They're only kids, we can't take them back . . . not to that place on Christmas Day, be reasonable.'

'Reasonable! Who does all the work to make Christmas nice for everybody? Who makes dozens of mince pies and a cake and puddings and . . . and does all the decorations and the shopping and gets up at six for the kids and sorts out their fights and cooks the bloody meal? While you pour a few sherries and play the cheery host. I'm sick of it. Sick of it . . .'

She grabs the nearest Christmas log and hurls it. He ducks, catching the candle with one hand. Isobel sees Uncle Max go to clap then think better of it. Glitter flutters prettily to the carpet.

Aunty Iris dispenses with her cigarette holder and steps between them. 'There, Irene, I know.'

Isobel's mother collapses sobbing in her arms. Odd words escape – 'Going back . . . ruining Christmas . . . not fair to the girls.'

Teddy reappears, smelling of the garden, and sets the football in the middle of the carpet. Isobel is embarrassed by his air of cooperation – it does not stand up well beside Danny's withering scorn. Her father raises his hands in a gesture of helplessness. Uncle Max flicks glitter from his jacket. Danny glances from Uncle Max to Isobel's mother through narrowed eyes and Isobel can see that he hasn't finished yet.

'A thousand,' she shouts quickly, almost believing it. 'I got to a thousand hula-hoops.'

PART ONE

NEW ZEALAND 1964

Chapter 1

Isobel longed for the journey to be over. It was all so utterly intolerable that she could not understand why she didn't simply expire on the spot. To be dragged all this way, to be so ignominiously crammed in the back seat with Gillian and Cynthia and the dog, to have her view of the road ahead blocked for hour after hour by her mother's perm. Yet outside was even worse. The country looked as if its entire population had walked out leaving the door open. Only disgust stood between Isobel and complete despair.

Her mother kept up a stream of admiring little gasps – at the hills (as if there were none in England), the greenness (as if northern foliage were purple), the cloudless sky, even the few dreary inhabitants. Gillian said, 'I Spy with My Little Eye Something Beginning With H,' and when they all gave in, yelled H for holiday. Cynthia shoved her, Isobel elbowed her, and the dog growled and nipped her. Gillian wept. Their mother raised her voice, their father raised his voice even more. And Isobel pulled Buster onto her lap and imagined vivid scenes in which she walked bravely away from a tangled wreckage of car and family. She vowed to continue the journey in a punishing silence.

'Oh-tack-ay,' announced her father cheerily, as they swished down a long deserted high street.

'It's an I, not an E acute,' snapped Isobel. 'It's not French.'

'Daddy ought to know, darling,' said her mother. 'He was in France in the War.'

'God, the War!' exploded Isobel. To get away from it all, she pictured Rita at Clacton until it felt like toothache. And then it was happening again.

'*Please* don't make me go.' *I'll speak properly. Do as I'm told. Say thank you.* She is pleading, she never pleads.

'Pull yourself together, young lady. We expect you to be grown up about this, don't we, Daddy. It's a wonderful opportunity. A new start.'

'You'll like it, Izzy,' murmurs her father without conviction, slapping his pocket for cigarettes.

'No!' shouts Isobel, fists clenched. 'No, I won't! I don't want to go, I want to live here, we live here.' A promise has been broken, one all the more monumental for never having been uttered.

'That will do,' orders her mother. 'It's not the end of the world, is it, Daddy.'

'Yes it is,' rages Isobel, who got an A for New Zealand in Geography. 'I hate you! You don't love me, you don't even care about me.'

'Of course we love you, you stupid girl. And you ought to count your blessings, be thankful you're not one of those poor little Kennedy children.'

'Bugger the Kennedys! I wish someone would shoot *you*,' roars Isobel. But it's too late, the world has exploded like a dropped cup.

'Gidday, young ladies,' said the man behind the counter, 'and what can I do you for?'

It was called Des's Dairy but there was no sign of a cow.

'Three ice lollies, please.'

'Come again?' said the man – Des, presumably.

'Three ice lollies,' piped Cynthia, and Isobel was grateful for her resilience.

Des lifted a khaki hat, rubbed a hand through sparse khaki hair and replaced the hat. 'Now, we got lollies and we got ice blocks so what's it to be?'

'Could we just see?' said Isobel, as if humouring the little ones.

'Over there in the freezer, help yourself. On holiday from the Old Country, are you?' He seemed amused by the very idea.

Isobel, thinking they might as well be carrying a sign, chose raspberry. 'We're staying by the lake till our new house is built,' she said, trying to dignify her position.

'In a bach, are you?'

She pulled off sticky wrapping, licked and, to avoid providing even more amusement, thought fast. Maybe he meant a beach, but how could you stay *in* a beach, even if the lake had proper beaches which it didn't. *Beach* . . . it was like holding a shell to her ear – the Atlantic surf thundered, the undertow gnawed her legs and swallowed the shingle underfoot. It is green and smelly in Teddy's tent. They lie side by side, close but not touching. Cigarette smoke filters through the canvas from the twilight outside, and the clinking of ice against glass. Uncle Max starts it, he always does. 'Ought to think about New Zealand, Dave. Man's country down there.'

'Aren't they all,' sniffs Isobel's mother.

'Land of opportunity, Dave. Flowing with milk and honey. Don't know what's stopping us.'

'What?' But it's only Des. *Speak properly, Isobel.* 'I mean, I beg your pardon?'

'In a bach, are you?'

She nodded. She would learn everything there was to learn as fast as possible and soon they wouldn't be able to tell she was different. One day she might even be able to say *gidday*.

Cynthia was still peering into the depths of the freezer. 'Picked a beaut time,' continued Des, leaning confidentially across the counter. 'Bet you didn't know there were two hundred and thirty-eight shakes in the last two weeks. Bet you don't get those back in the Old Country.'

Isobel smiled politely. A handwritten sign over his shoulder referred to shakes – vanilla, banana, chocolate and strawberry. '*Come on*, Cyn.'

'On the wireless this morning – two hundred and thirty-eight. Some bloke said the mountain might blow. Better keep your eye on it, girls.' And he chuckled and went back to his paper.

'Here we are,' announced Isobel's father. He knelt beside her on the stringy carpet, denting the map with his finger. She inhaled his scent of tweed and cigarette smoke. 'Mount Toe . . . Toe-hurrah.'

'Tauhara,' she sighed, fingering Buster's chest ruffles. The dog gave her a melting look and lowered his rump northwards. The floor beneath the map ran downhill to a dirty view of the garden, which was wildly overgrown – seed-heads around the sills, blowsy yellow roses bumping the glass. She looked quickly back at the map. She wouldn't look at the tree again, not yet. She would save it.

When her father had shouldered open the door a few days before, Isobel watched the serenity drain from her mother's face, saw her take in the dingy kitchen with its broken-down bench and cracked lino. 'Oh David,' she said, hand at her mouth. 'When you said a holiday cottage, I thought . . .'

Isobel knew exactly what her mother had thought – the kind of thing depicted on several Midwinter tea-towels and biscuit tin lids. Something English. Then, through the smeared window, Isobel had seen the tree. The word itself was wrong – *tree* evoked something leafy, branching, expansive. This was a

curve of skinny trunk and an exotic sprouting bearing no relation to leaves, no relation to anything. By then her father had
his arm around her mother in the kitchen, and her mother was
sniffing about the impossibility of preparing meals with such
dreadful saucepans, and what sort of a holiday would it be for
her anyway? The blades of the tree had gleamed and twisted like
knives, and Isobel's blood had raced.

'The Antipathies, eh, Izzy,' joked her father, giving the dog
a shove. Buster slouched off in an easterly direction, grumbling
under his breath.

The map's familiar symbols and swirls had a calming effect
on Isobel – reduced to these elements, one country looked
much like another. She fingered the contours. To the south they
clustered around three peaks.

'Gar-a-hoe,' mused her father. 'It's a volcano.'

The idea of a volcano was as thrilling as the tree. Any
moment your life could be blown to smithereens; it made the
English look pathetic.

'Campaigns were defeated by bad maps, Izzy,' said her father
with satisfaction, 'lives lost. Look, there's a path up Mount Toe-
hurrah, so if we take the car to here . . . It's a volcano too, an
extinct one.'

'How do they know?' scoffed Isobel. 'Just because it hasn't
blown up for ages doesn't mean it won't. Maybe tomorrow.'

'Anyone'd think you wanted us all swept away by red-hot
lava,' said her mother sharply, dumping plates of baked beans
on the rickety table.

The family fell on them. Isobel's mother chewed fastidiously,
crooking her little finger and replacing her fork on her plate
between mouthfuls. Isobel averted her eyes. It was unthinkable
that someone who ate in this manner in a decrepit house under
threat of volcano and earthquake should be in charge of
another person's whole life.

'Whoa,' said her father through his beans, 'here we go
again.' The family stared up at the bare bulb over the table. It

swung with captivating grace. When it stopped, he pushed his plate away with an aggrieved expression and asked if there was some ham in the fridge for a sandwich.

'I don't know,' said Isobel's mother, delicately wiping the corners of her mouth. 'Why don't you look?'

'Oh David, it's lovely,' said her mother, tucking her hand through her husband's arm and offering him a delighted smile. He grinned back as if bestowing a great treat, and patted the hand, meatlessness forgiven. They strolled through a field dotted with clover and dandelion. A breeze stirred the wispy grass and drab little moths flitted at their feet. Dogs barked a long way off, and now and then, an odd musical chirrup piped up from somewhere unseen.

'Look at that wonderful watercress, just growing wild,' said Isobel's mother, as they leaped a stream. Cynthia and Gillian raced ahead, Buster yapping at their heels. Isobel maintained a dignified distance from them all. 'Look at that sky,' said her mother. Isobel grudgingly glanced upwards and was almost struck down by the fierce blue. They reached the top of the rise. 'Oh,' breathed her mother. 'Look at those mountains.'

Isobel stomped past, heading for the woods beyond the fence and longing for a radio, although what was the point when Rita had given her *Twenty-four Hours from Tulsa* as a leaving present and it still hadn't got here. Twenty-Four Hours from Everywhere. Panic gripped her – where would she be without Rita, without Rita's grin, her knowledge of pop music, fashion, sexual etiquette and human biology? But at least thinking of Rita stopped her thinking about Dan. *I love you, Isobel, you can't go* . . . She gritted her teeth and strode on. Cynthia had burst into tears on the plane when their father said her birthday had fallen down the dateline, and Isobel had produced a knowing older-sister grin. Yet several times a day now the dateline yawned, threatening to swallow something much bigger than a birthday. A terrible force – the undertow? True north? –

kept dragging her to the brink, and in her dreams she fell and fell.

There was ringing in her ears. It built in volume and intensity with every step until her legs and arms seemed to vibrate like violin strings. Her heart pounded but she kept walking, she wouldn't let them see.

'Grasshoppers,' said her father from behind. 'Rubbing their back legs together.'

This preposterous theory instantly turned her fear to scorn. She scowled up at the hill. 'Oh God' – 'Language, Isobel' – 'why do we have to go all the way up there?'

'Because it's there,' said her father with relish. 'Forward now. Legitimate order, that is, could be shot in battle for disobeying a legitimate order.' He separated the fence wires for her mother to clamber through.

'Goodness me, no stile. Come along, Isobel. The exercise will do you good.'

The air screamed between the trees. She wanted to clap her hands over her ears, she wanted to scream along with it. Then, just when she could stand it no longer, it ceased. The path was steep and rough, winding disconcertingly through tangled growth. Sunlight spattered the ground, but mostly it was deeply littered, dark and dank. Ferns sprouted from mossy banks and vines hung like nooses. This was nothing like the bluebell woods in Kew Gardens. This was jungle.

'Whew,' panted her mother, leaning against a tree and wiping her brow. 'You'd think it would be cool in here, wouldn't you?' She was resolutely jolly. Isobel's father stood hands on hips, gazing about with extreme satisfaction. They haven't noticed, Isobel thought, they think it's like England. 'Well,' said her mother, 'so long as there's a nice view from the top.'

In one spot they had to haul themselves up on hands and knees. Her father was studying the map at the next bend. 'Well, no view. That's rather disappointing.' Isobel's mother brushed twigs and leaves from her arms. She was spectacularly red in the face. 'Isobel, you should have worn your wellingtons. Look at your shoes.'

'No, Irene,' said her father. 'This isn't the top. Look . . .'

Her mother's eyes ran uncomprehendingly over the map. 'How much further then?' she asked with undisguised dismay.

'Hard to say.' He squinted at the map.

'Only you said not to bring lunch and the children must be getting very tired.'

He stuffed the map back in his pocket, undeterred by reminders of parental responsibility. 'Onward and upward.' Then, as Isobel trudged alongside, 'Ed Hillary's a Kiwi, Izzy,' he said, in his faraway voice.

Some time later there was a cry from behind like an injured bird. 'Mummy,' said Isobel. The long-unused word clogged her mouth.

'Mmm?' said her father.

'David, I can't go on,' her mother gasped. She clapped a hand to her brow in a portentous manner. 'I feel . . . most peculiar. I really do think we ought to turn back. And the children . . .' Her mother had no faraway voice, she was always right there.

'I'm not tired,' said Isobel. 'Nor am I,' said Gillian.

Their mother made a strangled sound, hinting at profound but bravely born suffering, and hauled herself to a fallen tree beside the path.

'Come on, Irene,' urged Isobel's father, as if they were playing French cricket on the Woodland Rise lawn. 'Not far now.'

'You haven't a clue how far,' burst out her mother. 'You've no idea where we're going or how far it is.' This criticism seemed to encompass a good deal more than an unexpectedly long walk and to cost her mother dearly. Isobel crossed her fingers tight so her mother wouldn't cry. 'Well, I'm staying here if you insist on going on.'

'Jolly good,' said her father.

Now the danger of tears had passed, Isobel regarded her mother with disdain. Never had she seen anyone so ill-equipped to camp on the side of a jungle-covered volcano, dormant or otherwise. Buster was considering his loyalties. Isobel called entreatingly and he scampered up the path after the rest of them.

Eventually the trees untangled, shrinking to shrubby undergrowth. The four of them plodded up a tight gully carved into the hillside, the sun beating on their heads. Their progress struck Isobel as ignorant, foolhardy. *Forgive us our trespasses.* Cynthia whined steadily – she was thirsty, she was tired, she wished she'd stayed with Mummy, she wished she'd stayed at the cottage. 'Bach,' said Isobel. Gillian trudged on, uncomplaining. Buster, too, was clearly regretting his decision. They clambered over vast moonlike rocks blotched with lichen.

'Victory!' shouted their father. They found themselves on a plateau the size of a hockey pitch. At their feet brooded the dark jungle green. Beyond, everything dissolved into blue. A long way off, a snowy peak glistened. 'Marvellous, isn't it, girls.' His eyes glistened like the peak.

Isobel shifted her weight from one foot to another. She grabbed his wrist and frowned at his watch. 'Half past four. We left her hours ago.'

'Let's just enjoy it for a minute, Izzy. Mummy would want us to.' They both knew this was untrue.

Isobel squinted into the sun at Cynthia who was waiting behind a rock to ambush Gillian. A few of the closer hills exhaled puffs of steam like sleeping animals. Beyond, they ranged away to the horizon. Suddenly she knew that from up here she would be able to see England. She turned slowly, trying to calculate in which direction it lay, then faster. She was quivering the way her compass used to quiver until it found the right way. But there was no right way, not now. The world was round so England was in all directions, which made it worse, put it more utterly beyond her. She stood stock still, overwhelmed by the awful rolling vastness that had nothing whatever to do with her.

Cynthia limped over, blood dripping from her leg. 'Come on,' said their father, administering absent-minded pats all round. 'We've left Mummy long enough.'

They tumbled downhill in a silent rush. The sun had slipped away and it was gloomier than ever, but the afternoon heat was still trapped in the tangle of growth. Isobel got there first but maybe she had made a mistake. 'No, Izzy, there's the log by the path. She must have gone back to the car.'

She scarcely heard the screaming this time. Their shadows stretched across the field and Cynthia and Gillian whooped and plunged while Buster limped in the rear with an air of reproach. Isobel's father said, 'I suppose we were away a while. You know how she worries. Can you see her down by the car? Perhaps she's sitting in it.' She didn't point out that the keys were jingling in his pocket.

Heat rushed from the car like a caged beast. Cynthia and Gillian collapsed, their faces red and shiny. Buster sank the three inches between him and the ground and sighed deeply. Isobel and her father leaned on the car roof, staring back up the hill. The gullies darkened before their eyes. 'Stay here,' he said heavily. 'I'll go back up and find her.' Isobel stared in disbelief – her own legs were throbbing unbearably – but he was already striding back across the field. She stretched out on the cool grass and closed her eyes.

There was a blank, then she heard Cynthia's piping voice. 'We've lost our mother. Up the hill.'

The man's eyes were buried deep in leathery furrows. An excited black and white dog was licking Gillian's hand. 'Ged-in,' thundered the man, and they all jumped violently except the dog. Buster slunk under the car, whimpering. The man prodded the ground with a long stick as if assessing its worth. 'Be dark soon.'

'Our father's gone to find her,' said Isobel officially, as the oldest. 'She must have gone the wrong way.'

'Ged-in! Bloody well hope not. You know the bush.' Apparently it wasn't obvious to him that they didn't. 'Not going to eat that watercress, are you? Dead ewe upstream.'

She wished he would go away. She wanted to be alone with the churning in her stomach which made it feel as if she cared her mother was lost. The man was leaning on his stick, poking the grateful dog with the toe of a huge unlaced boot. There was a silence as long as the shadows.

'There they are!' cried Gillian. Two figures appeared at the top of the ridge, the smaller leaning into the bigger.

'I'm all right, kiddies, really,' gasped their mother, as soon as she was within earshot and it was perfectly clear that she wasn't. She wiped her eyes and blew her nose in a charade of self-control that made Isobel simultaneously want to slap her and burst into tears herself.

'Gidday,' said the man without expression. 'Thrown a bit of a wobbly, has she, mate?'

'Just a misunderstanding, you know how it is.' He smiled man-to-man.

Isobel's mother jerked away. 'You left me up there for hours. I was worried *sick*. You had no idea at all where you were going. The children . . . no lunch . . . getting dark . . . trees, horrible trees . . .' She sobbed. The girls shuffled. Their father grinned sheepishly.

'Righto then,' concluded the man. 'Ged-in!' They watched him shamble off. 'By the way, mate,' he called back, 'private property, this. Not a public path. Lambing season, I'd've shot the dog.'

Chapter 2

STEAM BILLOWED INTO THE DARKNESS, UNFOCUSING THE STARS, but the warmth of the pool still came as a shock. It looked like used bath water and gave off an unappetising smell. Isobel shrank against the side as Cynthia and Gillian gleefully spluttered and thrashed. Their parents had opted for a private facility, their mother still limp from her *experience*. She would be gazing up at the stars, and saying *look at those stars*. And Isobel lovingly constructed a picture of her mother stumbling hungry, thirsty and exhausted, possibly injured and certainly scared through the dense bush. *Think of fairies in a bluebell wood*, she called out cheerily.

A small brown child shot overhead, bobbed up in front of Isobel, then climbed out and did it again. Boys were executing rowdy honeypots in the deep end. Two old people sat on the steps, the woman's head sprouting orange rubber daisies. 'Race,' gasped Cynthia, scarlet with heat. 'Come on.'

For the sake of the boys, Isobel feigned deafness. She watched Cynthia surge through the water in pursuit of the brown child, and thought, it's not fair. *Life's not fair, Izzy,* came her father's perennial response. All her life she had waited for him to elaborate on this bleak theme, since, honoured as she felt to receive it, it always alarmed her – what did he think parents were for but to enforce fairness? *To thine own self be true* was another of his favourites. But she had no idea what her own self was except things that were not allowed to count – black underwear, the radio loud, staying in England.

And then she was gulping mouthfuls of smelly water, blowing fat bubbles, struggling for her life. She broke the surface, gasped steamy air, and went down again. This time she would kill Gillian. She lashed out with her foot, dislodging the hand on her ankle. *Hah, she bet that hurt.*

A boy was grinning inches from her spluttering face. His eyes glittered like blue glass and his grin wiped everything else from her mind. 'Thought I'd cheer you up.'

Gillian dog-paddled over. 'You look funny, Isobel.'

'Isobel,' said the boy, intensifying the grin. She tried to smile in spite of thumping heart and burning lungs. The effects of near drowning were becoming muddled with the effects of the boy and his Cheshire cat grin.

'Hey, Gil,' yelled another boy. 'Whoa,' chorused the others. Isobel blushed deeply and the boy swam off.

The girls turned their pale English backs to one another in the corrugated iron changing shed. Isobel examined herself in the shiny sheet of metal that substituted for a mirror and tried to lift her wet hair from her scalp. She touched up her Outdoor Girl mascara, powdered her nose and cheeks with Rimmel Wild Rose, and whitened her lips with Rimmel Snowflake.

Her father was leaning on the little bridge when they emerged. Their mother rose from a bench. 'All right, poppets? Lovely, wasn't it? Don't get cold now.' She seemed magically recovered.

'There was a boy,' Gillian informed them. And Isobel

shot her a look that made Gillian stumble and drop towel and swimming costume in the dirt.

'Hey, kids, come and look at these trout,' called their father. Fish, thought Isobel, God, who cares? 'See, down there, under the bridge. This young man's been telling me all about them. Down there, Isobel, you're not looking. My word, they're beauties.'

'Catch one,' shouted Cynthia, jumping up and down. 'For breakfast.'

'Your father can clean it,' declared their mother.

'Protected,' said the boy, blue eyes glinting at Isobel. 'They like the warm water. There's a thermal spring just over there, see?' The Midwinters obediently saw. 'Come back in the daytime and see them better.'

'Well, thank you,' said their mother, making shepherding movements. 'Very interesting.'

'Tantalising,' said Isobel's father. 'I'd want to land one.'

'You can haul them up by the ton out on the lake trolling.'

'Catch a troll, catch a troll,' yelled Cynthia, who was seriously overheated.

'No boat, I'm afraid.' Their father shook his head sadly.

'Come out with me. Mate's got a jet boat.'

'A jet boat, eh.' He rubbed his hands and grinned. *Man's country.*

Isobel stared into the murky water, resisting her mother's efforts to move her on. 'The children are getting cold, David.'

'Your daughter could have a crack at water-skiing.' The boy was grinning right at her.

'Water-skiing, eh, Izzy. How about that?'

'David, Isobel's shivering.'

'Where're you staying?' said the boy. 'Pick you up tomorrow, early. That's the best time.'

'Very kind,' said Isobel's father. 'But . . .'

'Giltrap,' said the boy, extending a hand. 'Clyde Giltrap.'

'David Midwinter. And this is Mrs Midwinter, er . . . Irene. Oh, she's gone. And these are the kids.' Isobel glared at his terminology.

'Come over to the wagon and I'll get your address,' said the boy.

The glitter of blue and the grin hovered above Isobel's lumpy bunk as she fell asleep. That night there was no dizzying fall into the dateline.

Next morning, the grin performed introductions by the wharf. 'That one – the one playing pocket billiards – that's Rats. And this is Janola, it's his old man's boat.' The boys shambled and grinned, as if they shared a really good secret. She wondered why none of them had real names. 'Janola's cunt-struck,' said the boy with the grin.

'Fuck off,' bellowed Janola, and thumped him.

Isobel cast an apprehensive glance along the beach. But her mother was stretched out on a towel in the sun, and for reasons unknown to Isobel, off sentry duty. Cynthia and Gillian splashed in the shallows, and her father crouched on the wharf with a large knife and three dead fish. The sky was an unbelievable blue. And at last, something interesting was going to happen. The boys tangled on the stones at her feet, emitting grunts, bellows and curses. She stood politely, waiting for them to finish.

'We going bloody water-skiing or not?' demanded Janola, extricating himself and running a hand through white-blonde hair. 'Dad wants the boat after lunch.' They pounded down the wooden wharf and two of them leaped into the boat, rocking it wildly. The one with the grin was untying the rope when he called back to Isobel, 'C'mon, rattle your dags.'

She stepped on board. The engine roared and the boat shot forward so fast that the bow reared up. Isobel pitched backwards, cracking her head. 'Fuckin' hell, Janola,' roared the other two appreciatively. Isobel tried to look appreciative too, while surreptitiously examining her skull. Her family shrank as the boat skimmed over the glittering water. Until now the lake had left her unimpressed, its only interesting feature being the way rocks bobbed on its surface, defying the laws of nature. Pumice, her father told them, but bearing little relation to the intimate chunks in Andrea Dodds' soapdish. A rainbow formed in the spray and silvery water ran through her fingers. The boat slewed maniacally and stopped dead. 'Okay,' said the boy with the grin when Isobel had picked herself up again. 'Out you hop.'

The lake was icy. It hurt her bones. She clung to the bar at the end of the rope as if it would stop her sinking, and the skis stuck out stupidly from her feet. The boy with the grin shouted instructions – 'Hold on, stand up when you start moving. Piece of piss. Sorry, I mean it's dead easy, just relax. Right, gun it, Janola.'

The boat moved off in what Isobel now appreciated was a sober manner. The rope snaked away from her. She was abandoned, treading water in the middle of a lake on the wrong side of the world. She squinted despairingly at the dots that were Buster and Gillian and Cynthia and her parents. The rope jerked. There was a momentary release, then a hideous wrench. She was ripped along on her belly at a hundred miles an hour. Water tore at her mouth and eyes, knocked unrecognisable sounds out of her. She thumped like a sack of coal across the wake and the bar flew from her hand.

Peace. She wallowed, too relieved to care about drowning. In the distance, the boat slowed and turned. 'Forgot to say,' shouted the boy with the grin, 'if you fall over, let go.'

It was on her sixth attempt, humiliated by her ineptitude and on the brink of giving up, that she found herself skimming over the water. She looked down in wonder, wobbled dangerously, and recovered. There was whooping from the boat; the boys were watching her, waving their fists. She flew over the lake, a spotless wind streaming past her cheeks and through her hair. She stared triumphantly at the raw folded hills and bare blue sky. Then water slammed into her like a wall.

The boy with the grin hauled her into the boat. Rats said, 'Pretty good, for a Pom. Pass the jar, Gil, you prick.' They were guzzling from a huge bottle, laughing as its contents poured down their bare chests. The boy offered her a cigarette. 'No vices, eh?' he said.

'Whoa!' exclaimed the others. 'Gil'll soon change that.'

Some time later the boy slung an arm around Isobel's goose-pimpled shoulder and she understood she was to be his girlfriend for the duration of the holiday. And why not? She couldn't be faithful to Dan forever.

Her mother was waiting on the wharf, packed into a navy swimming costume. The flesh on her shoulders and arms was round and pink, her breasts of another order altogether than what was concealed beneath Isobel's tiny bikini. *Two eggs in a handkerchief,* quips her mother with a little laugh. *Late developer,* murmurs Andrea Dodds in convent tones. 'Isobel, are you all right? You didn't seem to be wearing a life jacket and Daddy said . . .'

'Course I am,' scowled Isobel, knowing only too well that personal injury meant public shame and parental inconvenience.

'Only, Mr Midwinter was adamant about life jackets, Clyde,' said her mother, struggling to reconcile good manners with public safety. 'And I didn't see . . .'

Clyde grinned. 'She's right.' This seemed to carry far more weight than Isobel's first-person statement.

'Well, thank you so much for taking her out. Say thank you . . .'

Isobel had stalked off.

'We're going to Mark's for some tucker,' she heard Clyde say. 'Can Isobel come?' She halted halfway down the wharf.

'I think that's really rather up to Mark's mother.' Her mother's sunburned back was turned but Isobel pictured the condescending smile.

'Mum loves feeding people,' said Janola.

Isobel cringed in anticipation of a waspish response. None came, only laughter – her mother's and the boys' – and then her mother was picking her wedge-heeled way down the wharf with quite a different expression on her face than the one Isobel had imagined. The three boys watched her go. Isobel saw Clyde grasp an elbow then clench his fist and shake it with an ugly grimace. She had no idea – and every idea – what the gesture meant.

When Clyde caught up with her, she said airily, 'Don't take any notice of her. She treats me like a child.'

He grinned again. 'Your old lady? Looks like a goer to me.'

Janola's mother was decently covered in a tatty towelling beach robe and had several homely varicose veins. She fussed around the boys as if they were grown men, sitting them at a table under a tree and bringing out plates of food. Pressing a third grilled sausage on Isobel, she inquired of Clyde, 'And where did you find a nice girl like this?' Clyde forked lettuce smothered in mayonnaise and tomato sauce past his grin. Gillian, Isobel supposed, was a nice girl, and Andrea Dodds, of course. Yet she couldn't suppress a twitch of pleasure.

'So what are you all up to for the rest of the day?' said Mrs Janola, finally sitting down with a cup of coffee. She seemed to inquire out of genuine rather than managerial interest, and Isobel felt a sudden overpowering desire to be a boy, a beery boating boy whom a mother would take seriously. She tried to concentrate on what they were saying, to detect how far their plans included her, but the air was hot and heavy and scented with cut grass. There was chirruping at her feet, and further off, the screech of the bush. Already it had lost its power to unnerve her; it was a constant backdrop, the shrill of summer in mid-winter. December, January, February – the words evoked cold like a knife, bare branches, puddles that creaked and cracked when you stepped on them. Here, even her name – Midwinter – had lost its meaning. She fixed her eyes on a tree like the one at the bach and felt the blood race in her veins. There was a sound like a drop of pure water. She held her breath for it to come again, but it was drowned out by a rumbling belch from Clyde, as a heavy blackbird flapped overhead.

'Seen a cicada?' he asked. She shook her head. He came back from a flowerbed with cupped hands. She just had time to calculate that it was alive and not a mammal when he opened his hands and something veered out, colliding with her nose. Something greenish and horrible. She squawked and jerked away. Rats hooted. Mrs Janola said, 'Clyde, jolly well be nice to her. She's just out from Home.'

'Hold still,' said Clyde. Isobel barely suppressed a shriek as he fumbled in her hair. He held the thing by her ear so she could hear the terrible muffled flicking. Then he raised his hands to his mouth and displayed empty hands. He grinned, mouth shut tight.

'Shit, you're a dag,' said Rats with utter joy.

Clyde leaned down as if to kiss her. Inches from her face, his grin opened wide and the thing lurched out and away.

Chapter 3

ISOBEL CONCENTRATED ON ARRANGING HER GLASS ANIMALS
nose to tail along the shelf in her new bedroom, and tried not
to think of her mother down the other end of the house, crying
in the built-in pantry. The new place reminded Isobel of the
forts they used to build at the bottom of the garden at Woodland
Rise. It smelled raw and had a temporary feel, as though the
builder might come back at any moment with a better idea of
how to arrange its constituent parts. Only her parents' bedroom
was bigger than the smallest at home, and the dining room and
lounge ran into each other in a way that seemed particularly to
distress her mother – the term *open-plan* had been spluttered
into a handkerchief. Glass sliding doors opened onto a glaring
expanse of hardened clay. Beyond lay a dismal pine forest.

The view from her window continued to take her by surprise,
as if she still had the right to expect the Woodland Rise pavement, Mrs Runciman-Brown on her majestic bicycle, the elm
across the street. *I watch your house, I hide behind that tree, and I
know you haven't got a boyfriend so will you go out with me?* She sat

down hard on the bed. *I love you, Isobel, you can't go*. She shook her head, trying to clear it. It was the past, twelve thousand miles away, gone forever. By sheer force of will she banished Dan's face. But the old place came back – the landing with its gloomy Rembrandt print, the little brass knocker on each bedroom door, the raspberry patch where William was buried . . .

There was a shout, a crash and a slammed door. Isobel gave her door a shove and delved determinedly into her tea-chest. She stuck her *West Side Story* record sleeve to the wardrobe door at a jaunty angle. She pulled out matching volumes of *Black Beauty* and *Alice in Wonderland* and put them on the bottom shelf. Then she tore at a mysterious floppy parcel and a hank of coppery hair fell across the bed. She shuddered – it was like digging up a dead person. Cutting it off was her fourteenth birthday present.

Crunch, crunch go the scissors and the hairdresser holds out something shining which isn't so awful now it's no longer Isobel's. 'Keep it tidy and she can sell it, Mrs Midwinter,' says the hairdresser, so it is still Isobel's. But, 'Oh,' cries her mother and the hair slips through her hands and spills across the floor, worthless as water.

'Wake up England.' Her father stood at the bedroom door with hammer, screwdriver and stern expression.

'I was just thinking,' said Isobel, jumping up.

'Wish I had time to sit and think. Come and give me a hand.'

'I'm small but willing,' said someone behind him. She had a covered dish and a chiffon scarf around stiff blonde hair.

'Pat,' said Isobel's father, a broad grin replacing the frown.

'Just a chicken casserole, where shall I put it?' She led them down the hall and made a couple of circuits of the chaotic kitchen. Isobel's father looked helpless. 'And who is this attractive young woman, David?'

'Who? Oh, Isobel, our oldest. Isobel, this is Mrs Lambert. She's . . .'

Isobel knew exactly who she was – the wife of her father's

new boss, consort of the trouble-maker who had hypnotised her parents into believing the job he was offering was a blessing for them all, and worth dragging the Midwinter family round the world for.

Her mother bustled into the kitchen, straightening apron and hair. She was faintly tear-stained. 'Pat – how kind. Isobel, put the kettle on, darling, and find some cups and the teapot – no, the nice one. Oh dear, no milk.'

'Here' – Lambert's wife thrust a bunch of keys at Isobel – 'take my car and nip down to the dairy.'

Isobel gazed blankly at the keys. 'I can't drive, I'm too young.'

'Surely not!' exclaimed the woman, and Isobel didn't know whether to be pleased or ashamed. 'You can get your licence at fifteen here, you know. Never mind, put the jug on, Irene, back in half a mo.'

Isobel went back to her bedroom and began corralling her glass animals for immediate delivery to Cynthia, or, since things had taken such an unexpected turn for the better, possibly even Gillian. She unpacked more childish stuff, amazed that only months earlier she had believed she needed it. What use were Snakes and Ladders, metal puzzles and jigsaws to someone old enough to drive? Her fingers found the last small object on the bottom of the tea chest. Instantly she saw sky the colour of rabbit's blood, the shadow of Uncle Max and his gun stretching towards her.

Here you are, lass, for luck. She flicks away tears and takes the poor silky thing, knowing it will never bring her luck. Midwinters don't believe in it, they leave nothing to chance. But she will keep it forever, so she never forgets Uncle Max is a murderer.

'Here you are,' said Lambert's wife. She put a cup of tea on the bedside table and Isobel shoved the rabbit's foot under her pillow. 'Tell you what, come and have a swim in our pool. We're just down the road. Bring your sisters, Penny'll be there.'

Her mother was emphatic. 'Not this evening, darling. Mrs Lambert's seen quite enough Midwinters for one day. Now, lay the table.'

'She invited me,' said Isobel half-heartedly, intimidated by the prospect of Penny.

'You're old enough to know when people are just being polite, darling. Anyway, it's school tomorrow, you need an early night.' And Isobel slammed down a handful of cutlery for appearances' sake.

Chapter 4

THE CIRCLE OF GIRLS IN THE DUSTY YARD REGARDED ISOBEL with frank curiosity. Their faces were scrubbed, without a trace of illicit makeup between them, their hair brutally parted and scraped back. There were no disobediently patterned stockings or hitched-up skirts, no surreptitious jewellery, and their bare feet were buckled into the kind of sandals Isobel had spurned since she was ten. 'Have you seen the Beatles?' asked one of them, biting into a beetroot sandwich.

'No,' said Isobel, disturbed by the very idea of a beetroot sandwich. 'They never came to where we lived.'

'What's television like in England?'

'We didn't have one.' *You're snobs, you lot.*

'Why not? We've got it,' said another. 'So have we.' 'So have we.' They chewed thoughtfully. 'Why don't you talk like they do on *Coronation Street*?' 'Have you got a boyfriend?'

'Yes,' said Isobel, at last spying an attractive opening.

They drew closer. 'What's his name?' 'Where d'you meet him?' 'How old is he?' 'Has *he* seen the Beatles?'

I love you, Isobel, you can't go . . . 'I met him at Taupo. He's nineteen.' She saw no need to mention that Clyde's status had expired with the holiday, no point at all in mentioning Dan.

'Nineteen!' Their response was everything she had hoped for.

'Janice's got this book,' chirruped a girl with sallow skin that a little foundation would have done wonders for. 'There's this bit in it. About this man and woman in bed and he bites her breast.' She giggled. 'Why would anyone do that?'

They looked hopefully at each other and Isobel's heart sank further still. Andrea Dodds had spoken properly, owned a national doll collection and an air of convent-induced propriety, but even she had not wallowed in this offensive state of innocence. Andrea had had a little book.

One day when Mummy and Daddy loved each other very much . . . Isobel tumbles over the words, fearful of what she will discover, more fearful of not discovering anything before Andrea reappears. *And he put his* . . . *into Mummy's* . . . It gets worse, far worse. *Mummy pushed and pushed, and suddenly* . . . Isobel's stomach heaves but she can't stop reading. *If you're a boy, when you grow up you'll look like Daddy. And if you're a girl, you'll grow up to look like Mummy, inside and out* . . . *inside and out.* So it's not just Midwinter that's written right through Isobel but . . . *Mummy.* Andrea puts the book back on her shelf. 'I thought you didn't know the facts of life. Mummy says you're a late developer.' If it were Gillian, Isobel would thump her. She vows she will never be caught not knowing things again. It is a Fact of Life.

She caught the train home. Reeking of hot grime, it trundled down the valley through dull back gardens. She squinted through the grubby window and turned over in her mind the only useful fact she had learned that day – that you could go to university straight from the lower sixth. Life was Snakes and Ladders, and since you never knew when a snake might raise its ugly head, you had to seize every available ladder

– learn to drive, get a boyfriend, learn to smoke, leave school, leave home. The ladders would take you from nought (the indignity of family life) to a hundred (freedom).

At her station, a crowd of girls from another school swarmed off a train going in the opposite direction. They wore panama hats and white gloves, and called to each other in fluting voices. Isobel trudged up Balmoral Road behind several of them. She realised now why at lunchtime the girls' expressions had shifted when in answer to yet another question she had told them where she lived. These houses were bigger than those she had seen from the train. They were set back from the road on sweeping lawns edged with trees, and the splashes and yells of hidden swimming pools carried over the hot afternoon air. By moving south the Midwinters had come up in the world.

'S-o-o-o boring,' trilled one of the girls ahead. 'And you know what Simon's like. Honestly, it was such a hoot.' Their careless confidence made Isobel feel simultaneously beneath notice and a public spectacle.

Half an hour later, with Gillian and Cynthia, she retraced her steps, looking for ninety-six. 'Come in, dears,' urged Lambert's wife, whom it was becoming increasingly hard to despise. She wore a striped cover-up thing that didn't quite, allowing glimpses of rolled flesh. The girls followed her through a black and white tiled hall into a gleaming kitchen. The pool shone a glamorous turquoise beyond french doors. Gillian was struck dumb. Cynthia, maddened by the sight of water, began ripping her clothes off in the middle of the floor. 'Regular little water baby,' smiled Lambert's wife, as they emerged into the glare. Isobel was about to apologise for her sister when she noticed three lounging figures at the far end of the pool. Relentlessly, Lambert's wife marched her towards them. 'This is my Penny,' she announced.

Lambert's daughter – minus panama hat, white gloves and a good deal else – raised her sunglasses and issued a languid, 'Hi.'

'This is her friend Fiona. And this' – the dark-haired boy stirred in his deckchair in minimal acknowledgement of etiquette – 'this is Simon, Simon Ratner.'

'Gidday,' said Rats, but with such a well-mannered smile Isobel almost failed to recognise him. 'Small world, eh.'

Chapter 5

'SO CAN I?' DEMANDED ISOBEL FROM THE DOORSTEP, HEART IN her mouth. Her mother was installed in a deckchair on the baking patch of concrete. She wore shorts and a skimpy top, and had a pot of tea at her feet and a cigarette in her hand. She spent a good deal of time in this state, as if New Zealand were an antipodean Debworth Cove. Buster snored in her shade, barely registering Isobel's presence. She clicked her tongue, compelling him to open one eye.

'I don't see why not, darling. We'll have to speak to Daddy, of course, but if Mrs Lambert knows them and Penny's going too, and as long as you're back at a reasonable hour, well . . .' She petered out – she never petered out – and her eyes closed again.

Isobel steeled herself. 'What's a reasonable time?'

'If it's a dance, I'd say eleven, eleven-thirty's reasonable, wouldn't you?'

It was so reasonable, Isobel couldn't speak for several minutes. When she did, she threw caution to the wind. 'I need a new dress.'

'We'll see,' consented her mother, without opening her eyes.

Isobel turned away. Was her mother undergoing some sort of personality change as the result of emigration? Was this what people meant by a new start? And where did that leave Isobel?

That Friday evening her father parked their car – a green Morris Oxford which he repeatedly told them compared unfavourably to the black Austin A90 they had left in England – outside Edser's, the town's only department store. Its window contained an artistic display of hedge trimmers, posthole diggers and chainsaws. Isobel had never been shopping in the dark before – it lent an exotic air to what by day was a charmless main street. They bought a pop-up toaster like the Lamberts', three candlewick bedspreads in lemon, pink and blue, and three matching lampshades. They left Isobel's father in Hardware selecting tools capable of converting their clay pit into a flourishing garden, and Gillian and Cynthia fidgeted while Isobel and her mother flicked through the racks in Womenswear.

'Hmmn,' frowned her mother. 'Well made, I suppose, but . . .'

'Horrible,' despaired Isobel. 'Hopeless.' A dowdy assistant shot her a look.

'We'll just have to make you something,' decided her mother, and Isobel followed her gratefully into Fabrics.

At a place down the street, her father handed over money for three milkshakes and two teas with the air of a man who knew how to give his family a good time. Isobel noticed too late that this establishment was a hub of youthful activity and not the place to be seen with one's parents. She organised her expression into one of pained aloofness. Vast rumbling cars cruised by, leaving a wake of blaring music and exhaust fumes. Her sisters and parents stared. Isobel contrived to look at nothing.

'Gidday,' said a voice. The beetroot sandwich girl.

'Hello,' said Isobel, refusing to dismantle her expression.

'You shopping then?'

'Yes,' said Isobel. She wished the girl would go away.

'Aren't you going to introduce us to your friend, darling?' said Isobel's mother. Isobel winced at the *dahling*.

'My name's Jackie?' said the girl. 'Isobel's in my form at college?'

'That's nice. Why don't you come and visit Isobel after school one day. She'd like that, wouldn't you, darling?'

Isobel snatched up the aluminium beakers and returned them to the counter. Really, if her mother were to persist in this chronic good mood, life would become unmanageable.

Rats gunned his car down the Midwinters' drive at horrifying speed. 'How're going?' grinned Clyde from the front seat, and Isobel hardly dared speculate why he was there. At the end of Balmoral Road, the railway crossing lights began to blink and the bells to ring. 'Plant it,' ordered Clyde. The car shot under the lowering barrier, clipping its radio aerial, and the boys whooped.

'Where's the dance?' asked Isobel, feeling she should contribute. And then, 'Where's Penny?'

'Penny?' echoed Rats. 'Oh, Penny.'

'Yeah, Penny,' said Clyde, swigging from a bottle. ' 'Bout time you cracked her, mate. Bet she'd go off.' Isobel caught their joyous grins in the flash of a street lamp. They headed down a street of houses like packing cases. Rats screeched to a halt and jammed his palm on the horn. A girl teetered out of a nearby house, waving and yoo-hooing. 'Lurlene,' explained Clyde. 'Ratsie's on a promise.'

The girl slithered onto the back seat and smiled generously at Isobel. They drove out of town, Rats deafening them with incoherent blasts from the radio. Clyde offered Lurlene a cigarette and lit it for her. Then after much cursing and slopping, he handed over two paper cups of something frothy. 'Oooh, lovely,' said Lurlene. 'Fallen angels.'

Isobel sipped. It was milkshake with a jab of alcohol. 'Drink up, girls,' encouraged Rats.

At last he swooped through a gate and bumped across a paddock. Dozens of cars were parked around a brightly lit hall, and figures clustered at the door. Clyde said, 'Over there, mate, under the cabbage tree, gotta water the horse.' He got out and Rats followed.

'How d'you meet Gil?' inquired Lurlene, twitching her hair. Isobel told her, omitting any reference to Penny out of respect for Lurlene's feelings. 'So Rats must have told Clyde I was coming to the dance and . . . '

Lurlene was impressed. 'He must really like you.'

Isobel wondered if she dared believe it. 'Do you think we'll go in soon?' She wanted to show off her new dress.

Lurlene shrugged and sipped. 'Depends on the boys.'

'N'other one, girls?' said Clyde, getting back in the car.

By the time she picked her way across the paddock to the hall, Isobel was overrun by fallen angels. The lighted doorway danced before her eyes and she clung to Clyde. 'Hey,' he said, grabbing the paper cup and flinging it into the darkness, 'can't take that in.'

She blinked like a creature that had dug itself up in the wrong spot. Five or six men and their equipment were crammed onto a tiny stage, sweating out a ballad. Couples of all ages, even children, were shuffling around the floor. Others sat at tables covered in white paper, with candles in bottles, dishes of crisps and overflowing ashtrays. A man in a crooked bow tie leaped onto the stage. 'Now, ladies and gentlemen and the rest, take your partners for the Gay Gordons.' He leaped off to a chorus of catcalls and whistles.

'Hello there, Clyde,' said a woman in a dress from Edser's. 'How's your Aunty Joan keeping?'

'Good, thanks, Mrs Everett.'

'This your new girlfriend?' She peered at Isobel at close range. 'Come on then, dear.' She gave Isobel's hand to the red-nosed man next to her and grabbed Clyde's for herself.

'I don't know what to do,' Isobel yelled above the pounding from the stage. The man shouted something back and caught her in his arms. Before she'd recovered, he flung her on to the next man. 'Enjoying yourself?' this one shouted, seizing her waist authoritatively. 'Hot, eh?' gasped the third, lunging for her hand. 'Haven't seen you before,' bellowed another. His face was streaming, his nylon shirt clung to his chest. On and on it went until just when Isobel thought it would never end, it did.

She felt the imprint of a hundred hot hands on her body as she and Clyde moved around the hall, people calling out to him as they went. He was well-mannered and personable with those who addressed him as Clyde, but as Gil he was boisterous, uncouth, his speech almost incomprehensible to her.

'Ladies and gentlemen,' shouted the man from the stage, 'take your partners for the supper waltz.'

Clyde – or rather, at that moment, Gil – let out a 'Bloody oath,' and steered her onto the floor. She had learned ballroom dancing by letting her father propel her around the lounge to *The Music of Joe Loss and His Orchestra*. To her surprise what she had learned worked equally well with Clyde. But as the melody neared its end, he confined their activities to one corner until they were practically dancing on the spot. The music stopped, a side door opened and with Clyde grasping her hand, they led the stampede towards the supper table. With the crowd pressing forward, Isobel grabbed the closest items. 'Want tomato sauce with your sav?' bawled Clyde. His paper plate was loaded to buckling point. A starving elbow caught her in the ribs, a ravenous foot pinned one of her own to the floor. Finally, they beat a retreat to chairs backed against the wall.

'Try this,' said Clyde, offering something with his fingers. 'Roast wild pork. And venison. Bet you never had this back Home.' She nibbled dutifully.

'Want some pavlova and fruit salad?' he asked eventually. He returned with two more paper plates buried under a snowdrift.

Spoonful after spoonful of sweet meringue and cream melted on her tongue. Her eyes fluttered with bliss. Clyde belched and rubbed his stomach. 'Won't wait for tea,' he said, getting up. 'Have a few spots in the car.'

Men all over the hall were having the same idea. They grouped around each car, now and then tipping back their heads. Isobel stared up at the cold moon and shivered. Dimly she recalled breathless English nights when the air lay like a quilt. 'That tree,' she said, pointing, 'what's it called?'

'That one? Cabbage tree. Hey, Rats, give us the beer, you bugger,' and he rapped on the car window. Isobel considered what her mother did to cabbage and swallowed disappointment. Clyde was rocking the car. 'Come on, you randy bugger, give us the beer.' An arm and a bottle appeared. Clyde thumped the arm and seized the bottle, then steered Isobel towards a grassy bank.

'Is she Rats' girlfriend?' she asked, staring up at the face in the moon and wondering what nationality it was.

Clyde swigged. 'Lurlene? Shit no, Lurlene's, well . . .' He seemed struck by a fleeting sense of propriety. 'Lurlene's the town bike.'

Late developer. 'I'm going to learn to drive,' she said.

He exhaled smoke. 'Teach you, if you like. Rats'd lend us his wagon, if I twist his balls. Or I might buy one, especially if he's going to take all bloody night.'

His arm had found its way around her shoulder with refreshing ease. He smelled sweet and strong, and when he kissed her, she inhaled Old Spice, beer and tobacco. He put the bottle down, and minutes later, a hand on her breast. To her great relief, he did not snigger.

'Hey, Gil.' Rats emerged from the car, followed by Lurlene struggling with her skirt. 'S'all yours, mate.'

It was stuffy in the car and the windows were fogged. When they paused for breath, Clyde mixed another fallen angel. Her skin was singing where he had touched her. She wanted to slow down, take stock, not rush like this through thin air at a thousand miles an hour. It was like being in a plane tearing into the unknown. But he was stroking her leg, and his hand had found the gap above her stocking. *Stop him*, said Rita, *you've got to stop them.* The hand reached her pants. Still kissing, he slipped a finger inside her pants and then to her utter astonishment inside her. No point stopping him now. His kiss ran out and his breath rasped in her ear. She opened her eyes, glimpsed his arm working like machinery. It was nothing like kissing or stroking which resembled the bliss of pavlova. This was grim, driven. She closed her eyes, searched for his mouth. They kissed, and they stopped kissing, and they kissed again, and all the time the arm cranked the finger in and out of her until something gripped her abdomen like steel and she was a machine too. She heard herself panting like she had in the Gay Gordons, wanted to shout *stop* and *don't stop* but the words couldn't find her mouth and on and on it went until just when she thought it would never end, it did.

Chapter 6

The Monday after they met Jackie Beetroot in the Comet Milkbar, she called to Isobel before their first class and patted an empty chair. And Isobel sat, knowing that since she could no longer have Rita, she ought at least to pretend to have a best friend. So now she and Jackie went to the Comet most days after school and giggled at the boys from St Pat's and told each other everything. Although Isobel did not tell Jackie what Clyde had done to her in Rats' car because she was sure no other sixth former in the southern hemisphere – possibly the entire Commonwealth – had discovered this phenomenon, not even Andrea Dodds, for all her convent education. Even more significant was the fact that once a boy had shown you how, you could do it yourself. It was like having a passport to your own secret place and you could go there as often as you liked, without money, new clothes or parental permission. And while you were there, you never ever thought of England.

One day during break, the girls had a discussion – hypothetical, Isobel was entirely sure – about sex before marriage. 'You wouldn't go all the way with Clyde, would you?' someone asked Isobel, wide-eyed.

'Why not? We wouldn't be hurting anybody.' She was already establishing a reputation as a freethinker.

'What about . . . you know . . . falling for a baby?'

'You don't have to, you can be careful,' she said airily. She had no idea how but was sure Clyde would know. She dimly recalled, too, some piece of wisdom about only nice girls getting caught which, in spite of Mrs Janola's judgment, surely guaranteed her own safety. In any case, the rules of reproduction didn't apply to her; they were merely a maternal phobia. She was incapable of ever harbouring another human being.

'Don't you want to save yourself for your husband? Your husband's your destiny,' said someone dreamily.

They moved on to glory boxes. 'Granny gave me half a dozen tea-towels. And I've got my other gran's china and some ribbon-edged blankets.'

'I got some sheets the other day in Edser's sale – lemon flannelette with rosebuds. What's in your box, Isobel?'

She gaped. What did a sixth former want with sheets? 'Nothing. I mean, I don't have one.'

'Maybe they don't have them in England,' said Jackie, as a best friend should.

'No,' said Isobel, rallying. 'Anyway, you don't *have* to get married, and even if you do, you've got to have a *life* first.'

It went without saying that you were not going to have one afterwards. You only had to look at her mother, who sometimes paused long enough between chores to tell the girls of the days Before Daddy and I Married, of well-heeled admirers with MGs, underwear stitched from parachute silk, and crucial responsibilities in a munitions factory. And how it had all come to an end When Daddy Came Home from the War. Isobel refused to devote *her* life to emptying ashtrays and forcing small children to eat brussels sprouts and speak properly. She hated Domestic Science, it was a Fact of Life.

Yet her mother, too, seemed to be enjoying a change of heart. She sat down more and smiled more. Meatless meals were delivered to the table more often and with an air of bravado, and Isobel suspected her sheets were no longer being changed on the firm weekly basis of top to bottom, bottom in the wash. Her mother also seemed to be best friends with Lambert's wife; she had not had friends in England, only relatives and neighbours. The two women chattered and giggled the way Isobel and Rita had, and sometimes Isobel found herself joining in.

That first summer, the sun forgot how to stop shining. One evening, as her mother was soliciting Isobel's opinion on curtain fabrics, she nodded outside in mock disapproval, 'Look at those little monkeys.'

Gillian was holding the hose as Cynthia ran squealing through the spray. Gillian started guiltily when her mother tapped on the window then, catching her mother's expression, grinned and turned. Water cascaded down the glass and her mother reeled back with a yell of laughter. She watched from the step as Cynthia played the hose on Isobel and Gillian, then without warning, Cynthia turned the hose on her mother. She dropped her sodden cigarette and rushed at Cynthia, screeching like a mad woman. The girls shrieked. The older two grabbed her arms and she wailed as water rained down. She got free and lunged for the hose, and they all stood transfixed as water gushed overhead in a glittering column and fell with a sigh on their father coming home from work.

'Hey, watch it!' he shouted, briefcase over his head. He wheeled away, his face black.

Isobel's mother stood dripping by the door, suppressing laughter, then followed her husband inside. The words *hard day* and *bit of moral support* carried down the hall as Isobel surveyed her homework. She opened her new history textbook. 'Ever since the late nineteenth century,' she read, 'New Zealand has commonly been considered the most dutiful of Britain's daughters.' She gritted her teeth and pressed on. She hated history, there was no point in it. It was the past, dead and gone.

Her mother's voice sailed down the hall, amplified by shock. 'Oh, David, that's not fair. The girls are . . .'

Isobel slipped from her room and flattened herself against the wall outside the lounge door. Shut up, she told her thumping heart, this is an intelligence-gathering operation.

' . . . what we came here for, isn't it?' Her mother was attempting to hold her ground but her voice wobbled danger-ously, her guilt seeped through the wall. 'I'm home every day when they get in from school, and . . .'

A paternal rumble, like distant thunder.

'Oh, David, that's not true. Anyway how would you know, you're not here, we hardly ever see you.' A pitiful outflanking manoeuvre. Isobel pressed her back and palms to the wall.

' . . . bit of gratitude . . . pull your weight . . . running round like wild animals.'

'David . . .' A muffled sob. Isobel clapped a hand over her own mouth.

'Old Lambert . . . the dance . . . that girl needs . . .'

Isobel fled. She was innocently studying North Island climate patterns when her mother burst in without even a token knock. 'I've a bone to pick with you, young lady.' She looked anything but guilty now. 'Mr Lambert told Daddy that Penny didn't go to that dance, so who exactly were you with?'

'I never said Penny.' Isobel was instantly battle-alert.

'You certainly implied, and Daddy and I thought . . .'

'I told you – I went with some people.'

'Don't raise your voice to me.'

'I'm not. You're calling me a liar.'

'You're only sixteen and we must know where you are and who you're with. You can't go gallivanting . . .'

'Seventeen. Nearly seventeen. And I wasn't gallivanting!'

'We trusted you, Isobel. We let you stay out till midnight.'

'Half past eleven. It was half past eleven!' Rage surged

through her as if it had come all the way from England in the tea chest. 'Get out and leave me alone! Get out of my bloody room!'

Buster trotted up, brown eyes brimming with concern.

'It's not your room, my girl,' growled her father from the doorway. 'The money I bring home pays for it, and as long as you live in this house you'll do as you're told. And that includes language.'

'Bloody's not language! You treat me like a child.'

'Well, she certainly sounds like one, doesn't she, Daddy?' Her mother made a point of catching her husband's eye. 'You can stay in here until you decide to tell us the truth about that dance.' And she shut the door a split second before Isobel could slam it.

Isobel let loose a stream of abuse, flung open the door and charged down the hall, Buster yipping at her heels. It was a tactical error – her father appeared in the kitchen ahead, her mother cut her off by coming from the bathroom behind. '*I said . . .*' began her mother with terrible emphasis.

Isobel feigned indifference to the menace in her mother's eyes. Buster flattened his ears and put his tail away.

Her father addressed his wife coldly over Isobel's head. '*Now* perhaps you see what I mean, Irene.'

'Back to your room!' ordered her mother with renewed commitment. 'Do . . . as . . . you're . . . told.'

Strategic withdrawal was the only sensible tactic if there wasn't to be unthinkable loss of life. But . . . *into the valley of death rode the six hundred . . .* her mother was blocking her retreat. 'Let me get past,' said Isobel, wishing her voice wouldn't quiver like that.

'Get to your room!' Buster growled and bared two neat rows of teeth.

'You'll hit me.'

'I will not, you stupid girl. Now do as you're told.'

The blow caught Isobel on the side of her head, making her

ears ring. As she shut the bedroom door, her mother was trying to pry Buster's jaws from her ankle.

The chimes of Big Ben heralded the BBC news as Isobel crept past the lounge door. She prodded the puffy flesh under her eyes in the bathroom mirror and splashed on cold water. The newsreader was booming about hostilities in the Middle East when she slipped back again. Her father was slumped in his chair, dusted with cigarette ash. Her mother stabbed a needle in and out of an old sock. They were like something dead behind glass in a museum.

Back in her room, she seized a blank sheet of paper. *Dear Rita*, she scribbled furiously. She wrung out a few sentences then flung the balled-up paper to the floor. It was like shouting all the way to Woodland Rise. Rita had forgotten her, Rita might as well be dead.

Dear Dan, she began again. But hope curdled immediately to despair. Dan was dead *and* going out with other girls. And Isobel was alone on the summit of Mount Tauhara, the hills rolling back and back to England.

Inert on her bed, she heard the small change from her father's pockets hit the bedroom floor, the settling of bed-springs. The Curse of the Midwinters. She had known all along it would be no different here, that it would always be them murmuring in the dark together, her alone in this narrow bed – their daughter, their colony. She tried prodding her anger back to life but it refused to stir. The dateline cut through her, creaking and tearing. She wailed into the pillow.

She scuttles along the landing under the looming picture. The bad dream comes with her. She reaches for the doorknob. Her parents' bedroom is dark, the bed miles across the floor. 'Whatever do you want now?' The voice issues from the single bump in the bed. Isobel shivers at the door. The bad dream is fading, her mother's sharpness has done the trick. Now she has no reason for being here, no excuse. 'Nothing,' she says in a small, middle-of-the-night voice. 'I don't want anything.' 'Back

to bed then, at once,' orders her mother, then, as a concession
when Isobel turns to go, 'Think of fairies in a bluebell wood.'

Isobel heard scratching. She opened the door and Buster
trotted in. She hauled him illicitly onto the bed and let him lick
her salty cheek, then fell asleep with him snoring in the crook
of her arm.

Chapter 7

THE FOLLOWING SATURDAY AFTERNOON AS SHE SAT AT HER dressing table desultorily inventing new hairstyles, the doorbell rang. 'Izzy,' bawled Cynthia. 'It's that boy.'

Isobel yanked out the pins and dragged a comb through her hair. She put her hands in her lap and waited for the flush to fade from her face and the blood to stop pounding in her ears. By the time she reached the kitchen, her mother had ushered Clyde in, reprimanded Cynthia for lack of manners, and was offering a choice of tea or coffee. 'Hello,' said Isobel, to distract Clyde's glittering eye from her mother's rear view as she bent for cups and saucers. This official home visit was a masterstroke.

'Clyde's offered to take you out for a driving lesson, darling. Mr Midwinter's going to look into getting a car for me,' she told him. 'Then I'll be having lessons too.'

'Take you out, too, if you like,' he said, offering her a cigarette. 'Just say the word.'

'Well, that's very . . .' She exhaled so competently, Isobel had to avert her eyes.

'A van,' said Isobel, when she saw it at the bottom of the drive. Rita's mum had issued humorous warnings about boys in vans.

'A Traveller,' said Clyde. 'Hop in. No, the driver's seat.'

They bunny-hopped through sleepy streets. Penny Lambert sped by in her mother's red Mini, a tanned elbow out of the window, but Isobel didn't care – she was driving, and it was like water-skiing and the Gay Gordons and that other thing, unstoppably easy once you got the hang of it.

'Touch it,' he said. 'Go on.'

After the driving lesson and the movies – an outing for which he had cleverly asked and received maternal permission – he had driven down a rutted track behind the railway station and nosed into a small clearing in the gorse. They had kissed for some time, but then suddenly the teeth of his unzipped fly were glinting in the half-light like crocodile jaws. 'Go on, touch it.'

Teddy stands in the greenish gloom, asking with his eyes, asking so it's easy to say no, as girls are meant to. He thinks for a minute, then slips into her sleeping bag with her. 'S'all right, Mum says we're like brother and sister.' She decides to ignore the thing poking into her leg.

'Delicious, Irene,' booms Uncle Max, in the twilight outside. 'I thought I used a little too much thyme,' says Isobel's mother, in a pleased voice. Murderers, the lot of them, thinks Isobel, seeing rabbit's-blood sky and a pile of picked bones and gravy. Teddy snuffles then breathes evenly. She doesn't know where the idea comes from but slowly, carefully, so as not to wake him, so he'll never know, she lifts her nightie right up to her chest. She gasps at the sweet shock of him, her Isobel edges melt like milk and honey . . .

'Touch it,' said Clyde. It was taking all her strength to resist the force of his hand on hers. Rita's moral code had not even contemplated this turn of events.

'I don't want to.' It was war again.

Clyde released her hand, lit a cigarette and glared into the dark for several unpleasant minutes. Then he regarded her through narrowed eyes. 'I do it to you.'

Ah, so it had nothing to do with wanting, it was to do with fairness. She took a deep breath and plunged in. He gasped. She gasped. All the geography texts in the world could not have prepared her for this. When she took her hand away, she thought, good, I'm glad, it wasn't a snake after all but another ladder. Clyde wasn't glad, though. On the contrary, he seemed more agitated than ever. 'Touch it again,' he pleaded. 'Move your hand up and down on it. Come on. Other girls do.'

She braced herself and reached out again. *Half a league, half a league, half a league onwards, Into the valley of death rode the six hundred* – and she imagined the faces of the six hundred girls who did pressed up against the window. Penny Lambert, she was sure, was not among them. Penny had no need to be fair. And as for Lurlene, she apparently did this sort of thing and more for pleasure.

In the end it resembled driving – wrestling with the gear stick, Clyde issuing urgent instructions – but was rather less thrilling. 'Not so fast, faster, that's it, harder . . . aaargh.' And considerably more messy. Mess had not been something covered by Andrea Dodds' little book. Clyde slumped as if he had been punctured, and she began dabbing with her handkerchief in a housewifely manner.

Chapter 8

THERE WAS WILD HOOTING, A METALLIC GRAUNCH, AND THE face of a man unnaturally close. Isobel was paralysed in the driver's seat. 'Didn't you see me?' he said, once he had extricated himself. He seemed surprised rather than furious. 'You all right?'

She struggled out of the passenger door, as he had done. 'I looked before I pulled out, honestly I did.'

'Don't cry, I don't think there's much damage, you just gave me a scare.'

They peered down the inch-wide gap between the two cars. His own big cream shiny vehicle wore streaks of pea green from her mother's Ford Prefect. She gasped and covered her mouth. 'They'll never let me take it out again. Oh bugger blast shit bugger.'

The man looked taken aback. But when her tears started again, he put an awkward arm around her. She sniffed on his lapel, then pulled away, wiping her nose on the back of her hand. Tears stained her school uniform. 'Sorry.'

He had kind crinkles around his eyes. He was broad rather than tall, making him look as if nothing could knock him down, the opposite of her father, whose height made him seem to sway in the breeze a long way off. 'It's only money.' The man said this rather proudly. 'Look, I live just along there. Why don't you come in for a cup of tea before you drive again. I'll move the cars.' When she didn't budge, he added, 'My wife'll be there. You can ring home if you want.'

She waited by a stone wall in front of a two-storey house while he parked both cars in the drive. 'Do you think . . . if there's any damage, could I just pay you for it and you not tell my parents?' A dim hope. However kind, he was an adult and would almost certainly take the view that her Parents Must Be Informed.

'Not a mark on the Prefect. Solid old cars.' He rubbed his own paintwork with a finger. 'Should come off with a cut and polish. Come on, I'll get Jo to put the jug on.'

The path around the side of the house ended in a wide lawn. A copper beech rustled overhead, dappling the grass, and small children were playing in the far corner. Isobel was dismayed to find herself close to tears again. A woman rose stiffly and came towards them, trowel in hand. She had filthy bare feet and looked at the man as if trying to work out who he was. 'Put the jug on, Jo, we need a cup of tea. Adrian Glossop,' he said, offering Isobel a hand as if she were a business acquaintance rather than a tearstained girl. 'And this is my wife, Jo.'

'Hello,' said the woman neutrally, and disappeared inside the house.

'She's a great gardener,' said the man, as if something required explanation. 'She forgets the time when she's out here. I'll show you where the phone is.'

The rooms were large and shabby and the telephone had to be unearthed from a heap of gardening magazines. 'Hello. It's me.'

'Where are you? I'm waiting for the sugar.' Her mother was

peremptory rather than frantic. Isobel had not been gone as long as she feared.

'I met a friend from school at the dairy. I'm in Springfield Road, won't be long.' She hoped the man and his wife could not hear. Lies were more undignified than a gymslip and sensible shoes; lies told the truth about how little freedom you had.

'I wish you'd ask first, Isobel. I might need the car.' Isobel swallowed a scathing retort – as if her mother had anywhere to go.

The woman had put a tray on the grass and was pouring tea. 'Why didn't you use the other pot, the nice one?' the man was saying in an undertone. 'And we really must get some garden furniture, you can't expect people to sit on the grass.'

'But the grass is lovely,' said his wife, holding out a cup to Isobel, who had not known a man could care about such things. Two small grubby boys ran up for biscuits, then away again.

'You live in Balmoral Road, do you? I'm a real estate agent,' said Adrian Glossop. Isobel sipped her tea. 'Been out here long? Do you know anyone?' She could hardly be bothered conversing. She wondered if this profound sense of peace was actually shock.

Adrian Glossop drained his tea and asked his wife if she knew where the car polish was. She sighed and followed him into the house, extremely reluctantly, Isobel sensed. She lay back on the grass, staring up at the house. She was on the lawn at Woodland Rise, the air soft on her arms, the sunshine mild. Gillian and Cynthia were murmuring beneath the apple tree. There was the distant shsh-whirr of a mower, her father warbling in the raspberry patch – *Home, home on the range* . . . The world still beyond the fence, still whole and undreamed of.

'It's all come off, no worries.' She blinked up at the male figure. She struggled upright, disoriented, and said the first thing that came into her head. 'We don't have a garden anymore.'

'Come back whenever you want. Jo's always home and I'm in and out. Here.' He brushed her back and plucked something from her hair. She felt in danger of leaning into him again and stiffened her spine. 'Jo! Isobel's going. I've told her to come and see the garden whenever she wants.'

'Yes,' smiled his wife vaguely. 'It needs a lot of work.'

'Thanks,' said Isobel. 'For the tea, and . . . everything.' And the peace of the Glossops' garden lingered as far as the Midwinter letterbox.

'How is a ball different to a dance?' she said, swinging her legs from the kitchen table.

Clyde shrugged. 'When's your old lady home?'

She looked down at the skirt which ended closer to her bottom than her knees and recalled her mother's face shining above folds of green velvet, her father tall and handsome in black. 'I'd never have gone to a ball in England.'

Clyde was propelling her up the hall. She managed to kick the bedroom door shut as he pulled her towards the bed. Cynthia was asleep, Gillian reading, those were the rules. 'They'll never give me enough for anything decent to wear,' she said, as Clyde burrowed in her underwear. 'But I've got nearly ten pounds saved.' She gasped as he slipped two fingers inside her.

'Come on,' he moaned. 'You know I love you. You'll like it. It won't hurt or anything, not after all this. It makes my balls ache, not doing it. It's bad for me.' His fingers marked time with the familiar litany.

Eventually he sat up and appeared to be studying the record sleeves on her wardrobe door. 'If you won't, I'll go out with someone who will.' She felt a tremor of panic and he sensed his advantage. 'We can use French letters and stuff. Come on.' He launched himself at her again.

'I don't want to.'

'Why not?' His jaw was rigid with annoyance, his hand in her pants again.

'Want a drink of water,' called Gillian.

'Get one,' gasped Isobel.

'My turn,' said Clyde.

'Not here.' She shoved him down the hall.

The basement was cool and dark and she used the time to plan her Thomas Hardy essay. The second he went limp in her aching hand, her parents' car changed gear at the bottom of the drive. Something glistened on the dusty floor and she stepped forward, covering it with her bare foot. 'Clyde's asked me to a ball.'

'What on earth are you doing down here, are the girls all right? Good evening, Clyde.' The outing had clearly not been a success. Her father headed for the BBC news. 'Your first ball, darling, how lovely.' A memory of green velvet flickered across her mother's face.

Next morning, she called Isobel early to the telephone. 'A letter for you too, Miss Popular. And how many times do you have to be told *not* to let the dog on your bed.'

Isobel put the letter in her dressing gown pocket, refusing to satisfy her mother's curiosity, and headed for the phone.

'Hope you don't mind me asking,' said Adrian Glossop. 'Jo's idea really, she thought you could do with the money. I said you might already have a job after school, but I said I'd call and . . .'

'You want me to babysit for you?' asked Isobel. 'When?'

Chapter 9

'DOESN'T SHE LOOK A PICTURE, DADDY? TURN ROUND, DARLING.'

Isobel paraded the length of the lounge, listening to the rustle of her gown and the hiss of air through her hairdo. Petals, the hairdresser had decreed, then clamped each one with a hairpin and armour-plated the lot with spray so that the result bore little relation to anything in the natural world.

'Shantung,' declared her mother with satisfaction. 'See how it changes colour when she moves? We dyed the gloves to match, and look at the rose, Daddy. It came out very well, I think, don't you? Oh, do you remember going up to London for the do at the Dorchester?' She sighed painfully but he was deep in his newspaper.

Adrian Glossop stood at the door in a bow tie. Isobel stood next to him and her parents inspected them until there was a collective fidget and everyone reminded themselves he was ten years her senior and had a wife waiting in the car.

'So kind of you both to pick Isobel up,' said her mother. 'Say thank you, Isobel. Goodness me' – she raised an eyebrow – 'that face certainly doesn't go with that pretty dress.'

Isobel almost dragged Adrian from the house. 'You do look very nice, Isobel,' he said, holding open the car door.

'Lovely,' echoed Jo.

Clyde was waiting outside the Majestic, unnaturally plastered down to the same extent that Isobel was unnaturally teased up. His eyes glittered approval. 'Here,' he said. He handed her a bottle of screwdriver and two more of beer which they proceeded to hide in and around her gown. There had been no bottles concealed in her mother's gown at the Dorchester, she was sure. They joined Rats and Lurlene inside. 'Cracker dress, Iz,' said Lurlene.

'Shit hot,' said Rats. 'Pass the bottle, Gil, you bastard.'

'You look nice too,' said Isobel. In fact, Lurlene was blinding. Her dress seemed to be made of oven foil and flashed as she moved. Things also flashed at her ears, throat and wrist. Her eyelids glittered. Her hair, piled higher and woven even more elaborately than Isobel's, was liberally sequined. Gazing around the ballroom, Isobel realised identical conversations were going on at every table – women paying minute attention to each other's appearances, men desperately trying to counteract the effects of their own by barking and knocking the tops off bottles. The band struck up an over-confident rendition of *Blowing in the Wind* and Isobel waited for Clyde to ask her to dance. Inspired by the music, Rats lit a paper napkin from the candle in the bottle, held it to his dinner-suited crutch and farted. Even Isobel was impressed by the resulting sheet of blue flame.

She danced twice with Clyde, once with Adrian who propelled her around the floor at a gentlemanly distance, once with Rats' knee wedged between her thighs, and once with Lurlene, Isobel being the man. In between, she sipped screwdriver from a soggy paper cup. When Rats eventually said, 'C'mon, girls, we're off for a burl,' she was relieved. She waved to Adrian and Jo as she crossed the floor. They piled into Rats' car, Lurlene in front fondling Rats' neck, Isobel and Clyde in the back. 'Where are we?' she asked some time later.

'Airport,' said Rats, gunning the car at a gravelly incline. Runway lights converged in the distance and a windsock flapped turgidly. Isobel was reminded of it minutes later as Clyde nudged her hand towards his fly. 'You look terrific tonight,' he whispered. 'Your hair and dress and everything. Let's go all the way. Come on. Please.'

Rats appeared over the front seat. 'Everybody out.'

Isobel folded her arms against the wind, inhaling sea spray and jet fuel. Black waves crashed behind her. She stared down the runway, outlandish in her gown and hair. Gusts filled the wide skirt, whistled through her petals and on through the chain link fence where bits of rubbish flapped. 'Jeez, Isobel! What'ya doing?'

The configuration of the car seats had changed. Rats and Lurlene were squirming on what appeared in the gloom to be half a bed, and Clyde was pulling her down on the other half. Rats could be heard negotiating Lurlene's oven foil. 'Come on,' urged Clyde. The car rocked as Rats and Lurlene manoeuvred into position. 'You know I love you.' Lurlene moaned, Rats grunted. There was a general air of urgency. 'You'll like it. Lurlene does, don't you, Lur?'

Isobel slammed out of the car and stomped along the bank, tears stinging her eyes. Maybe her mother was right after all, maybe she was *completely* unreasonable. Why else did she persist in stopping Clyde from doing what he so badly wanted to do? Particularly since it was what her mother most dreaded her doing, and the girls at school believed she was doing already. Yet there was something about Clyde's threats and cajoling and sulking which provoked the same reaction as her mother's demands to lay the table, speak properly, say thank you, made her want to defend to the death some desperate little bit of territory she couldn't even name. Her mother had to be stopped, the way her father said Hitler had had to be, but why was she making an enemy of Clyde? Why did she risk driving him away when his blue eyes and his grin were all that kept her here, and the past on the other side of the world where it belonged?

He was urinating on the far side of the car when she got back in. Lurlene was repairing her makeup in the rear mirror and shot Isobel a curious look. 'Don't you ever let him? Shit, he must really like you.'

Chapter 10

THE SHOES WERE THE SORT LURLENE WORE. ISOBEL COULD NOT remember exactly how they had found their way from the shelf to her feet and wondered if Clyde were trying to transform her into a girl like Lurlene, a girl who would. She had tottered around Edser's Footwear section under his glittering eye, said thank you when he handed her the box, and half hoped to lose it on the way home.

'Look,' she said, wobbling across the lounge where both parents were installed in their armchairs. Clyde grinned from the doorway.

Her mother gave Isobel's feet a fleeting inspection. 'Very generous of you, Clyde. I hope you said thank you, Isobel. Look, Daddy, what Clyde bought Isobel.' Clearly she disapproved of their spiky heels and pointed toes, equally clearly she had decided it would be bad manners to say so. The newspaper rustled minimally. Isobel veered in the general direction of the door, uncertain whether she could make it down the hall, let alone onto the street. Maybe Lurlene would give her lessons.

'Isobel!' Her father's roar threw her off balance and she clutched at the doorpost. He crushed the paper in his lap and rose abruptly in a shower of ash. *Who says it's dormant just because it hasn't erupted for ages?* 'Get them off,' he thundered.

Astounded, she flicked the shoes from her feet. They lay on the carpet like the football when Teddy brought it in from the garden. *I bet you do it, you two.* The other three watched Isobel's father as if a troll had emerged from under a bridge. 'Here, young man.' He jabbed the shoes at Clyde. 'Take my advice, return these to the shop and buy Isobel something more suitable.'

Clyde's bewilderment stung her. 'You can't say that! They were a present. How can he say that?' She appealed to her mother's code of etiquette.

Her mother looked equally stunned. 'If Daddy thinks . . .'

'What's wrong with them? Why can't I keep them?'

Isobel stood her ground as her father loomed over her. His face was black, his tone icy. 'In my day we only gave presents like this to *girls we slept with*.' The last four words were loaded with contempt.

When she kissed Clyde goodnight at the front door, she apologised for her father. He shrugged, the shoes under his arm, as if it were no more than he expected from fathers.

Her mother came to her room, pausing long enough to knock but not long enough to be granted or refused entry. 'Sit down, Isobel. I need to talk to you. Daddy and I think you're seeing too much of Clyde.'

'You don't think he's right about the shoes, do you?'

'He's unsuitable, Isobel.'

'You don't, do you? I know you don't. You think I ought to be able to keep them, don't you?' She would go on seeing Clyde whether they let her or not; she was more anxious to get her mother to declare her real beliefs.

Her mother examined her fingernails. 'Mrs Lambert knows him. He left school at sixteen and didn't go to university and he's much too old for you, Isobel.'

'*You* like him, I know you do. I've seen you.'

Her mother was startled. 'Daddy and I think it's best if you don't see him anymore.'

She mistook Isobel's long silence for resignation. She reached out, although her hand failed to make it all the way to her daughter's. 'Oh, darling, you'll get over him. In my day, you know, we used to get around in a crowd, not just attach ourselves to one person. Spending too much time with someone . . . of the opposite . . . at your age . . .' She was turning pink and her tone had become several shades brighter. 'When you're married . . . I hope . . . all the right responses . . . but till then . . .'

She rose from Isobel's bed with a deep sigh as if something crucial had been accomplished. 'Good. I'm glad you understand, darling.'

Chapter 11

ISOBEL WENT TO A PARTY WEARING HER FIRST TAMPON. 'IS IT mod, the way you dance?' inquired a boy with a furious pimple on his neck.

'You haven't pushed it up far enough,' hissed Jackie, when Isobel edged back onto the couch. Isobel grimaced and plucked at the frill of her Fast and Easy Mary Quant dress, wondering what Clyde was doing and with whom. She was only here because Jackie had begged and bullied, and because it provided a convenient alibi for time with Clyde later in the evening. The boys had baby faces and limbs that behaved as if they were still in school shorts. They tipped back glasses of beer down one end of the room, while the girls – all giggles and inexpertly applied makeup – congealed at the other. Sheer boredom compelled Isobel to drain her glass of horse's neck and, in spite of the tampon, go in search of more. A boy found her the right bottle on the kitchen table. He was ludicrously young and reeked of bad aftershave but he made conversation without reference to England, and after a decent interval kissed her. She kissed him back. He knocked a bottle to the floor but did not take his mouth away. People came and went, clinking bottles and glasses, and guffawing, and the kissing went on. They kissed until the universe was one giddy kiss with Isobel spinning inside it.

From a long way off someone shouted, 'Break it up, Mum and Dad'll be back soon.' Isobel and the boy fell apart. Dizzily she found her coat. His mouth was waiting at the gate and only a long blast on a horn startled her out of his arms. She ran towards Clyde's car, slammed the door, and saw the boy leap from the path of Clyde's screeching U-turn.

'Slow down,' she demanded. He overshot Balmoral Road and careered up the hill. 'I told them I'd be home by twelve.' His eyes were narrowed, his jaw rigid, his hands clenched on the wheel. He looked as if he might crack or explode. 'It's not what you think . . .' He yanked the car into a lay-by at the top of the hill and cut the motor. 'I don't even know his name, I won't see him again, honestly.' She was bemused by how much he seemed to care.

He lit a cigarette, inhaled hungrily and glared out of the window. 'Any other girl, that'd be it,' he said through gritted teeth. Then his demeanour crumpled. 'You're different, I knew that right from the start. We should get married.'

She nearly laughed out loud. Then because something else was called for, she kissed his cheek. His bristles were a shock – the boy's cheek had been smooth as her own. 'I'm not even allowed to be seeing you,' she reminded him gently. 'They'd never let me get married.' Married . . . *Like Mummy, inside and out* . . .

He looked at her for the first time since she got in the car 'Engaged then . . .' She kissed him again and reached for his zip.

Ten minutes later at the top of the drive she sank onto one of her father's heaps of clay and began to weep. Maybe her mother was right, maybe she would get over Clyde, maybe there was a chance, a slim one, that she would be able to face the dateline without him now. She got to her feet and went indoors.

'Isobel?' Her mother looked up with a tremulous expression, and Isobel knew it was safe to sink into her father's chair. Buster careered across the carpet and threw himself at her, licking and wagging.

'Why aren't you in bed?'

'I don't sleep until you're safely in.' Isobel refrained from observing that coming in was usually the most dangerous part of the evening. Her mother released a sigh that sounded almost like a sob and blew her nose. 'Daddy's just gone. He's been talking about work all evening. Things aren't going at all well.' She seemed to have forgotten she was speaking to her daughter. 'He doesn't want me to see Pat Lambert anymore.'

'What?' She would write – *Dear Clyde, I'm sorry but* . . .

'Things haven't worked out the way Daddy was promised. He says he's been stabbed in the back and he doesn't want me to have anything to do with Pat.' She pulled herself out of her reverie. 'Did you enjoy the party, darling?'

'It was all right. It's just . . .' She glanced at her mother and considered, just for a moment, presenting her dilemma over Clyde the way she had once presented daisy chains and powder paint pictures. Instead she said, 'But it's not fair, Pat's your friend.' *Nothing's fair, Izzy.*

Her mother got to her feet and began picking up cups and straightening cushions with the air of someone who had gone too far. 'Some good news tonight, darling – Aunty Iris and Uncle Max are coming out next year. That'll be nice, won't it.' When Isobel did not respond, she said, 'I know you miss Clyde, darling, but there'll be other boys and you're an attractive girl.' This startled them both.

As they headed for the door, her mother frowned into Isobel's bag. 'What are those?'

'You know what they are,' said Isobel, pushing the tampons out of sight.

'You shouldn't be using those, should you, darling? They're

for married women, surely?' She looked so pink and flustered, Isobel was tempted to ask for details, yet temptation was quickly followed by a pang of pity. What was wrong with her mother? What compelled her to avow beliefs any sensible person would scorn – that a plug of cottonwool was a sign of moral decay, a process hastened by accepting a gift of footwear? It was just as she had always suspected, Domestic Science killed off your brain cells. And Isobel switched off her bedside lamp determined never to see Clyde again.

Chapter 12

SHE WAS ASTONISHED WHEN HER CAMPAIGN TO GO STRAIGHT from the lower sixth to university was victorious. Astonished and, every morning as the train doors closed with a desolate thunk, aghast. The first day she had even hoped to see Penny at the station, but no doubt Penny had been whisked to university by more glamorous means. As the train rattled towards the city, she could not help wondering if her victory didn't have certain characteristics of a defeat. For a start, she had absolutely no interest in a tertiary education, it had simply been her only presentable excuse for leaving school. And then, there was the unsettling memory of that skirmish in the kitchen.

'You see,' she had said equably from the sink, where she was washing up Saturday lunch dishes unasked, 'I know what I want to *do* – Geography and English – and the vocational guidance lady said you didn't *need* another year at school for those, so . . .'

Parental silence as Isobel wiped down the benches and draped the dishcloth over the taps in the prescribed manner. She hoped her mother was noticing. 'Penny's not going into the upper sixth,' she remarked, seating herself at the table and hoping to convey that this was a casual family conversation rather than an ambush. 'Neither's Jackie.'

She and Jackie had been to see the vocational guidance lady together. She had asked which number came next in the series 3, 7, 15, 31, then told them they both showed aptitude for university study. Isobel had been put out, though, to learn that Jackie had returned to the vocational guidance lady and been encouraged to apply for a scholarship for disadvantaged girls. Surely the aptitude for claiming disadvantage meant you were not disadvantaged at all?

'So the upper sixth would just be a waste of time really,' Isobel concluded blithely.

'David,' began her mother. 'David, what do you think?'

'Mmm?' He was slapping his pockets.

'About Isobel going to university?'

'Well . . .' He found his cigarettes on the table in front of him, lit up and exhaled smoke with a thoughtful frown. He pushed out his bottom lip and stretched his legs full-length under the table. 'She's a girl.'

'Daddy and I never had the chance of an education, you know,' she told Isobel for the millionth time. 'I left school at thirteen and went behind the counter in Perks, and Daddy left at fourteen. He had to get all his qualifications at evening class. In our day . . .'

Well, it isn't *your* day anymore, Isobel wanted to yell. But she kept her mouth shut, determined to stick to diplomacy. Her mother went on, this time addressing her husband who was gazing into the middle distance through a haze of smoke. 'I think she should have a chance, don't you, Daddy? The chance of an education we didn't have?'

Isobel felt stirrings of unease.

'She's a girl,' said her father again with the suggestion of a shrug. 'She'll get married.'

Her mother's back stiffened and her tone became edgy.

'Your life doesn't stop when you get married. You still have a brain, you'd still like to be able to use it. I want all the girls . . .'

Her father narrowed his eyes. 'You'll be talking about going out to work next, Irene.'

'And why not,' demanded his wife angrily. Under the table, Buster growled and her father hastily retracted his legs.

'So can I?' said Isobel, who was beginning to feel it was she who had been ambushed.

'*May I*,' snapped her mother. 'Speak properly.'

'For crying out loud,' cried Isobel loudly.

'Well,' said her mother, pursing her lips and raising her eyebrows, 'she'll never get a man with a tongue like that, will she, Daddy?'

She was expelled into the racket and grime of the city station. She plodded up Lambton Quay remembering the first time she had seen it on a shopping trip with her mother and Pat Lambert. Its hunched buildings, sparse traffic and dowdy pedestrians made her think of an old lithograph – of a Scottish city, perhaps, although she had never seen a Scottish city. Now she had lost all basis for comparison, forgotten what cities were meant to look like. She turned into Cable Car Lane. Young people – all alarmingly confident and attractive – were converging on the ticket office, the really charmed ones in groups of three or four. She bought her ten-trip ticket in an undertone, determined not to give herself away as a first-year.

She and Jackie had set out the day after school broke up to do the rounds of government departments. The man in Defence had said come back tomorrow when the boss would be there, he was crook today, something going round. The man in Motor Registration had said, 'Okay, girls, you're on.' They had giggled behind ceiling-high shelves of manila files, looked up the car numbers of everyone they knew, and every Thursday for ten weeks, taken home little brown envelopes containing nine pounds fifteen shillings and threepence. And in the tea breaks,

Isobel had learned to smoke – a preparation for university every bit as vital and daunting as university entrance.

She took an outside seat on the cable car and it heaved its arthritic way up the hill. The city spread out below and Isobel wanted to dive from her seat and pierce the smooth skin of the harbour. Up and down cars nudged alongside each other as if for some awkward mating, and she found herself nose to nose with passengers in the outside seat of the other car. She studied a pair of pinstriped knees, a dowdy pleated skirt, some self-assured brown thighs. The motors were silent. Nobody budged or spoke. Fifty or so people were clinging at a mad angle to the side of the hill in a silence so excruciating it enveloped the cars like fog. Isobel was scared she might scream or fart, more scared someone else might. She stuck a cigarette in her mouth and lit it with unconfident fingers. The filter flared spectacularly. She gasped and flung it away. Pinstriped knees grunted and swatted the smouldering thing from his lap. She grimaced an apology and struggled to light a second cigarette. The cable car gave a lurch. The matchbox executed a devilish flip and emptied itself down the track, and Isobel gasped again, this time with a mouthful of smoke. It filled her lungs, her head, her entire being. As the car rumbled on up the hill, she was wracked by coughing so violent, she thought she might die before she could get off.

'Hi,' called Jackie, her 'i' piercing the dense fug of the caff. While Isobel had been learning – not so proficiently, as it turned out – to smoke, Jackie had been perfecting her vowels. 'This is Roger, this is Keith, that's Trish, this is Melody, and that's Ross.' The introduced faces smiled and immediately blurred into one dull wholesome entity. Isobel knew exactly who they were – they were the gang her mother wanted her to get around with. Well, she was trying, wasn't she? She had not seen Clyde for months and months, and though she was still plagued by dreams of falling, the days passed without undue hazard.

'What subjects are you doing?' inquired the boy on her left. He had a turned-up nose, lush hair and eyelashes, and was dismayingly sincere. Penny and her friends were occupying their usual table, the one around which the entire caff seemed to orbit. The boys over there were less sincere, more confident – clearly you could not be both. When they weren't guffawing, Penny's boys sprawled and sucked on cigarettes with sardonic grins, while the girls flapped their hands and wore a lot of camel.

'. . . and Pol Sci,' Isobel concluded without enthusiasm. The subjects she really needed – Triumphing Over Your Family, Stages I, II and III; Becoming Popular and Confident, An Introduction with Compulsory Field Trips – were not on offer.

'Have you got all the books yet?' Ross or Roger was asking. 'They told me in Whitcombe and Tombs . . .'

Penny greeted Rats with squeals of glee. She wore a camel suit and a string of pearls, and her sunglasses were perched on her bouncily coiffed head. As usual, Isobel pretended not to recognise Rats. 'Sorry, what?'

'I said, are you English?' repeated Ross or Roger, who probably never sprawled.

'No?' said Isobel as if he were mad to think so. 'What subjects are you doing?' She forgot to listen to his reply.

'I'm doing Education, Psychology and Anthropology,' Jackie informed the table at large. This high-minded list, Isobel supposed, was the result of more encouragement from the vocational guidance lady.

'I'm doing History . . .' offered Melody.

'Yeuch,' said Isobel and turned her back. 'Where do you live?' she inquired of Ross or Roger.

He looked gratified. 'Eastbourne. Have to stick it out this year but I'm going flatting next year.'

'Me too,' said Isobel with instant enthusiasm.

Jackie looked sceptical. 'They won't let you.'

'They won't be able to stop me.'

Melody patted baby-fine hair. 'I'm in Helen Lowry Hall. My parents live in Masterton.'

'What's it like?' said Isobel. Maybe her parents would be fooled by a hall of residence.

Melody looked wistful – 'Not as nice as home' – and Isobel disregarded her from then on.

Penny snapped the gleaming catch on her pigskin bag. 'Hi,' she said with a flap of her hand as she glided past Isobel's table. Isobel expelled some gratifyingly expert smoke in her direction.

Sometime later, Ross or Roger leaned towards her and said, 'Do you want to come to the movies Saturday night?' It was the thought of his future flat that made her say yes.

He arrived at Balmoral Road in his father's car, extended a hand to Isobel's mother and said, 'How do you do, Mrs Midwinter. I'm Keith Barraclough.'

She beamed on his good manners. 'How do you do, Keith. So nice of you to come all this way to pick Isobel up, isn't it, Isobel? Her father would have dropped her off normally' – Isobel gaped, her father had never dropped her off anywhere – 'but today's been one of those days. We had to go and watch Cynthia swim – that's our youngest, she's a Wellington representative . . .'

'Is not,' muttered Isobel furiously. 'Am so,' said Cynthia from the dining room.

'. . . and we have friends arriving from England tonight. I thought Isobel might want to stay in and see them but . . .' She beamed again to indicate Isobel had made the only sensible choice. 'And what subjects are you doing at university, Keith? Do sit down.'

It occurred to Isobel that her mother had never beamed at Clyde, that when she had smiled at him at all it had been with head cocked, cigarette at a jaunty angle and a certain challenging glint in her eye. The suitable boyfriend material was listing his chosen subjects. If he had said Outer Mongolian

Culture and Language, her mother would have continued to beam, but he didn't, he said, 'I'm going into law.'

Her beam took on a distinctly hungry aspect. 'Your father's a lawyer, is he?'

'No, Mum is. Dad's an architect.' She struggled visibly with awe, envy and bewilderment, and Isobel mentally slapped her for her own good.

Keith said, 'She's nice, your mother,' as he sailed the Rover down Balmoral Road. So it didn't come as a complete shock when, three hours later as they emerged from *The Sound of Music*, he said sincerely, 'Fabulous, wasn't it.'

'Stupid, I hated it. Families aren't like that.' He looked startled then hurt, and it occurred to her that his family and possibly everyone else's was exactly like the Von Trapps', that only the Midwinters were cursed.

He pulled up the Rover on the foreshore. There was a minute's respectful silence then he lunged and fixed his lips on hers. 'Arrh,' she cried, wriggling off the handbrake. The inexpert lip friction continued. Across the harbour, the lights of the city winked as if it were all an enormous joke. His hand quivered on her breast but it lacked conviction so she flicked it off. It returned, and she let it stay for a second or two to make up for *The Sound of Music*. She sighed. Mistaking it for a sign of pleasure, Keith withdrew his lips and said, 'Can I put my hand up your skirt?'

'*May* I.'

'What?' The hand in question trembled on her knee, sprouting black hair in as fine condition as that on his head.

'You *can*,' she said ferociously. 'But you *may not*.' She took a last disgusted survey of his earnest features then flung herself from the car.

'Where are you going?' he cried. 'I'm sorry.' Whether for his grammar or his intentions was unclear. 'You can't go, Mum's made up the spare room.'

If he thought an argument for maternal convenience would

89

save the day he was sadly mistaken. He was still pleading when she slammed the door and strode off down the parade, praying he would not pursue her. The wind was sharp and insistent, reeking of dead seaweed. As she headed towards the station, a Saturday night stream of cars emitted hoots and catcalls, and one even slowed and opened a door. She scowled at its occupants, making it clear she wasn't asking for it.

The wind moaned down the deserted platform. She glanced into the black gulf where the rails ran and flinched. Too late. She sat on a narrow bench, but no matter how hard she gritted her teeth and stiffened her shoulders, there he was, looking the way he had looked as he came towards her out of the fog that day. She retreated to the barren waiting room, but he was in there too.

'Isobel?'

'Danny?'

'Dan,' he scowls, looking again like someone who would make her mother cry on Christmas Day.

They walk side by side down Aldenham Road, making their own small space in the fog. 'Where were you going?' she asks.

'Your place.' He is uncharacteristically sheepish.

'What for?' She tries imagining her mother's expression as she opens the door.

He kicks a stone and it disappears off the edge of the world. 'Often do,' he says.

'No you don't. What do you mean?'

'I watch your house. I stand behind that tree on the other side of the road. I've seen you playing the piano, and dancing in your bedroom, and once your mother yelled and you ran out of the house crying and I know you haven't got a boyfriend so will you go out with me on Saturday night?'

The station at the other end was equally desolate, and she was the only passenger to get off the train. She stared at the spot where Clyde and she used to park and strode off down the platform. But the mile of Balmoral Road ahead of her was dark and haunted and she was terrified Dan would step out from behind a tree. Without thought, she plunged into the warmth of the call box outside the dairy, and found her fingers on the dial.

'Mrs Fisk? Is Clyde home?' *Other girls do. I'll go out with someone else.*

There was a sniff of recognition from Clyde's aunt. 'Hello, Isobel. Yes . . .'

'Can I speak to him, please?' *Clyde, it's me, I miss you. I think this feeling is called missing you.*

'He's asleep, dear,' Clyde's aunt informed her coldly. 'He went off on the couch after tea and I wouldn't like to wake him.'

'It's important.' She hated the way her voice shook.

'Yes dear, I'm sure, but he needs his rest.'

For a moment they each contemplated Isobel's helplessness, then she hung up. With every step she pounded another portion of Joan Fisk's corseted anatomy. As the trees of Balmoral Road closed in around her, a car slowed. She strode on. It pulled up and the passenger door opened. 'Want a lift, Isobel?'

She fell into the passenger seat. 'Oh Adrian, thank you. I went out with a boy my mother thinks is *suitable* and the film was stupid and then . . .'

He fumbled with the cigars he had bought from the dairy. 'Why didn't your father pick you up or your mother lend you her car? Surely they don't want you walking up here this time of night. I wouldn't if you were my daughter.'

But I'm their daughter, and that makes all the difference. Besides, she understood perfectly why her mother would not help her escape on a Saturday night when she herself was trapped at home. She leaned into Adrian's warm upholstery.

'Don't you see Clyde anymore?' he inquired politely.

Rather than explain, she said, 'I just phoned but his aunt wouldn't let me speak to him. She's doesn't like me, she sent me an anonymous letter last year. It said, "I know what you and Clyde are doing and if it doesn't stop, I shall be forced to tell your mother." She signed it, "A well-wisher." But it was her.'

Adrian pulled up at the bottom of the Midwinters' drive. He was shocked. So was she – she had told nobody about Joan Fisk's letter, not even Clyde. 'How bloody cowardly.'

She swallowed and stared into her lap. 'And it's not even as if we were, you know . . .'

He threw his cigar out of the window, went to put an arm round her then thought better of it. 'You're not happy, are you, Isobel?'

Happy? She was offended – she *managed*. She offered a minimal thank you for the ride and ran up the drive.

Jailhouse Rock boomed from the sitting room and Buster was sulking under the kitchen table. Isobel slunk up the hall.

'Izzy,' boomed Uncle Max. 'They said you wouldn't be home. Look, boy, look who's here.'

Isobel heavily retraced her steps as Elvis gave way to Acker Bilk and *Stranger on the Shore*. Her father and Aunty Iris and Aunty Iris' cigarette holder were rotating in an exaggeratedly dignified manner on a small patch of carpet. Her mother was slumped in a chair, gasping pleasurably. There was a half-familiar blur in the corner that began unwinding from a chair then changed its mind. 'Hello,' she said reluctantly to the room in general.

Uncle Max clapped a murderous hand on her shoulder. 'Izzy,' said her mother with unnatural goodwill. 'Izzy,' chimed her father and Aunty Iris.

'I thought you were staying the night at Keith's,' said her mother. 'Such a nice boy,' she added for Aunty Iris' benefit. 'Doing law.'

'Boring,' snapped Isobel. 'And stupid.' The adults exchanged amused glances. Teddy stared and she felt precious years slipping away. She gripped the back of a chair.

'Try to get his hand up your skirt, did he?' inquired Uncle Max, reasserting his own.

'Max!' scolded the women.

'We went to *The Sound of Music* and he liked it.'

Her father threw back his head and burst into song. 'Old Lambert's a prick and . . .'

'David!' laughed her mother. '. . . and his promises bullshit.'

Isobel escaped Uncle Max by slipping to the floor. Her father scrabbled destructively in the record pile. *Let's Twist Again*, despaired Isobel.

'Let's twist again!' roared Uncle Max, doing unspeakable things with his hips.

Teddy stood over her and for a confused second she thought he was asking her to dance. In the kitchen, she slouched against the bench and he sat backwards on a chair. She was too proud to stare. 'You at university or what?' she asked, in a manner intended to show how little she cared.

He shook his head. 'Nah. You are though.'

She radiated confidence and success. 'Couldn't wait to leave school.'

He grimaced, screwing up his freckles. 'I dreaded it. No idea what to do next. Still haven't. That's why I said I'd come here with the olds.' His air of affectionate detachment from his parents was demoralising and she turned away to fill the kettle.

'Got a boyfriend then?' He was putting on that accent, he had to be.

'Oh, not him tonight, he's just . . . I used to have a proper one. He was twenty, nearly twenty-one. His parents have a farm and Clyde's going to have it one day.'

'Banned him, did they?'

'*They* couldn't stop me. I decided, because Clyde wanted . . .' What had begun as a brag risked ending up lame and childish.

Teddy raked his hand through red curls that were almost ringlets now. 'Yeah, well that's what blokes want, innit.'

'Not that,' she muttered, embarrassed. 'I meant, married. He said we should get married.'

'Said you'd marry a farmer.'

She banged cups on the table. 'Well, you were wrong, weren't you. Why does everyone go on and on about marriage?'

'Listen to your accent. You sound like a New Zealander.'

She spooned instant coffee into cups. 'I am. You don't have to be born here, you can . . . make yourself one.' She paused, spoon in mid-air – England and childhood, time and distance were so hopelessly muddled that surely it meant she was a New Zealander.

He pulled a face. 'Old-fashioned here, though, innit. Behind the times.'

'No,' she declared hotly. 'You know what they call England? The Old Country, because it's old and dead.'

Aunty Iris and her mother came into the kitchen. 'Arguing already, you two?' They exchanged amused glances as her mother put out more cups. 'He's nearly driven me mad, Iris. On and on about work and old Lambert. I can tell you' – she adopted a stage whisper – 'it was touch and go at times. One evening I couldn't stand it a minute longer, I said, "David, you've got to get a sense of proportion – you're not putting a man on the moon, you're just making dog biscuits." I think it brought him to his senses, I really do.'

'Well, all that's behind you now, Irene,' soothed Aunty Iris.

Isobel escaped down the hall as Chubby Checker trumpeted again from the lounge. She only realised Teddy was following when she pulled up at her bedroom door and he banged into her. It was his warmth, his Teddyness – her arms tightened before she could stop them, so quick as a flash, before he could think she wanted to hug him, she pushed her tongue in his mouth. She'd show him old-fashioned!

He pulled away, wiping. 'Don't be daft, Iz.'

Uncle Max flung open the lounge door. 'Come on, young Isobel. Come and twist again, like we did last summer.'

'Nobody does that anymore,' she told him through gritted teeth.

He hauled her into the room. 'Show me what they do then,

94

come on. Should be getting in practice, you know. Lots of this sort of thing on the ship.'

'Max,' warned Isobel's mother, coming in with a plate of cheese and pineapple cubes on sticks.

'Have to get yourself in trim for Swinging London, girlie,' panted Uncle Max, gyrating in front of her.

'Max!' cried her mother. 'Max, we haven't told her yet.'

Chapter 13

ISOBEL MET HER MOTHER FOR LUNCH BETWEEN LECTURES AND they queued in Kirkcaldie's coffee lounge with brown plastic trays. Her mother wore a hat. 'What would you like, darling? My treat, to make up for everything.' Isobel helped herself generously as if sausage rolls and buns would make a difference. Her mother clicked her tongue over an inefficient teapot. 'Did you speak to anyone yet, darling, about universities back Home?'

'Not yet,' said Isobel through a ham roll. She despaired of the way her mother used that word – England *had* been home until they had forced her out of it. She would not go back, she would not plead. These were Facts of Life.

'The next few months'll fly by, darling. You really ought to make inquiries.'

Isobel gulped tea and changed the subject. 'What did you buy?'

Her mother looked animated. 'Nothing much. A little dress in a sale, and some sandals. Max and Iris said it's very hot in the tropics. And I thought . . . oh look, isn't that Jackie. Hello, Jackie. And Roger too, how nice.'

'Keith,' mumbled Isobel.

'Do join us,' invited Isobel's mother. 'You're looking well, Jackie. Are you enjoying university?'

'Yes, thank you,' said Jackie. 'You're looking well too.'

'How are you?' Keith asked Isobel warily.

'Fine,' said Isobel.

'Well,' said Isobel's mother. 'Isn't this nice?'

They all agreed it was. Jackie watched Isobel's mother cut her egg sandwich in two before eating it. Keith watched Isobel chew until Jackie told him to come with her and get her some coffee.

'Sorry, darling,' said Isobel's mother. 'It must be difficult for you with Jackie and Keith, I didn't think.' She nibbled through an asparagus roll and a lamington. She wiped the corners of her mouth. When the other two returned, she spoke of going Home, of Isobel's father's wonderful new job, of the ship and its splendid facilities, and how excited the girls were. Everyone was excessively polite, everyone except Isobel's mother seemed to be waiting for someone else to leave.

When she went to the Ladies to reapply her lipstick, Jackie hissed, 'I've got to talk to you. Keith, I've got to talk to Isobel. About . . . you know.'

'Oh,' said Keith, regretfully. 'Right. See you later then.'

'See you tonight,' said Isobel, thrusting her mother's parcels at her.

'Keith borrowed his father's car,' continued Jackie urgently, 'it's a Rover . . .' – 'I know,' said Isobel – '. . . and we went for a drive through the Wairarapa and round, and we did it. At Otaki Forks. It was lovely. Otaki Forks, I mean, not . . . I can't stop worrying about being pregnant and I knew you'd know.'

Isobel was gratified. Not since school had anyone consulted her on such matters. 'I don't think it was the dangerous time,' Jackie went on, wringing her hands. 'My period finished the day before so it wasn't right in the middle.'

'Hmmn,' considered Isobel in a tormenting manner.

'So I must be all right, mustn't I? Oh God, I'm never going to do it again. Imagine having to get married now, just when everything's starting to go right.' She meant university, her new vowels and the right way to deal with an egg sandwich.

Isobel made her wait. 'I expect you're okay,' she said finally.

'Thank God.' Jackie sagged in her chair. 'I told Keith you'd know. I told him you were an expert. I don't think he believed me.'

Isobel poked her doughnut. A wild possibility flickered in her fingertips.

Jackie bit into louise cake. 'Weren't you scared of getting pregnant when you were with Clyde? Imagine if you'd had to . . . you know, get married. You wouldn't have been able to finish university or go back to England or anything.'

The possibility reached Isobel's brain and the force of it almost stopped her heart.

'I want to go to the place we went with Rats and Lurlene,' she said, getting into the Traveller on a Friday evening when her mother believed her to be babysitting for the Glossops. 'That place by the airport.' She fondled Clyde's neck as she had seen Lurlene fondle Rats'. 'I want to do it.'

The Traveller veered over the centre line. 'Tonight?' They drove the rest of the way in silence.

Two or three other cars were on the bank overlooking the runway. 'This do?' said Clyde, cutting the motor. She patted his leg and the bloated windsock convulsed. In the back seat he took off her pants and she felt a fleeting shiver of excitement. But what followed was as impersonal and absurd as having something repeatedly inserted and retracted from her ear. Or someone else's ear. She was embarrassed for him – it was such a small thing to have wanted so badly. Maybe Lurlene was right, maybe it did mean he really liked her. She made noises like

Lurlene had, and Clyde certainly liked those. He wrenched himself away to reach for something in the glove box. 'Don't stop,' she whispered, and he groaned and sank back.

When he got out for a leak, she smelled sea spray and jet fuel, recalled the feeling of the wind in her gown and hair. She would not go back. Campaigns were defeated by bad maps, lives lost. She would not be a lost life.

'Girls never forget their first,' declared Clyde sentimentally, stopping the car a safe distance down Balmoral Road.

'No,' she said, 'they don't.' *I love you Isobel. Please don't go . . .*

'And I really love you.'

Of course we love you, you stupid girl. 'Good,' she said. 'Now it's time I met your parents.'

Chapter 14

IT BORE NO RESEMBLANCE AT ALL TO THE IDEA OF FARMHOUSES Isobel had gleaned from Ladybird books. Built of sickish green brick, it squatted close to the road on a barren lawn, looking like a public toilet in the middle of nowhere. As the car scrunched to a halt by the back door, a hand tweaked a net curtain. Clyde sucked on his cigarette like a condemned man and seemed reluctant to get out of the car. A little grey woman in a flowery pinafore was flapping her hand from the back door as if she were similarly disinclined to leave the house.

'Mum,' muttered Clyde, stubbing out the cigarette. It was the closest he came to an introduction all weekend.

'Bring her in, Clyde, bring her in,' trilled Mrs Giltrap. 'Hello, dear, how nice. Clyde says you're English. Did you know the town's laid out like a Union Jack? The jug's on. Would you like to wash your hands? The bathroom's through there, there's a guest towel, the apricot one. We'll have a nice cup of tea then I'll get tea on. Jacko's killed a lamb, he killed a lamb specially, Clyde, isn't that nice? When you've had a cup of tea, Clyde can show you round, won't you, Clyde? I hardly see him these days. How's Aunty Joan, Clyde? There's the jug. Do you have milk and sugar? I don't suppose so, you're so slim, isn't she slim, Clyde?'

'Jeez, Mum.' Clyde eyed a plate of scones overloaded with jam and cream.

'Offer them round, Clyde. And wash your hands. You'd better move your car out of the middle of the drive. You know Jacko doesn't like it. Here, take the tray.'

Clyde ignored all these instructions. His mother put the loaded tray on the kitchen table and Isobel sat. 'Not here, dear, the front room.' She struggled with the door. 'Jeez,' sighed Clyde. He wasn't Gil at home, yet he wasn't Clyde either; he was nobody Isobel knew. They passed into a room shrouded in brown blinds, net curtains and drapes. For the first time in her life, Isobel reflected admiringly on her mother's taste.

'Pull out the nest of tables, Clyde,' said Mrs Giltrap. 'There now, isn't that nice?'

The scones were. But biting into her second, Isobel understood they were a ploy to keep her stationary and speechless while Mrs Giltrap regaled her with excruciatingly detailed accounts of people she would never meet. Mrs Hirini and the mongol daughter she wouldn't part with even though there was a lovely home not thirty miles away. Mrs Pardington and her three sons who were so good on the farm *and* helpful to their mother. Mrs Giltrap took a scone for appearances' sake and delicately spat bits of it into Isobel's lap while passing seamlessly on to Mrs Dudley who found time to bottle in spite of a senile father who wet the bed and wandered.

A Toby jug leered at Isobel from the china cabinet. A plate on the wall commemorated the 1954 visit to New Zealand of Her Majesty and Prince Philip. They looked young and hopeful. The fire screen depicted a lady in a crinoline stepping from a horse-drawn carriage, leaning on the arm of a man smirking in lace cuffs. A relentless line of waves threatened to break over the mantelpiece. As Isobel stared at this grim patch of ocean, Mrs

Giltrap's voice and the deathwatch tick of the clock receded. She seemed to be staring not at a picture but at a chink in the wall through which escape seemed distinctly possible.

A sound from the kitchen halted Mrs Giltrap in mid-sentence. Clyde's expression shifted. 'Move your bloody car,' someone growled, and Clyde exited fast. His mother made a flurry with the crockery as if caught in some forbidden act. Even the clock seemed to falter. Isobel reached for a sixth scone.

Clyde was gone for an appallingly long time. 'Had to give Jacko a hand in the shed,' he said when he returned. The sharp blue light had gone out of his eye, and Isobel considered a seventh scone.

'You're bleeding on the carpet,' fussed his mother, although the drops were swallowed up by rampant foliage. She handed plaster, Dettol and cottonwool to Isobel, as if she were now Clyde's mother.

'Needs a wash,' decided Clyde, peering at a cut between his thumb and forefinger. He locked the bathroom door. 'Quick,' he said, turning on the tap with the injured hand and unzipping his fly with the other. Isobel worked efficiently, avoiding the eye of another lady with a toilet roll up her skirt. Once she judged him past caring, she manoeuvred the end of his penis over the handbasin.

'Clyde?' chirruped his mother. 'Isobel?'

Isobel, content that Mrs Giltrap was quite incapable of imagining what was going on on the other side of her apricot bathroom door, kept going. 'Just coming, Mrs Giltrap,' she called, as Clyde jerked labour-savingly down the plughole.

A man in a grubby woollen hat and checked shirt was carving a joint of meat at the kitchen bench. He glowered at Isobel and resumed peeling off slices. Clyde's mother was scraping the bottom of a meat tin on the stove top and shaking in flour in an inept manner. 'Smells lovely,' said Isobel, hopelessly stuffed with scones.

The man looked at her again, then at his wife. 'Where's the potatoes and pumpkin?' His monotone electrified the air in the overheated kitchen.

'In the oven, Jacko,' twittered Mrs Giltrap.

'How many times d'you have to be bloody told? Get the vegetables out of the bloody oven before I start carving the meat, otherwise they're burning hot and the bloody meat's stone cold. Do you want us all to burn our bloody mouths?'

'No, Jacko,' said Mrs Giltrap into the oven.

Isobel glanced at Clyde, expecting a flicker of irony if not outright rebellion. But he hovered by the table, wordlessly allying himself with his father against scalding vegetables, cold meat and foolish women. Isobel stepped towards Mrs Giltrap, now poking at roast vegetables with a fork. 'Do you have a fish slice? You'll get all the lovely crunchy bits then. Have you got a dish or shall I put them straight on the plates?'

Clyde and his mother ate in silence. Now and then, they glanced at Isobel as she rattled on, reaching for green beans and carrots and gravy, as if it were she who was dangerous. The man put his unsanitary hat beside him on the table and surveyed the plates. 'Where's the silver beet?'

Mrs Giltrap put down her fork and said, 'Oh.' Isobel half expected her to look for the missing vegetable under the table.

'Where's the bloody silver beet?' The growl intensified and Clyde too put down his fork.

'Jacko, there's pumpkin and carrots and potatoes and green beans, and I thought, really, that was enough, don't you?'

'I don't grow a garden full of bloody vegetables to have them rot in the ground. I plant them, weed them, water them. Least you can bloody do is . . .'

'I've never had silver beet,' said Isobel brightly. 'What's it like?' The man weighed her question for treason. 'May I have more beans? They're lovely.'

'How long you been out from the Old Country then?' said the man.

Clyde and his mother resumed eating and something like a conversation ensued. The man interrogated Isobel about England – annual rainfall, unemployment and emigration rates – then supplied his own answers, expanding at length with particular reference to the stupidity and arrogance of Poms. Isobel smiled to show she was used to being teased. Mrs Giltrap was also smiling. 'Isn't this nice?' she remarked to the bamboo wallpaper. As she gathered up the plates, the man was ranting about the Common Market and the likely fate of New Zealand should the bloody English decide to join. Isobel opened her mouth to tell him what she could remember of her father's view, then pushed in bottled peaches and ice-cream instead.

'Common bloody Catholic Market.' He cleaned his bowl with his finger and stabbed it at Isobel. 'Italy, France, Spain – all bloody Catholics. Won't be happy until they've taken us over.' Isobel smiled. 'No laughing matter. Half the bloody state servants in this country are Doolans. Only a matter of time before one of them's prime minister and then, look out.'

Since the peaches and ice-cream were finished, Isobel said good-humouredly, 'You make it sound like a plot.'

He clenched his fist and lurched at her. Clyde started and pushed back his chair. 'Too bloody right it's a plot. Don't you give a damn about bloody history? It's bloody apathy like yours that'll let the Catholics take over and then . . .'

Isobel was still smiling when something – it could only have been Mrs Giltrap's slippered foot – came down hard on her sandalled toes. It stopped her smile but it was too late to stop the man. His face swelled and darkened, he sounded like an aircraft winding up for take-off. Clyde and his mother stared straight ahead, eyes glazed. Eventually he pulled on his hat and stood up. 'Call me for coffee,' he growled, and walked out.

Mrs Giltrap sagged and Clyde began whistling tunelessly through his teeth. 'We don't argue with Jacko,' said Mrs Giltrap. 'If you argue, he goes on longer.'

Isobel got up to stack dishes at the sink to hide her flush. 'I wasn't arguing, it was a discussion and it was interesting,' she lied.

'Not to those who've heard it a hundred times before,' said Mrs Giltrap with surprising dryness. Clyde picked lamb off the bone as if it had nothing to do with him, and Isobel crashed the meat tin into the sink. It was almost better when the man was there, when the tension was palpable and Clyde and his mother on their guard. The relief when he left shamed them all.

'He gets violent,' said Clyde, sucking on a furtive cigarette behind a hawthorn hedge. His father forbade smoking in close relatives.

Isobel was bewildered by Clyde's resignation. 'But you've left home. They can't tell you what to do when you've left home.' She sat on the cool evening grass, and squinted into the sun setting behind a row of pine trees. Black and white cows flicked their tails and chewed across the fence. She tried another tack. 'What do you mean, violent?'

'Knocked this tooth out.' He waggled pink plastic and wire on the end of his tongue.

'When?' Isobel didn't believe him.

'Couple of years ago. He goes berserk. I took off and he came after me, laid me out on the road outside Pardingtons'.' He shrugged.

'Didn't you hit him back? Didn't you want to kill him?' He looked at her as if she were a long way off. 'You have to fight back. You can't let them win.' Her limbs tingled with the necessity of it.

He shrugged again, threw his stub into the hedge and said, 'Told you, he goes berserk,' as if that's all there was to it.

The sunporch was narrow and chilly. Isobel waited on the thin mattress for Clyde who had said goodnight in front of his parents without even a kiss. Gingerly she reached for the nearest blind. It shot from her hand and clattered upwards. The country sky was pitch black, except for the stars twittering like Mrs

Giltrap. Her heart thumped – *he goes berserk*. She saw the man lean across the table, eyes narrowed, and the hectoring voice drummed in her ears. She saw Clyde laid out – wasn't that what they did to dead people? – on the hard road, a bleeding hole in his mouth. The Curse of the Giltraps. Yet poor Clyde had no concept of warfare, no idea of freedom or how to fight for it. She would have to show him, it was up to her. She longed to go to his room and take him in her angry arms. Her stomach churned.

She crept across the sitting room and felt her way around two sides of the hall. Noises were coming from the main bedroom, gruesome farmyard noises. Her stomach churned again. She fell through the bathroom door and threw up violently in the toilet. She fumbled in the lady's crinoline for toilet paper to clean herself up, then wobbled back to the sunporch to wait for Clyde. But he never came.

Chapter 15

'I'LL TAKE YOU HOME AGAIN, IRENE,' CROONED HER FATHER inaccurately. He was scouring a greasy meat tray before he had dealt with the cutlery, an oversight not lost on his wife and oldest daughter at the kitchen table. Isobel's mother sipped coffee. In spite of her husband's good humour, something was badly wrong – her spine and mouth had lost their air of command, there were two lines of suffering between her eyebrows, and when she raised her cup to her mouth, she forgot to extend her little finger. Gillian and Cynthia, excused dishes, were in their rooms pushing battered books and toys back into tea chests. Isobel's tea chest waited by her bedroom door, exhaling old tea leaves and disruption.

'Irene, goodnight, Irene. Irene, goodnight. Goodnight, Irene, goodnight, Irene. I'll see you in my dreams.' Her father finally clattered the smeared cutlery onto the bench and her mother winced.

'Buster!' called Gillian. 'Here, boy.' She came into the kitchen brandishing an unsavoury rubber bone. 'Look what I found, won't he be pleased. Where is he?' Her mother winced again and took her cup to the sink.

'Well,' said her father, letting the washing up water go with a slurp, 'how's the packing going, girls? This time next week and . . . A life on the ocean wave, something the bounding main.' He conducted himself with the dishcloth and Isobel's mother managed a brave smile. 'Come down to the basement, Izzy, we'll bring up more boxes.'

The basement ought by now to have realised its potential as a family room, but was still just a hole in a clay bank. Isobel recalled the glistening blob on the rough concrete and squinted, half expecting something indelible. How much more convenient it had been over the last few months, with Clyde disposing of all that mess inside her. She stood uselessly while her father rummaged in a corner, interspersing bars of *Hearts of Oak* with optimistic remarks about his future in plastics.

'What's up, Izzy? Not looking forward to going Home? Here, take these two.' She took them. 'Pity,' he said. 'Chance of a lifetime.'

She regarded him wearily – how many chances of a lifetime could one be expected to endure, and how could he believe they were all so neatly reversible? 'I'm not going.'

He straightened and rubbed his back, regarding her with mild exasperation. 'Now look here, Izzy, we've been through all that. You're too young to stay on your own, and the other two have come round. You'll enjoy it, you know, Swinging London and all that.'

'I'd be no good at swinging,' said Isobel, momentarily wistful. 'But anyway, I can't come because I'm pregnant.'

He froze, a box in his arms. Around them the basement dissolved then re-formed. The box slid to the floor and he dropped heavily onto a sawhorse, head in his hands. Overhead, her mother's feet crossed and recrossed the kitchen – hanging up tea-towels, wiping down benches, restoring order.

'How far gone?' said her father eventually.

'Nearly four months,' supplied Isobel.

'Too late for an abortion then.' He returned his head to his hands. 'If only you'd come to me sooner . . .'

She stared. She had had no idea he was a father who could – or would – arrange such things. Why had he not conveyed this to her at some earlier point in the last seventeen years? They heard the feet again, caught each other's eye in the fluorescent glare – equals at last, conspirators, this fact on their hands like a murder weapon.

'She's had a bad day,' he said dully. 'Took Buster to the vet. We can't take him back because of the quarantine so he's being put down. Stay here, Iz. I'll talk to her.'

She took her father's place on the sawhorse. Overhead the feet kept up their innocent tattoo while his trod the outside steps. The back door opened and shut. Chairs scraped lino, voices murmured. The feet stopped and Isobel waited. A cup hit the floor and exploded.

The music was deafening and jangly, some jolly folk tune magnified a hundred times and distorted beyond recognition. It was a huge wild party, and on the wharf the partygoers waved and shoved and yelled. Some were dancing, bottles at their mouths. They hurled streamers until the chilly air was plaited up green and red and yellow. Balloons rose majestically. And over it all, a thousand portholes winking like a magic city, towered the ship. As they struggled through the crowd, Isobel saw a young man tie the end of a flesh-coloured stocking to an immense ring low on the ship's flank.

'This way,' called her father over dozens of riotous heads. He pushed on, baggage sprouting from his arms. Near the gangplank, the partygoers separated into those who were leaving and those who were staying. People held onto each other. Isobel watched a girl her own age laughing and crying in the arms of a boy. She'd go to London, get a job as a barmaid or a nanny, live in a flat with other girls, go camping on the Continent. And two or three years from now she'd come home, marry this boy or another, settle down, have children, keep a house clean. Like a child keeping the best to last. Isobel pitied her.

At the top of the gangplank an olive-skinned sailor in whites saluted the Midwinters. Isobel's father gave him a comradely grin. They forged on down low corridors, reading numbers off doors. 'Here we are,' said Isobel's father.

The cabin had a porthole opaque with salt, four narrow bunks, and a shower and toilet in a cupboard. Her mother surveyed it all with pinched lips. As usual, it was less than she'd hoped for. As usual, she didn't know how they were going to manage.

'Good job I'm not coming,' said Isobel far too heartily.

Everyone looked at her. The ship throbbed and people banged down the corridor. Clyde produced a bouquet of limp red roses for Isobel's mother who endured a silent struggle then thanked him sparingly. Cynthia and Gillian claimed the top bunks. Their mother seemed about to countermand their choice, then sank onto a lower one, at a loss for a configuration she liked any better.

'The ship will sail in twenty minutes,' crackled a voice. 'All visitors ashore.'

Everyone looked at Isobel again. She wanted to say, 'Bye,' with a little wave, and slip out of the door. She hugged her mother first, to get it over with. Her mother gripped hard and let go suddenly. Gillian and Cynthia looked like frightened strangers but she hugged them anyway, as if it were a normal thing to do.

'The ship will sail in fifteen minutes. All visitors ashore. All visitors ashore.'

Her father bent towards her, face twisted, eyes pink and watery. He put his arms around her and said, 'Goodbye, girlie. Take care.' And she found herself blurting out, 'Thank you, thank you for everything.' She backed away in confusion.

Back on the wharf the partygoers went crazy each time the

ship hooted. Passengers crowded the rails, and the young man with the stocking had rigged up several more and was checking his knots. She was wondering how much they would hold the ship back when she realised it was already moving, slipping diplomatically from the wharf as if to avoid hurting anyone's feelings.

'There they are,' cried Clyde. 'Look, on that upper deck at the back. See them?'

'No,' she said.

'They're waving,' said Clyde. 'Wave back.'

'No point,' she said. 'I can't see them.'

They stood as the ship shrank and the partygoers drifted away. 'Come on,' said Clyde.

'Not yet,' she said. The stockings were fleshy no longer but taut, lethal as wire. One by one they snapped. 'There,' she said, and turned away.

PART TWO

NEW ZEALAND 1966

Chapter 16

'WELCOME, EVERYONE. YOU HAVE COME TO THIS REGISTRY OFFICE today – all those to whom Clyde and Isobel are dear – to witness the formalisation of those private vows of love this young couple have already made to one another, and to wish them well as they stand on the brink of a new life, ready to set out on that long journey of exploration that is' – the registrar came up for air – 'marriage. All, that is, except Isobel's parents, David and Eileen Midwinter and their two younger daughters Gill and Cindy, whose absence must undoubtedly be a cause of sadness to you all, but an absence that only makes the role the rest of you must play that much more vital, here, as you are, to witness the solemn promises Clyde and Isobel are about to make . . .'

'Excuse me,' whispered Isobel. Two pallid rose petals fluttered to the tabletop.

'Isobel and Clyde have made the brave choice to marry in this office, the honest decision that a church wedding was inappropriate for them – a decision we can only admire and respect . . .'

'Hmph,' said Joan Fisk.

'. . . but the vows Clyde and Isobel are about to take are no less binding, the bond forged between them no less mysterious or sacred for the fact that they have chosen to make it . . . them . . . here, in this humble office, rather than in the splendour of St Alban's next door, and every one of you. . .'

'Excuse me,' said Isobel again, more urgently.

'. . . every one of you, by being a witness here today, will become party to the vows they are about to take. Every one of you has a part to play in helping this young couple – Isobel and Clyde – keep their vows, for we all know – don't we, those of us who are older, those of us who are married perhaps – that the happiness Clyde and Isobel undoubtedly feel today . . .'

Faces spun at Isobel as she backed away from the table – the murdered rabbit eyes of Clyde's mother, Jacko, throttled by a furious tie, Jo, dreaming in suspiciously muddy shoes, the boys swinging their feet. A dozen indistinguishably wrinkled Giltraps.

'. . . will sometimes falter, sometimes fail, and there will, won't there, be days when Isobel or Clyde will undoubtedly wonder . . .'

She fled. The hallway was clogged with another wedding party. It parted and curious eyes followed her downstairs. She spied the half-open door and dashed through, hauling up her dress as she ran. She sank onto the toilet with a groan and peed wildly.

'. . . and I know I speak for all of you when I say to you – Isobel and Clyde . . .'

'Sorry,' whispered Isobel, resuming her place.

'. . . that marriage is not always easy, but perseverance and compromise bring their own rewards, and any one of these people, in the years to come, will undoubtedly regard it as their solemn duty to remind you of these vows made here, today, and of the feelings that led you here. Clyde and Isobel.' At last the registrar stopped, and beamed radiantly. 'Now, who has the ring?'

Rats swaggered forward, leered at Isobel, winked at Clyde and produced something from his pocket. She gaped, astonished that this vital prop had materialised without her supervision. And when, at the prompting of the registrar, Clyde slipped the gold ring onto her finger, she sent him a smile of such approval, the registrar clucked happily and said, 'Yes, please, do kiss the bride.'

Clyde's kiss was stale and inaccurate. He was cripplingly hung over. Rats wrenched her from Clyde's arms and worked his tongue into her mouth. She spat it out. The registrar shook her hand.

'Lovely, dear,' remarked Clyde's mother to no one in particular. 'Clyde, you look terrible. He should get more sleep, Isobel.'

Joan Fisk adjusted her hat with deadly intent. Jo and Adrian's boys chased each other round the table. Giltrap relatives stood about uncertainly in their best clothes. Adrian cleared his throat. 'I know Clyde and Isobel decided against a reception. But we would like to think . . . that is, Isobel has been staying with us since her parents left for England and we'd like to invite you all back to our home for a drink or a cup of tea. So, please, feel free . . .'

There was a murmur of begrudging approval from the extended Giltraps, a drift towards the door. Clyde was becalmed in the centre of the room. 'We'll have to drive your aunt, your parents' car's full. Have you invited the registrar? You ought to thank Adrian and Jo. How are you feeling?'

'Erghk,' said Clyde, leaning heavily as she propelled him to the door.

'Come with us,' said Isobel to Joan Fisk, determined to swamp the woman's disapproval with her management skills. 'Clyde's just going to get the car, aren't you, Clyde?'

As the last Giltrap inched downstairs, clutching the banister, Isobel heard the registrar begin again. 'You are all here today – all those to whom Kevin and Sharon are dear . . .' She was sorry not to be able to stay and observe Kevin and Sharon, to see how real newlyweds behaved, but the geriatric Giltrap tweaked her arm impatiently.

She stood for some time on the pavement until Jo and Adrian appeared, the boys rounded up. 'I think Clyde's gone without me,' she said. 'Can I come with you?'

Adrian looked distressed, she could see it wasn't his idea of a wedding at all; neither was it hers, she was pleased to say. The five of them ran through the rain to Adrian's car and Isobel piled in the back with the boys. 'Brides ought to have the front seat,' protested Jo mildly.

Isobel snorted. 'I'm not a real bride.' *Say thank you, Isobel.* 'It was nice of you to ask everyone back to your place.'

'Was that a wedding or not?' The youngest Glossop, Christopher, dumped himself on her lap and slipped a hot grubby hand into hers.

'Well, yes,' said Isobel, wriggling to make the most of what lap she still had.

'Was your wedding like that?' he piped in his mother's ear.

'No,' Jo sighed. 'Adrian's mother made us do it all properly. Oh, sorry, Isobel, I meant . . .'

'It's all right, I know what you mean.'

'So are you married or not?' demanded Christopher.

'Undoubtedly,' said Isobel. Jo giggled.

'Why aren't you in a big dress with white icing all over it?'

'This dress is quite big enough, thank you, and I like blue.'

'You didn't get much presents,' remarked Martin.

'I told you we shouldn't have brought them,' said Adrian, frowning at his wife as he changed gear.

'Shh, leave Isobel alone.' Jo pulled a wry face of apology.

Isobel smiled again and shook her head. The passing scent of a takeaway filled the car. 'God, I'm ravenous.'

'Chips, chips!' squealed the boys.

Adrian flashed them a stern look then caught Isobel's expression in the mirror. 'We could . . . if you want . . .' he offered.

She opened her mouth to utter a polite disclaimer, but the boys were bouncing madly and she didn't feel like being the only grown-up on the back seat. 'My shout then,' said Adrian, fumbling for change as he got out of the car.

Martin said, 'Dad doesn't use'lly let us eat in the car. It's because it's you.' He was half accusing, half respectful.

The windows steamed up in the silent chippy fug. Isobel licked her fingers and Christopher burped. 'Chips are better than wedding cake, aren't they, Is'bel?'

'Much,' she said.

'How did she get here?' she hissed on the threshold of the Glossops' sitting room.

'Who?' Clyde was a rather less intense shade of grey but no less bewildered. His perfectly knotted tie had slipped to the right exposing an inch or so of white plastic-encased elastic. She wondered if he fully comprehended that they were now husband and wife.

She snapped, 'Penny Lambert. I never asked her.'

Clyde flinched – 'Rats asked if he could bring someone' – then shrugged. 'She'll be right. Least it's not Lurlene.'

Isobel gritted her teeth and stalked off. She would have infinitely preferred Lurlene.

'Quite a nice frock, dear, in the circumstances. Good job those smock things are in, isn't it.' Joan Fisk held a sherry glass in her white-gloved hand and was wearing an outfit that as far as Isobel knew had not been in since Hillary conquered Everest. The dreadful woman bobbed an inexpertly lipsticked mouth at her glass, then said, 'Big place they've got here, your friends,' as if it were the fruits of crime.

'They're not friends. Adrian sold my parents' house and I used to babysit for them. They let me stay with them.'

Joan Fisk looked puzzled by this clarification, and Isobel took the opportunity to turn her back and sit down.

'Hi,' sang Penny. She was perched on the edge of the next

119

chair, legs crossed at the ankles, pigskin bag in her lap. She wore a shiny cream straw hat not much different from the one she had worn to school. 'You don't look at all pregnant,' she continued chattily.

'Well I am, nearly six months. That's why it's too late for an abortion and why my breasts are full of milk.' Penny's discreet makeup failed to camouflage her distaste.

'Will you introduce me to your friend, Isobel?' said Adrian.

'She's not . . . This is Penny Lambert.' Penny offered a ladylike hand and a smile that said she refused to take Isobel's churlishness personally.

Isobel found Jo in the kitchen feeding the boys baked beans. 'Sorry,' said Jo, shamefaced. 'I'm not much good at this sort of thing, and the boys were still hungry so . . .'

Isobel cut up Christopher's toast. 'Adrian is, though.'

Jo sighed. 'He always has been. Sometimes . . .' She drifted to the sink without finishing the sentence. It soothed Isobel, watching the boys wolf their beans.

'Will you live somewhere different now?' said Christopher, sawing his last bean into quarters. Younger sisters had inured Isobel to the charms of small children, yet it was impossible not to like Christopher, so confident was he of his own likability. Martin was more of a struggle. He had, more than once, told Jo that Isobel was his favourite babysitter, but he treated her with something close to suspicion.

'We're going to live with Clyde's aunt,' she told Christopher, 'till we can go and live on the farm.'

Jo meandered back, drying her hands. 'Oh dear, I'll miss you,' she said, sending Isobel an uncomplicated smile.

Rats burst in. 'Speeches! Come on, Mrs Giltrap.' He hauled her across the room to Clyde, and they stood side by side like two children at the front of the class. The guests backed against the walls as Rats pulled a leather pouf into a commanding position. 'Quiet,' he bellowed unnecessarily. He surveyed his audience unsteadily from the pouf, bottle in hand. 'Ladies and gentlemen, I've known Gil here – that's Clyde to you – I've known Gil – but not in the biblical sense . . .' Joan Fisk frowned into her second 'wee' sherry. '. . . I've known Gil for – ooh, bloody yonks, I'd say.' He slurped from the bottle. 'And I'd like to tell you a story to ill . . . to ill . . . to show what a great mate he is and how lucky Mrs Clyde Giltrap over there is to be getting this great bloke for a husband.'

Clyde's relatives began to take a lively interest. His mother smiled up at Rats as he swayed on the pouf. 'We were up the back of Campbell's bush this particular day. Still wet behind the ears, then, not the sophisticated men of the world you see before you today.' He congratulated himself with another swig. 'We were after a deer. Or a pig. Or a possum. Any bloody thing that moved, in fact. If it was on four legs we'd've shot it, eh Gil.'

Clyde grinned proudly at the carpet. Isobel's smile began to ache.

'We were slogging up this hill, bush-whacking like buggers, you know what it's like up the back there, when . . .'

'Aah,' exclaimed Isobel. Faces turned, some clearly resentful at this interruption to Rats' narrative. 'It kicked,' she said. 'Sorry.'

Adrian took her arm. 'Better sit down.'

'I'd like some fresh air. Carry on, though,' she told Rats pleasantly. 'You don't need me.'

'When all of a sudden . . .' continued Rats.

The garden reeked of rain and the grass soaked her feet. She lowered herself onto the garden seat Adrian had recently installed under the copper beech. The tree dripped on their shoulders and thighs. 'I hate speeches,' she said.

Adrian looked troubled. 'He's just a boy,' he began. She had no idea whether he meant Rats or Clyde. She breathed the garden air and somewhere a blackbird chortled. 'Did you really *want* to get married, Isobel?'

'I had to.' Sometimes she wondered how bright Adrian was.

'But what about . . . Well, I know you don't get on very well with your parents but . . .'

'They've gone,' she said simply. There was a postcard from Tenerife in her handbag. *Isobel darling, Having a wonderful time. Shipboard life is . . .* She had absolutely no idea where Tenerife was.

'But your sisters too, you must miss them. It's family, isn't it. Clyde's not a bad boy, but . . .'

She was overtaken by a wave of something painful. 'He couldn't even get a real tie for his own wedding. He's got something horrible on elastic.' She was startled to find herself complaining about Clyde. That triumphant young woman in her mother's wedding picture would never have dreamed of complaining about her brand-new husband.

'Lots of people wear those,' soothed Adrian. 'They can look quite smart.'

'My father wouldn't wear one,' she scoffed. 'Neither would you.'

There was another silence filled by the blackbird, then Adrian said, 'What about university, aren't you sorry to give it up?'

She shrugged. 'It was just like school. I'm sick of being told what to think, what to do. When you're married no one can tell you.'

He looked even more troubled. 'Marriage is . . . is more than that, Isobel. Clyde does love you, you know, and he's . . .'

'Not a bad boy.'

He frowned up into the tree, he disliked being teased. 'Anyway,' he said after a while, 'I took it seriously what the registrar said about helping when things get difficult.'

'Reminding me of my solemn vows?'

He was undeterred. 'I want you to know I'm your friend, Isobel. And I hope you'll always be mine.'

She kept silent – it was his house after all, and it might have been rude to point out that she had no need of friends, that the assumption she did rankled as much as the idea of marriage once had. But that night, as she and Clyde prepared for the sagging three-quarter bed in Joan Fisk's spare room, she said with a snigger, 'Adrian swore undying friendship today.'

Clyde watched her take off her bra and somewhere under the multicoloured peggy-squares, farted. 'Bloody Glossop, probably fancies you. Your tits look great now, come here.'

The night wore on and on. With Clyde beside her, lost in sleep, she felt more alone than she ever had in her single bed. Some time in the small hours she heard a peculiar sound, painful and insistent. She propped herself on one elbow and studied Clyde in the gloom. He was unrecognisable, his grinning daytime face gone. His eyelids fluttered madly as if behind them he were reliving horrors, his cheek muscles jerked, and his hand was a fist on the pillow. He was grinding his teeth with such ferocity she feared that if she woke him he might fly at her. She rolled away, clamping the pillow over her head.

Chapter 17

THE MORRIS CLAMBERED UP THE DARK DIRT ROAD WITH CLYDE at the wheel, whistling through his teeth. It bottomed on a bump and he cursed good-humouredly. 'How far?' she asked.

'Couple of miles. We'll work our way down from the top.'

She was proud Clyde considered her suitable company for this expedition, relieved to escape domestic imprisonment with Joan Fisk, which three months of married life had only rendered more and more deadly. Shocked, Joan had said, 'You can't take her up there, Clyde. Not in her state.'

'She'll be right, Aunty. If she goes into labour, I've delivered enough lambs and calves.'

Joan had taken a sip of sweet tea to eradicate these unpleasant animal associations that had nothing to do with crocheted pram covers. 'Isobel,' she appealed. 'You can't.'

'I'll be fine,' she breezed, delighted by the degree of good cheer you could maintain in the face of someone with no real power over you. As a concession, she added graciously, 'I'll be careful.'

'Would you really know what to do if I went into labour?' she asked, as a wheel thumped into a pothole.

'Nothing to it.' He pulled up. 'Out you hop.'

His confidence was exhilarating. That this boy – her husband – could deliver his own child and shoot his own dinner linked her to something elemental, something that revealed her old life for the pitiful suburban sham it had always been. She zipped up one of his jackets and pulled on a woolly hat. Clyde was doing something with a firearm on the other side of the car. 'Okay,' he said. 'Get behind the wheel, go real slow and when I say stop, stop.'

She steered the car back down the road, window open, on the alert for any ruts and bumps that might tip Clyde from his perch on the bonnet. He hung on with one hand, rifle tucked under his arm. The other swung the spotlight back and forth across the road and into the trees. The silence of the hillside filled the car and the town lights flickered below. When they moved to the farm, there would be no more lights, no more Joan Fisk, no more rules.

'Stop,' hissed Clyde. He raised the rifle to his shoulder. A crack split the dark, then another. 'Bugger,' he said. 'Big bastard too. Okay, drive on.'

She glimpsed several pairs of pink eyes in the glare a second before Clyde fired. Only once did she stop too abruptly and watch aghast as he slid from the bonnet. 'Jeez,' he said, picking himself up with a tolerant grin. Now and again possums had thumped on the roof of the house in Balmoral Road, gasped outside the window like psychopaths. Pests, Clyde declared, but okay if you cooked them right. She imagined something like a giant rat and shuddered. She called softly through the window, 'Can I have a go?'

She thought he would say no, but he hopped off the bonnet, blinding her with the spot. 'Yeah. Why not?' He seemed pleased. 'Should have given you some practice in the daylight, but you'll get the hang of it. Bring it up like this. Aim for that tree' – he flashed the spot on a trunk – 'and squeeze.' They left the car and continued on foot, Clyde swinging the spot. In her hands the rifle felt too clumsy to kill.

'There.' The beam caught the lower branches of a tree.

'Where?' But then she saw two bright spots of panic and she had to fight the impulse to yank up the rifle and fire wildly.

'That's it,' whispered Clyde. 'Nice and steady, now squeeze.' A crackle of twigs and a thump. 'Shit, you got him, you got him!'

Clyde bounded away, the spot picking out random pools of road and bush. She knelt and let the rifle slip from her shaking arms.

'Right through the bloody head, you're a natural,' Clyde said admiringly. 'A female, look, she's got a joey.'

The creature was upholstered in thick unratlike fur and a luxuriant tail lay across the stones. But its face was pinched and mean, its eyes stupid with death. She flinched as Clyde plunged his hand into the animal's abdomen and pulled something out, something ugly and unformed. 'People keep them as pets,' he said, cradling the thing in his palm. 'This one's too young, it'll die.'

'Yukh,' said Isobel, recoiling. 'It looks boiled.'

'Just a baby animal,' he said, reprovingly. 'They give birth to them real tiny and the baby crawls into the pouch.'

Isobel turned away, overwhelmed with envy for possum mothers. She no longer dreamed of falling. Now, night after night, she woke in a sweat of terror before that final unimaginable push, before she knew if she was giving birth or being born herself. *Like Mummy inside and out.* Her distended abdomen lurched and she yelped. Clyde reached out. 'A boy,' he said with a grin. 'For sure. Feel that foot.'

His confidence rattled her. 'How can you tell?'

He took her hand, neither tenderly nor roughly. 'Press there.'

She explored with reluctant fingers. It was unmistakably a small foot, and it lashed out again. Clyde flung the boiled thing into the bushes and led Isobel back up the hill to the car, swinging the dead mother by her tail.

Joan Fisk's kitchen was claustrophobic. 'That friend of yours rang,' she said, arms folded, hair netted for bed. 'He said it was important so I waited up.'

Isobel registered the familiar compound of martyrdom, disapproval and curiosity. 'Who?'

'That Glossop man. He wouldn't leave a message' – this, accompanied by a meaningful glance over Isobel's shoulder at Clyde – 'I told him I didn't know when you'd be back. I told him . . .'

'I'll be in the shed,' said Clyde, oblivious to innuendo. 'Skinning.'

Joan Fisk flinched from what he held up in the light of the porch. 'Very nice, dear.'

'I shot it,' said Isobel. 'I'm going to learn how to skin them too.' Halfway down the path, she called back, 'I'll ring Adrian tomorrow. They probably want me to babysit.'

She enjoyed being shut in the shed with Clyde knowing that Joan Fisk was alone in the house, preparing for an empty bed. The smell was nauseating but she lit one of Clyde's cigarettes and leaned against the bench. He peeled back skin like orange pith. It made a pithy sound and lay on the bench like abandoned pyjamas. The carcass was a reassuring lump of meat. 'I could find a recipe,' she conceded.

'Ask Mum,' he said, stretching the skin over a wooden frame and catching it at the edges with tacks. 'Good skin. It'll make a hat, for the kid.'

He's happy, she thought, marrying me has made him happy, and something inside her stirred and flexed. It felt like driving rather than having to submit to the back seat.

She was still in bed next morning when the telephone rang. She liked to hold the day – and Joan Fisk – at bay as long as possible since Clyde did not come home until after five. Joan Fisk disapproved of lying in bed in general, and dereliction of wifely duty in particular. 'He ought to have breakfast, dear.'

'He doesn't want breakfast,' Isobel repeated a dozen times. 'He only wants coffee and he can do that.' Joan Fisk would purse her mouth and turn away, and Isobel would hum resolutely as she tipped cornflakes into a bowl and the sombre oak clock on the mantelpiece struck nine-thirty.

'Poor Muriel's coming for a bite of lunch,' said Joan, bustling into the spare room with the merest of knocks. 'Jacko's going to drop her off on his way to Rotary. We'll make a batch of scones. She doesn't get out much.'

In fact, Clyde's mother stood on Joan Fisk's doorstep in a state of disarray at least once a fortnight as Jacko's car roared off down the road. Two hours later he would return, hoot peremptorily, and Muriel would scurry out, gathering up endless bags, issuing last-minute cautions to her sister and daughter-in-law.

Isobel got out of bed since it was the only way to get Joan Fisk out of her room.

Joan flicked her feather duster over the sitting room mantelpiece, faltering before a glum wedding photograph. Isobel sprinkled sugar on her cornflakes and considered feather dusters, hearing her mother's disdainful tones – *All they do is flick the dust from one spot to another.* In one of her intermittent attempts at galvanising the two of them out of their numbing daily routine, she asked Joan, around a mouthful of cornflakes, 'What was your husband's name?'

The duster froze like a startled bird. 'Noel,' choked Joan, then resumed flicking.

'When did he die?' Isobel moderated her tone, but only slightly. Flick, flick. 'Was it a long time ago?' Joan moved on to the spider plant. Its striped leaves rattled in alarm.

Joan turned a troubled un-Fisklike face. 'I'd better get along to the shops. You might carry on with the cleaning. I do like the place nice for poor Muriel.'

The venetian blinds parted with a hostile crack as Isobel monitored Joan's progress past the six cowed standard roses. She exhaled noisily, and made for the sideboard where Joan Fisk kept a half-empty bottle of Bristol Cream. She took a generous swig, gasped and took another. It filled her mouth as illicitly as communion wine and settled nicely on top of the cornflakes.

The telephone caught her red-handed. 'Isobel? It's Adrian.'

'Oh Adrian. Sorry, I forgot . . .'

'Isobel, I just wanted you to know, to hear it from me, Christopher is . . . was . . . he's . . . dead.'

'What?' The sherry blazed a trail down her ribs.

'Run over, outside the school yesterday. He saw a friend on the other side of the road and this woman knocked him down. The wheel went over him. I wanted you to know.'

The sherry reached her knees. She slid to the carpet, fumbling for words. 'Jo. How's Jo?'

There was an appalling sob. 'She's out in the garden, doesn't talk to me. Martin's gone to Mum's, it's just the two of us, Isobel. I can't bear it, please come over.'

I can't, I'm too young, I don't know about death. It's Mummy you want, she knows what to do. 'Of course. I'll be there in half an hour.'

Feeling simultaneously virtuous and reckless, she called a taxi, robbed Clyde's money jar and left a note for Joan. Purring importantly through the back streets, she recalled the set of her mother's shoulders, her air of suppressed excitement – *'Poor Celia Dodds' mother passed away. I'm just popping round to see what I can do.'*

Isobel walked down the side of the Glossops' house thinking, I'm just popping round to see what I can do. Jo lifted a stricken face from a flowerbed. 'I've been meaning to get to this for ages. It's choked with weeds, the spring bulbs will never get through.'

'I'm sorry,' said Isobel. 'I'm so sorry.' She was appalled by the futility of the words, yet surely, any second, Christopher would bound from the house to greet her as he always had, as Buster always had. 'I'm so sorry,' she told Jo again. Yet somehow, like Buster, Christopher was this thing called dead, which was like being sent to another country for ever and ever amen.

Jo got to her feet and put an awkward arm round Isobel's shoulder, as if Isobel were the one suffering, then dropped to her knees again on the damp grass. 'Adrian wants to keep talking about it but I feel better out here on my own.' She paused, studied her dirty cracked hands. 'I don't want him cremated, Isobel. Cremation is for getting people out of the way quickly. I want him put in the earth. The earth is good. People should never call it dirt.'

Her words hurt Isobel's chest. She watched Jo for a few more minutes – pulling weeds, shaking off soil, heaping them on the lawn – then took a step backwards and turned for the house.

Adrian was slumped by a cold littered fireplace, his hand clenched around a glass of something amber. His face was so socked by grief he had gained ten years, and she hesitated at the door, suddenly shy.

'Isobel.' He half lifted himself from the chair then sank back. She pecked his cheek, aware that something out of the ordinary was called for. 'Would you like one of these? He was eight, only eight, how can he be dead? Christ, it's so unfair. And the poor woman who did it, the mother of one of his friends, Chris'd been to her house, she says he's such a nice kid, always says please and thank you and makes her laugh. It wasn't her fault, he ran straight under her front wheel. Stupid little bastard, he's been told and told.' He emptied his glass and stood to pour another. 'Want one?'

She nodded because it was simpler that saying no. 'I saw Jo outside.'

He slumped again and stared into the dismal fireplace. 'She won't talk to me. She's been like it for years, it started after Christopher was born. We don't fight, not like other couples, but we don't do lots of things other couples do. Do you and Clyde fight?'

Fights between couples were what you saw on television –

they were raw and passionate, they had a certain splendour. 'No,' she said, not sure whether to be proud or apologetic. 'Not exactly.'

They both drank. 'I know I don't spend much time with them but it's because I'm working hard and that's for them in the end, isn't it? I did love him, Isobel. Sometimes I think Jo believes I didn't.' His eyes brimmed. 'There's a picture upstairs from when they were little. Christopher's the prettiest and the brightest.'

She winced. She remembered when it had been impossible to contemplate another day under the same roof, breathing the same air, as Gillian. Luckily for her, her sister had stayed in the land of the living. Poor Martin, your rivals were much less dangerous alive. Adrian was halfway to the door, motioning her to follow. Isobel clutched the banister, giddy from Bristol Cream, whisky and unknown territory. They passed the boys' room, lined with bunks and littered with toys and clothes, and what had for a few weeks been her room, now the spare room again. She hesitated on the threshold of the main bedroom. *What do you want, Isobel?* Adrian and Jo's bed was unmade, the floor on Jo's side spectacularly heaped with gardening magazines and catalogues. Adrian made for a framed photograph on the chest of drawers and handed it to Isobel. It showed two angelic babies in smocks, unrecognisable as the kids she had read to and whose noses she had blown.

'There's a picture of me and my sisters like this,' she mused. She meant idealised, sentimental, a parent's dream of children. Then, fearing she might have caused pain by denying his children's uniqueness, she added quickly, 'He was sweet.'

She returned the photograph to the chest of drawers and sat next to him on the edge of the bed. He reached for her. Their arms tightened and their mouths met in a disorganised way. His hand passed over her swollen breasts as if by mistake, then he pulled away. He stared at his hands on his thighs. 'Jo and I love each other. In our way. But' – he searched the room for the right words – 'there's no warmth. I need warmth, I'm shrivelling up,

Isobel. Sometimes when I'm driving home at night I wonder why, what am I coming home to? She's a wonderful woman, you know that. But . . . oh God.' He put his head in his hands and made a strangled noise. Tentatively she touched his shoulder. He took her hand and held it between his own. 'I just want us to be friends, Isobel,' he said urgently. 'Allies. I didn't mean . . . just now . . . I just want to know that when I'm in the office and sitting downstairs in the evening, someone cares about me, someone like you.'

She hadn't the heart to contradict him, to tell him he had misread her, that there was no one like her.

'Just friends though, Isobel. I didn't mean . . . That's Clyde's baby, and I'd never leave Jo, ever.' These melodramatics made her fidget. He put a hand on her swollen stomach. 'Do you think it's a girl? I always wanted a little girl. I'll help you, Isobel. I'll do whatever I can for you and the baby, I want you to know that.'

She bridled. 'I don't need help. I've got Clyde.'

There were footsteps on the stairs and Jo appeared in the doorway with an exhausted smile. 'I've put the jug on.' She had obviously decided to make an effort.

'I should be making you tea,' said Isobel stoutly, following her downstairs. She felt a pressing need to be what help she could to Jo. 'I'll clean the grate while the jug's boiling, then you can tell me what else needs doing. Anything at all.'

Joan Fisk looked up from bullying gladioli blooms on the kitchen table. 'There you are.'

'You saw my note, didn't you?'

'Muriel was so sorry you weren't here. I thought you'd at least get home for Clyde.'

'Where is he?'

'Not in yet, but . . .'

'Well then,' said Isobel with grim satisfaction.

' . . . I have to be out at flower arranging in just over an hour, and no tea on . . .'

'Jo and Adrian's son is dead,' Isobel told her coldly. 'He was eight, he was run over. I went to see what I could do.' She traversed the tense space between Joan Fisk and herself. 'As you're in a hurry, we'd better open a can.'

'Muriel's family now,' said Joan, shocked but still putting up a fight.

Isobel glared at her aunt-in-law. She stabbed the rusty point of the opener into the can and hacked her way around, thinking savagely, family? I've got rid of them, and you lot don't count, whatever makes you think you do?

Chapter 18

Isobel had regularly passed St Alban's on her way down the main street, and from the pavement the church's wooden construction seemed appealing, intimate and human after cold English stone. But now she halted on the threshold, and Clyde, in wedding suit and funeral demeanour, bumped into her. The interior was gloomy and smelled of commandments, the organ was churning out horror movie music. As her eyes adjusted, she took in bad hats and, at the far end of the aisle, a small white gleaming coffin.

As soon as she and Clyde were seated, her eyes went back to the coffin. It was banked with flowers, and propped at the end facing the congregation was a large photograph of Christopher. She was glad to be far enough back to be unable to discern his features in detail. The very idea of the photograph dismayed her, the way people sought to intensify their pain rather than avoid it. But even blurred by distance, Christopher's smile hovered like an innocent charming ghost. Her fingers played over a battered hymn book. White was for innocence – dead children, confirmations, brides, real brides. Andrea Dodds had been confirmed in white; her mother would have married in white had there not been a war on. Isobel recalled the sensible Marks and Spencer cream separates in which she had been confirmed, the useful blue wedding outfit. She had never warranted white. Because she had never been innocent, obviously. Because for as long as she could remember she had been too watchful and calculating to merit the term. Christopher had not been a good child – he had been exhaustingly lively and inquisitive, carrying out science experiments in the toilet and regularly running away. It was Jo's fierce love that had rendered him innocent.

Jo, Adrian, Martin and two older people Isobel assumed were grandparents trailed up the aisle and after some shuffling sat down. Jo was blessedly hatless. Martin – his head barely visible above the pew – was stationed between his parents. Isobel could not recall a single occasion when her own mother had allowed her children to come between herself and her husband. And she was shocked, in the middle of the vicar's sing-song opening remarks, to realise her parents had spent her childhood conducting an intense and not altogether happy love affair, and that she and her sisters were merely its by-products. Her mother's real life was her husband. It was he, of all the Midwinters, who had been rendered innocent by love. Him, and Buster.

A small knowing foot booted Isobel from the inside. Clyde fiddled with a pack of Pall Mall Plain. She heard sniffing and nose-blowing, and gritted her teeth. *Mummy's all right, kiddies – just a silly mistake.* Birth, death, love, hate, loss, joy – all the big things in life were silly mistakes to her mother, all except her own marriage.

The organ struck up again and the congregation came in late. *I vow to thee my country all earthly things above.* The women warbled beneath their hats; the men mumbled, shamefaced at surrendering to an unmanly activity. *Entire and whole and perfect, the service of my love. The love that asks no questions, the love that stands the test* . . . Isobel sang with gusto, and Clyde and several others shot curious glances in her direction . . . *that lays upon the altar the dearest and the best, the love that never falters, the love that pays the price, the love that makes undaunted the final sacrifice.*

She was seized by weeping. After fidgeting indecisively for a few minutes, Clyde steered her down the aisle past pews of whispers and pitying glances. He sat her on a low stone wall outside the church and lit up gratefully while she gave in to racking sobs. From time to time he squeezed her arm but he was remote, insubstantial, and she half-expected Adrian to abandon his son's funeral to comfort her. She looked up at Clyde, deluded by misery into believing he might for once understand. 'She killed him. I loved him and she had him killed,' she wailed.

Clyde scrutinised a passing pair of legs in a short skirt. 'Iz, Jo wouldn't . . .' He was out of his depth.

'I loved him and she had him put down, we could have had him, he could have lived with us, but she killed him.' Her voice rose on the churchyard air like a howl.

Someone put *Revolver* on the stereo and turned up the volume. The people milling about the Glossops' sitting room visibly relaxed, and there were gales of laughter as someone delivered a punchline. Isobel was on her third bacardi and coke, and, in spite of a vicious backache, feeling rather better.

'Mother won't approve of the music,' worried Adrian.

'Mothers don't approve of anything,' quipped Isobel, and several people chuckled.

Adrian said, 'Isobel, this is Tim Blackstone, our senior partner.' Tim Blackstone extended a pudgy hand and allowed Isobel to squeeze it. 'And this is Campbell Hurley.'

Isobel nodded politely at a stout man with a clownish expression who was wrenching at his tie and shirt buttons. Chest hair sprang out. 'Cam. How d'you do. Pretty thoroughly, by the look of you.' He grinned at her abdomen.

Adrian noted Tim Blackstone's expression. He seemed to have replaced the agony of grief with the anxiety of playing host. 'Campbell's an old friend, he's a vet, and chair of the local branch of . . .'

'Piss-takers and bullshit artists, and general all-round embarrassment,' said Campbell Hurley. 'More beer, Glossop!' Tim Blackstone – with a chilly glance at Campbell Hurley – walked off. 'Who are you?' demanded Cam.

'I'm married to Clyde Giltrap.' She knew by now that this was an acceptable answer.

'Aha, and a Pom, too. I see Glossop's taken a shine to you.' He leaned closer. 'Better watch him, bit of a stick man, you know.' Isobel shrank away, but the remark was made for the benefit of Adrian who had returned with beer.

'Isobel's one of the family now,' Adrian said, dropping an arm around her shoulder. 'She lived with us before she got married, and she's been great since . . . since it happened. We couldn't have managed without her. Ask Jo.'

Isobel blushed and stared at the floor. 'Ask Jo what?' demanded Jo. She held a drink, and her face had lost some of its strain.

'I was just telling Cam, Isobel's been a tower of strength.' Adrian didn't take his arm away.

'Mmm,' agreed Jo. 'I don't know how we're going to manage when you move away.'

'Isobel and Clyde are going to take over Clyde's father's farm at the end of the year,' explained Adrian.

'Landed gentry, eh,' said Cam.

'Hardly,' scoffed Isobel.

'Lovely to be on a farm,' said Jo dreamily.

'You all right, Isobel?' Adrian frowned.

'Fine, thanks, just backache. Actually, another drink might help.' She boldly handed him her glass. Cam sank into a nearby chair, pulling Jo onto his lap and burying his face in her neck with loud spluttering noises.

'You can always come and stay with us,' said Jo, flicking Cam's hand off her breast. 'When you feel like a day in town. Adrian likes to see you. And me too, of course.' She pulled away from Cam who let out an anguished moan.

'Bloody Hurley,' said a passing man. 'At it again.' Jo seized the chance to escape.

'I wanted to ask you since you're a vet,' said Isobel quickly, 'what happens when you put an animal down?'

Cam shot her a quizzical look. 'Painless injection.'

'I mean, to the body.'

'It's disposed of,' he said, with oblique professionalism. Then, 'All right, who's going to dance with me?'

'Mother's still here,' said Adrian, handing Isobel her drink.

'I'll ask her then.' He lunged across the room and Isobel saw Adrian and Jo exchange a glance. Impossible to imagine her and Clyde ever exchanging a glance. Whatever else Adrian and Jo did or did not do, they at least did this.

'I'll dance with you,' she called after Cam, putting down her drink. 'If that's all right, Jo?'

Jo managed a smile. 'We might as well enjoy ourselves if we feel like it. Christopher wouldn't mind.'

Cam was dragging Isobel to the middle of the room. 'Make way, make way.' People fell aside, grinning and shaking their heads.

'Don't drop it here, will you,' called Clyde. He had been drinking steadily and his grin was lopsided.

'Why not?' Isobel called gaily. 'You can deliver it on the carpet.' People laughed. Someone offered to boil water, someone else was keen to tear up petticoats. Cam gyrated unrhythmically.' Isobel managed what she hoped was a stylish but medically safe shuffle. A woman wearing a black hat with a veil as if she were in a movie about a funeral, was trying to dislodge a man from the couch. When the music ended, Isobel gulped from her glass and reached for Clyde. He brushed her off, slopping beer down his shirt. Cam dropped to his knees in front of Jo. Music filled the room again.

'The men are always hopeless,' said Jo, cuffing Cam. Always? thought Isobel. She felt suddenly greedy to be part of whatever it was. *In my day, we didn't tie ourselves down to one person* . . .

'Adrian,' she cried. 'You're not hopeless.' But he was, his limbs were wooden. Hoping to spur him on, she embellished her own style, raising her arms above her head, twirling, advancing and retreating. It increased his bewilderment; his arms dropped to his side and he seemed about to walk away. She caught his hand. 'Ballroom then. Only I'll have to do it side-saddle.' There were cheers and laughter as they hobbled around the room to an unsuitable beat, Adrian clinging rather than leading. The volume had climbed to the point that conversation was impossible. The woman with the veil had got Clyde on his feet and he was weaving about in a manner denoting serious drunkenness. Passing her glass, Isobel drained it, drowning a sharp pang. She shouted in Adrian's ear, 'I'm tipsy.'

It took her a second to understand that her voice was the only sound in the room, that the music had stopped dead.

'Mother,' said Adrian, abruptly releasing Isobel.

'It's like that game,' she cried. 'Everyone dances until someone turns off the music then . . .'

'Adrian!' exploded the short woman with cruelly styled hair who Isobel had seen in church. 'How could you?' Her manner was so theatrical Isobel expected someone to laugh. 'What about Christopher?' demanded the woman with a nicely calibrated sob.

Jo detached herself from the guests who were pressing themselves against the wall and studying the carpet. 'It's all right, Mother, Christopher wouldn't . . .'

'It's not all right, it's disgusting. That poor little boy, you should all be ashamed. And you, Adrian . . .' She swept her eyes over Isobel and back to her son. 'Disgusting.'

'Mother,' said Adrian and Jo together, advancing on her.

Around the room, people began to shuffle in the direction of spouses and belongings. Isobel sought out Clyde, but at some point he had slumped unconscious to the hearth rug. Jo was in the kitchen making tea as if there had been an accident. The woman with the hair was hunched over the table sniffing into a tiny lace handkerchief, while an ineffectual-looking man patted her hand.

'Jo . . .' began Isobel.

Adrian said, 'You should have left earlier, Mother, when you could see things were starting to upset you.'

'Driving your own mother out of your house on a day like this.'

'Not driving you out, Mother.' Adrian's fists were clenched. 'But if you don't . . .' The Curse of the Glossops, thought Isobel.

'Please, Adrian,' said Jo, putting a cup and saucer in front of the woman. 'She's upset.'

Adrian rounded on her. 'Whose fault is that? She could have . . .'

'Adrian . . . ' said Isobel, sinking into a chair. Someone was hacking through her spine with a rusty saw.

'Sorry,' said Adrian, suddenly noticing her. 'You haven't met my mother, Edna Glossop. Mother, this is Isobel. She's . . .'

'Yes,' said the woman, eyeing Isobel beadily and setting her lips in a grim line. 'And in her condition, she ought to know better.'

'Mother! And this is Dad.' The man held a liver-spotted hand across the table and gave Isobel a harmless smile.

'Adrian . . .' said Isobel.

'Sorry, Mrs Glossop,' boomed Cam Hurley, surging through the door. 'All my fault – the music and dancing and general debauchery. Please accept my apologies.' He grabbed her hand and kissed it.

'Cam,' remonstrated Adrian.

'More tea, Mother?' said Jo.

'Please,' said Isobel, struggling to her feet. 'Someone's going to have to take me to the hospital. I've started.'

The car swept up to the main door of the maternity hospital with an impressive squeal of tyres. It was a long, low, impermanent-looking building that might just as well have served as a school or an army barracks. Isobel lumbered at speed to the reception desk. 'I think I'm in labour,' she told the middle-aged woman scanning a *Woman's Day*.

'Did you ring? You're meant to ring.'

'It's just I've got this pain in my back, I've had it for hours and it's getting worse.' She heard a thin cry like a lamb in a distant paddock. 'It's probably not real labour, it might go away. I'll just . . .'

'No, don't go.' The woman grudgingly abandoned the *Woman's Day*. 'Sit over there, dear. I'll get someone to take a look.'

The light in the reception area was livid and surreal. A clock high on a wall said ten forty-two then made a frightened jump to ten forty-three. The jumble of magazine covers on the low table screamed irrelevancies. She wanted to sweep them to the floor. She heard another cry, a wrung-out guttural sound that fled down the corridor like a bad dream. *Think of fairies in a bluebell wood . . .*

'And you are Mrs . . .?' said a very small nurse. She had a bossy mouth and perky hair, as if it were ten in the morning.

'Giltrap. I don't think . . .'

'How long have you been having the pains . . .?'

'That's it, you see . . .'

'. . . and how far apart are they?'

'Look,' cried Isobel, towering over the nurse. 'I've just got bloody backache. Give me something for the backache and I'll bloody well go home.'

'Well,' said the nurse, not the least intimidated. 'There's no call for that tone. When did the pains start, Mr Giltrap, has she timed them?' She clearly set much store by male common sense.

'He's not my husband,' snapped Isobel, as the saw bit into her back. 'He's . . . a friend.' Cam seemed not to object to this description and offered an appropriately friendly grin.

'Single, are you?' said the nurse.

Isobel intercepted a glance between her and the woman behind the counter and wanted to strike them both. 'No, I'm bloody well not single.'

The nurse addressed Cam. 'Where's her husband then? We need some details.' She leaned towards Isobel and sniffed. 'Has she been drinking?'

'I've had four bacardi and cokes,' said Isobel, 'and I can still remember my name and address.'

'Yes, well,' said the nurse, with visible satisfaction. 'I'd better get Sister to come and look at you. Stay here. Please,' she added, for Cam's benefit.

'You might as well go,' Isobel told Cam with what she hoped was an apologetic smile. If he didn't, she would very soon attack him too. Fury boiled in her, great rolling waves surged through her body. She was furious with Adrian's mother, with the bossy little nurse, with that wretched foot under her ribs that never gave her a minute's peace, with the perfect placid faces on the magazine covers, with whoever had screamed. She hated them all. But then the pain knocked her back into the chair and she groaned.

Cam consulted his watch. 'Five minutes, tell them five minutes when they come back.'

She gasped and rocked. He fumbled for her hand but she clenched her fist and knocked him away. 'I'm all right. You should go. Sorry. Thank you.'

He stood uncertainly. 'I don't mind staying, we've had two kids.'

The vice released its grip. 'Really, I'm fine.' *I don't care how many bloody kids you've had, this is me.*

He shoved his hands in his pockets. 'Righto. Well. Nothing to it. And I'll . . . er . . . tell Clyde you're okay,' and he pecked her on the cheek.

'You can tell Clyde to get fucked,' snarled Isobel. Or maybe not, because the little nurse was back with an older one who stood smiling warmly.

'This is Mrs Giltrap. It wasn't her husband who brought her in and she doesn't know how often the pains are coming.'

'Five minutes,' muttered Isobel. 'Every five minutes.'

'And she's been drinking,' concluded the nurse with a meaningful look at the older woman.

'Righto, dear, up you come.' She leaned over Isobel and offered an arm.

'I don't think . . .'

'You'll be right, lovie,' said the older woman. 'Just come with me and we'll make you more comfortable. Shame hubby couldn't be here. That's it, lean on me.'

She smelled of warm lavender. But the corridor was long and empty, Isobel's legs wouldn't work properly and there was a terrible drumbeat in her ears. 'Like going to an execution,' she whispered.

The little nurse clicked her tongue. 'You shouldn't think like that, you should . . .'

'Thanks, Charmaine,' said the older woman. 'You can leave Mrs Giltrap with me.'

They reached a door which the sister pushed open. Beyond, everything was gleaming and brutal. Isobel could not go in. 'Someone screamed.' It hadn't been a scream, but there was no other word for that cry of agony and horror and despair.

'What's your name, lovie?'

'Giltrap.' But it wasn't. She had put on Giltrap like the blue dress she was married in. Now she was naked, exposed, Midwinter to the bone.

'No, I meant . . .'

'Isobel Irene Midwinter.' *Like pink rock.*

'Look, there's no one in here, Isobel. That was probably Mrs Dixon you heard, she always makes a fuss. It's her fourth, she's sitting up in bed now, happy as Larry.' She propelled Isobel towards a high bed. 'That'll be you in a few hours, a wee baby in your arms.'

'A baby,' gargled Isobel. 'I think I'm going to be sick.'

The sister put a tiny punnet by the pillow. Her badge said Sister Nell Bridges. 'Where are you from, Isobel?'

'Nowhere. I can't have a baby, I'm only eighteen, it's not fair.'

Sister Bridges pumped the blood pressure machine. 'Jolly good,' she said. The machine gave a long sigh. 'Now, let's have a look down here.'

'I never wanted a baby, why would I want a baby? I just wanted . . . Aaah!'

'You're well on, lovie. We'd better get Charmaine to prep you. Can you get yourself out of your clothes?'

Isobel looked down at her mountainous abdomen. 'It's too big. I can't.'

'Can't what?' inquired Charmaine crisply from the stainless steel bench where she was preparing instruments like a torturer.

'It's not fair,' wailed Isobel. 'It's not fair.'

'Lie back, I'm going to shave you.'

'What!'

'It's hygiene. Didn't you go to antenatal, you and your hubby? My fiancé and me, we're going together.'

'My hus . . . Clyde didn't need to. He's delivered calves and lambs, he could easily deliver a baby.'

'Pity he isn't here then, isn't it. Right, enema next. Ray and I are starting a family soon as we're married, one of each, we want.' She was pulling a long tube out of a packet. 'That's one good thing, you're starting nice and young.'

She advanced with nozzle and tube. Isobel arched her back as the pain attacked. She hissed into Charmaine's imperturbable face, 'I'm not *starting anything*, specially not a *family*.'

'Nonsense,' said Charmaine. 'Now hold still,' and she inserted the nozzle.

144

'What's the time?' Isobel inquired blearily. Hospital linen buried her like snow.

'Breakfast time,' said Sister Bridges. 'Hungry, lovie? Try something, you had a long night.'

Isobel tried to remember but what she had been through bore no relation to night or day, wakefulness or dreaming. 'I made a fuss, didn't I?'

Sister Bridges smiled. 'Some do, some don't.'

Isobel hated to be one who did. 'What did I do?'

'It's only a bruise, and Charmaine should have kept out of the way. She's young, she's got a lot to learn.' Isobel frowned. Charmaine looked twenty-two or three so why was Nell Bridges speaking as if Isobel were the older wiser one? She plumped Isobel's pillows and propped her up. 'Hubby rang, sounded a bit under the weather, but he'll be in this afternoon. And after you've eaten, we'll bring Baby in.'

Isobel sipped pale tea. The second bed in the small room was mercifully empty. Through the window she saw begonias in rows and a trimmed lawn. Gingerly she poked her abdomen. It was tender and extraordinarily empty. There were carnations and gypsophila on the bedside table, rammed into two ugly vases. She reached for the cards. *Congratulations and love from Adrian and Jo. Bloody well done, now on with the dance, from Cam (Hurley) and Cheryl.* She sipped more tea and thought about the congratulations – for surviving, she supposed. For descending into hell and coming back to sip tea and look out of windows. It was all right here, really, like a hotel. Although something wasn't quite right – her breasts, they were bruised and tender too, but rather than empty, horribly full. She shuddered and withdrew her hand.

'Here he is then,' said Nell Bridges, bustling into the room.

'Clyde!' breathed Isobel, wishing she had had time to comb her hair.

'A dear little boy. Just over nine pounds. No wonder you gave Mum such a hard time, you little monkey,' she cooed into the bundle of bedding in her arms. Isobel watched as the bundle passed from the beaming sister to herself. She peered into it. *Say thank you, Isobel.*

Nell Bridges chuckled. 'Don't thank me, lovie. It was all your own work. Now I'll leave you two to get to know each other. You might try giving him a bit of a feed and I'll come back in a wee while and see how you're doing.'

Isobel listened to the capable feet retreat down the corridor. The tiny red face in the blankets screwed itself up. It was far from lovely. Ages passed. Her arms ached but there was nowhere to put the bundle except on the end of the bed and she was sure that would not do. She tried to recapture her former serenity by gazing out of the window but she felt minute struggles against her aching arms and sore breasts. It was trying to get away, it didn't like her, and why should it? She wondered about ringing the bell, fetching someone, anyone. It gave a terrible squeak. Then another. The squeaks merged into a long piercing mewl and Isobel wanted to join in. It needed someone, she needed someone. Where was everybody?

'Well, for goodness sake,' trilled Charmaine, 'you can't sit there blubbing, you're a mother now. He's hungry. Up with that gown and try him on the breast.'

Isobel watched in mute dismay as Charmaine tweaked her nipple into the mewling mouth and the mouth spat it out. 'You see,' wept Isobel, and she held the baby out to Charmaine.

By the time Clyde arrived, they had wheeled in an ugly steel cot. 'They're modern here, you're lucky,' Charmaine informed her. 'It's rooming in.'

The baby had finally consented to suck. The sensation was akin to running her finger down a blackboard, and Isobel was absolutely convinced no milk passed between them. The very idea was ludicrous. Yet now the baby lay snuffling like a guinea pig in its layers of wrappings. Clyde squinted out from a severe hangover into the cot and extracted a tiny hand hooked tight around his finger.

'It likes you,' said Isobel, vaguely gratified.

Clyde grinned and his eyes went pink. 'A son.'

That night Isobel lay rigid, her nerves stretched to screaming point by a barrage of miniature snuffles and squeaks from the cot. She thought the night would never end. She prayed for someone to come and take the baby away. But as the sky leached to a cold grey she realised they never would. She was a mother now.

She slipped from the high bed, fearful of the effects of gravity on her loosened insides. She wheeled the clanking cot through the door and parked it in the dim corridor, then crept back to bed and fell alone into a pit of sleep.

Chapter 19

CLYDE SWUNG THE CAR INTO THE GILTRAPS' DRIVE AND ISOBEL rounded on him. 'You said they'd have gone. You *said.*' He crushed a half-smoked cigarette into the ashtray. 'You ought to be able to smoke if you want, it's your place now, you should stand up to him.' He wore no expression, bore no resemblance to a husband. The baby let out a demanding yell.

Clyde did not move. 'I'll just . . .'

"It's time for his bottle. You're coming in with me."

Clyde's mother made impotent little swoops from the top step. 'Aaah, the wee thing! Let me have him. What an angel.'

'He's wet and hungry,' Isobel informed her coldly. In the house, the floor and every other horizontal surface was clogged with half-packed boxes and heaps of ugly possessions. She thought to ask if she could heat the bottle then marched to the kitchen bench without a word. It was their house now, hers and Clyde's.

'Clyde's lost weight,' cheeped Muriel. 'Is he eating properly, dear?'

Isobel gripped the bench as Muriel and Jacko's clutter advanced like a tumour. She pictured her mother whirling through the chaos, ferociously establishing order. Muriel was incapable; Muriel, she realised with disgust, would foist this lot onto her and Clyde rather than dispose of it.

Her mother-in-law said, 'He's growing so fast, the dear wee thing. Have you got a name yet?'

'Dylan,' said Isobel, dripping warm milk on her wrist.

'Oh,' said Muriel.

'We like it, don't we, Clyde? Dylan David.'

Clyde was fiddling with a box of ornaments which included the leering Toby jug. 'Where's the old man?'

'Don't do that, Clyde. Killing something for tomorrow,' said Muriel, gasping with delight as the baby in her arms latched onto the teat. Then, with determined gaiety, 'We thought we may as well have Christmas as a family, now you're here.'

Isobel nearly burst into tears – not just at the prospect of Christmas with the Giltraps but because the incapable Muriel had outwitted her. 'Clyde said you wanted us to call the baby Jackson but we thought . . .'

'Jackson's the family name,' said Muriel. 'Do you want a cup of tea? Put the jug on, Clyde. We'll have a nice cup of tea.'

'Not your family though,' said Isobel sweetly.

Muriel looked bewildered. 'The family name,' she repeated. 'Isn't it, Clyde?' Clyde shrugged. 'It's been in the family for generations, and as it's a boy, Jacko and I thought . . .'

'What did Jacko and I think?' growled Clyde's father, kicking off his boots at the door. Clyde stood to attention.

'We thought, didn't we, they might call the baby Jackson as . . .'

'Suppose they can call it what they bloody well like,' said Jacko, splashing water over his hands at the sink.

'Yes, that's what we thought, didn't we, Clyde, so we chose Dylan.' Isobel tried to ignore the tremor that Jacko's arrival had caused, the tremor that made her a Giltrap.

'Sounds like the bloody Wild West. Where's my tea?'

Muriel bundled baby and bottle into Isobel's arms and scuttled to the jug. Isobel managed a hollow laugh. 'Not double l, i. It's got a y.'

Jacko's eyes narrowed. 'Never heard of it.'

Isobel said, 'I think he's had enough. Would you wind him, Clyde?' But Clyde was paralysed.

'Perhaps Jacko'd like to,' twittered Muriel, clattering cups.

'No,' said Isobel, pulling the baby against her. Jacko scowled, the baby burped.

'Aaah,' breathed Muriel.

'Bloody Poms,' snarled Jacko. 'Come over here and think they can have it all their own way.'

'Now, Jacko,' said Muriel, slopping tea. Isobel rubbed the baby's back too hard and Clyde shifted his weight from one foot to another.

Jacko slurped. 'Where's the bloody sugar? You haven't bloody sugared it, woman.'

Isobel's hand shook as she pulled off the baby's nappy in a clearing on the floor. 'We're all Poms really, aren't we?' she said around the safety pins. 'Unless you're Maori.'

Jacko leaned over her. 'Been to the cemetery, have you?'

'Clyde showed me the gravestones.' She refused to look at him, refused to show him the whites of her eyes.

'Six bloody generations of Giltraps in that cemetery, four of them Jacksons.'

Isobel straightened the baby's clothes and got to her feet with him in her arms. 'Yes,' she said brightly. 'And the first one was born in Lancashire and emigrated in eighteen fifty-three – a Pom, like me.'

Jacko turned purple and clenched the fist nearest to Muriel's flowery teacup. 'But you know better than six generations of Giltraps, you have to dream up some stupid bloody name.' The fist struck the table. The baby jumped and let out a bleat.

'Isobel,' murmured Muriel, twisting her cardigan buttons.

'You'll frighten the baby.'

Jacko whirled on Clyde. 'And you can bloody well come outside and help me load stuff in the shed instead of standing around like a bloody girl.' Clyde grinned like a caged primate and the sight of him forced Isobel to turn on her heel and leave the house.

Fluffy clouds were scattered across a nursery-blue sky, and the air was sweet after the foulness of the kitchen. She was hardly aware of Dylan still in her arms until she was away from the house. He snored in her ear as she strode past the tumbledown sheds and outhouses overflowing with rusting junk Jacko had hoarded for decades. The Giltraps, she decided grimly, should have been forced to emigrate – leaving your country of birth compelled you to leave your rubbish behind. The Giltraps never, apparently, let go of anything. She bent her head to pass through the sour wasteland under the line of macrocarpas behind the milking shed. With her free hand she yanked at the coarse greenery, crushed it and inhaled – Woodland Rise grabbed her by the throat. She pictured the bedraggled tree by the front door beneath whose scratchy branches she and Gillian and Cynthia had set up house, played shop, fought off Indians. Her mother had sent photographs of somewhere new and spacious with pale walls, she and Isobel's father smiling pleasantly like someone else's parents. Dylan's grandma and granddad, Dylan's aunts – terms made meaningless by distance. *So pleased to be Home. Daddy loves his new job, business trips to Paris and Budapest, maybe even Moscow, lucky thing. He'll write when things aren't so hectic. Gillian's planning for Exeter University, lovely boyfriend who's going to Oxford. Cynthia likes the grammar school. We love our new house but so much to do* . . . It was this gay style, quite unlike anything Isobel knew of her mother, which finally brought it home to her that now she was off the scene, now they no longer had her to contend with, the Midwinters could be a real family. It was Isobel who had spoiled it all those years, Isobel who had been the cuckoo in the nest, the odd one out, the silly mistake.

But now she was here and they were over there, and it was crystal clear that was how it should have always been.

She glimpsed grey water beyond the fence, heard a manic screech. The baby whimpered and blinked awake. She posted him between two bottom wires, then clambered over the fence next to a post, as Clyde had taught her. Picturing Muriel's horror at the baby resting even for a second on potentially damp grass made her smile as she bent to pick him up, and he beamed back a smile of such radiance, it felt like when he used to kick her.

The pond was punctured by desolate reeds, and half a dozen big birds sailed elegantly between them – sooty, with red beaks and perfectly coiffed tail-feathers. One stretched its neck and screeched at them. 'Swans, Dylan,' she whispered. 'Lovely black antipodean swans.' She stood for minutes, forcing herself to see these, and not the white swans of childhood, as real swans.

When she turned back, her shadow loped across the paddock ahead of her. The sheds loomed, their chaotic interiors dark and forbidding. The house crouched in its lifeless garden. She thought at first the growling was an animal, the dogs scrapping in their pen, maybe. Jacko was a dark shape by the back door, Clyde a lesser one. As she drew nearer, whatever they were carrying between them hit the concrete with a vicious crack. Jacko lunged, bellowing. His fist found Clyde's cheek with another crack and Clyde went down. Isobel froze in disbelief. Jacko vanished into a shed. Muriel fluttered in the doorway. Isobel broke into a run, thrust Dylan at Muriel and went to Clyde. He was blinking like the baby, trying to lift his head. Her tears wet his swelling cheek. 'I'm sorry, I'm so sorry, Clyde,' she said. It was his daughter-in-law Jacko had wanted to strike. But even his empire did not extend to her.

Muriel produced ice and a cloth. White and numb-looking, Clyde levered her off. She wrung her hands. 'Oh dear, the skin's broken. Does he need to see the doctor, do you think, Isobel? Sit down, Clyde. Perhaps he ought to lie down. Oh dear, what a silly accident.'

Isobel gaped. 'His father hit him!'

'Shh, dear.'

Isobel held the baby against her hammering heart. She understood now why Clyde looked nothing like a husband – because he was still a son. It was up to her to transform him into a spouse, a father. Dylan wriggled but she held him tight – he was hers, as much hers as Clyde's. She would not let him become a Giltrap. At the sink, Muriel rinsed watery blood from the cloth.

Chapter 20

THE FARM WAS EVERYTHING ISOBEL HAD HOPED FOR. ITS RULES were weather and season, sunrise and sunset; its absolutes, sex, food, birth and death. The cramped house in which Muriel had fussed her life away was merely a place to sleep and eat; real life lay beyond the garden fence. At Isobel's prompting, Clyde escaped the drudgery of twice-daily milking soon after they took over by selling the dairy herd and buying in beef cattle and sheep. His father was reportedly furious, but his father was hundreds of miles away, and it was Clyde's name on the title. The sheep ran through the old fences like water but Isobel outflanked them, shouting and waving her arms while Clyde hastily plugged the gaps. She rammed postholes and stapled battens, drafted beasts, grubbed ragwort and thistle, fed out silage. Dirty dishes piled up in the sink, beds stayed unmade, floors unswept. She wore dirty trousers and gumboots day after day, paid no attention to hair or makeup. Domestic Science paled into insignificance next to farm work. Never had she felt less like her mother's daughter.

They were late shutting up the paddocks for hay, the second

summer, and late getting it in. But the sky was a determined blue, the hills bleached corduroy. When the clanking mower moved on to the next farm, Isobel waded into cut grass like long hair. She saw it slip through her mother's fingers, spill across the floor. Clyde appeared beside her with two pitchforks. 'Have to turn the corners by hand,' he said, and the two of them moved rhythmically through the airy grass, lifting and turning, lifting and turning, while skylarks warbled overhead.

Next day another machine trundled over the paddocks, clumsily sweeping them clean, depositing neat bales in its wake. That night as a morepork called from the garden, she began a letter. *Dear* . . . she wrote, and barely faltered. Time and distance rendered *Mum and Dad* – even *dear* – acceptable options. She filled page after page with news of Dylan and Clyde, the farm, their neighbours and haymaking. She included photographs backed with sprightly captions. She read and re-read this version of her new life and days later dropped it in the letterbox in the centre of the town designed like a Union Jack.

When it was time to get the hay into the barn, Isobel took the wheel of a huge truck and Clyde and the boys from down the road hurled up bales to a boy on the deck who stacked them as lightly as kids' blocks. Clyde had done the same for them a few days earlier. The Birchall boys had polished chests and self-conscious grins. Bemused, they had watched Isobel struggle with a bale – their mother and sister stayed indoors, as Muriel had done. 'Green,' mumbled the oldest. 'Makes it heavy.' It was his idea she drive, freeing the men to load. She covered the paddocks in decreasing circles, stopping where she judged they could retrieve the greatest number of bales. As she hauled on the wheel, a car honked from the road. 'I'm not stopping,' she yelled at Clyde. 'Whoever it is.'

His face was streaked with sweat and dirt, hay stuck in his hair. She was proud of them both, of their teamwork. Sometimes she would look at him now and feel a flicker of hope, though for what exactly she could not have said.

'Gidday,' called Cam, stumping over the paddock. Behind him came Cheryl, a burly woman who moved like the Birchall boys, and two little girls tricked out in pastel dresses and frilly socks as if to compensate. Isobel proudly pulled the truck to a halt and gave them a welcoming smile, although behind it she was puzzled. Cam surveyed the paddock, hands in pockets. 'Good cut?' he inquired of Clyde. They moved off to poke bales and inspect stubble with manly grunts.

'This is Carmen and that's Amber,' said Cheryl. 'Don't do that, Amber. Where's yours?'

Isobel was prodded by guilt. 'In the house, asleep. I was just going to check.' But the paddock was golden in the late afternoon, the hay almost in.

'I'll take over,' said Cam, rolling up city sleeves.

'It's all right . . .' protested Isobel. But he was clambering up to the cab before she was even out.

'I'd kill for a cuppa,' said Cheryl, in her burly way, so Isobel gave in and turned for the house.

Dylan lay thoughtfully in his cot. 'Aaah,' cooed the little girls, just like Muriel.

'You're lucky he's so good,' pronounced Cheryl over folded arms. 'These two were a couple of whingers, still are.'

Isobel plucked him out. He was good, she supposed, if that meant he tolerated her clumsy efforts to care for him, her awkward gestures of affection. Yet sometimes when he turned his blue gaze on her she wondered if he were not merely biding his time.

Cheryl held out her arms. 'Bit hot, aren't you, pumpkin. Let's get this off you. Where are your clean naps, Iz? I'll see to him, you put the jug on. Didn't realise how bloody far it was over that hill. You can show me round while it's boiling. There, that's better, isn't it, tuppence-ha'penny. Blow your nose, Amber. Carmen, stop fiddling.' She planted Dylan on a capable hip. 'How'd you manage when he was born, Iz? Mum came for both mine. You must miss yours.'

Isobel murmured ambiguously. She filled the jug, grappling

with the notion that Cam and Cheryl believed she and Clyde were a real couple, and that they wanted to be friends, the way real couples were. She tipped gingernuts onto a plate and hoped nobody would notice they were not homemade scones or jam sponge. 'We're going to knock this wall out to make the living area bigger. Then we'll put ranchsliders in and build a deck. And there's tons to do in the garden.' She gestured at the scorched lawn and its few desperate shrubs. 'I want peonies and Russell lupins and lilac and Michaelmas daisies.' In her mind she filled the garden with flowers from her childhood, and imagining how it would all look one day – a kind of antipodean Woodland Rise – made how it looked now – the bleak Muriel and Jacko-ness of it – recede.

She and Cheryl returned to the kitchen and Cheryl flopped in a chair. 'God, I hope we can stay for tea. Can't face that drive, with the girls puking and whingeing in the back.'

'Of course,' said Isobel, as if nothing were more natural. She did a rapid mental search of the freezer.

'Been wanting to come over for ages,' remarked Cheryl, beefy arms on the table. 'You were great, the night of the funeral. I said to Cam, she's great, a real goer. Shall we take the boys out some tea or will they come in?'

In fact, 'the boys' did not come in until after dark. When they had drunk their tea, Isobel poured herself and Cheryl bacardi and cokes, feeling as if she were playing grown-ups. They prepared vegetables side by side at the sink and Cheryl wrote out two mince recipes and provided Isobel with a lurid account of both her caesareans. Dylan tottered across the floor under Cheryl's approving gaze, and Isobel watched as if he were someone else's child.

'Right,' said Cheryl, hands on hips. 'Bath, you lot.' She scooped up Dylan and shooed the grizzling little girls ahead of her. This, Isobel supposed, was the sort of thing Cheryl's mother had done. No wonder she had found it so helpful.

The Birchall boys gruffly refused to follow Cam and Clyde

inside. They sat on the step with bottles of beer and cast shy glances into the kitchen, while moths battered the porch light and Isobel felt light-headed with company.

'Great tucker,' said Cam, pushing back his plate some time later. 'You can cook as well, Iz.'

She made instant coffee and Cam offered Clyde a cigar. 'There's brandy in the cupboard, Clyde. Jacko left it.' She loaded a tray and led them into the sitting room. Any minute someone would put *Stranger on the Shore* on the stereo and her father and Aunty Iris would foxtrot into view.

'So,' inquired Cam soberly from the armchair, 'how's married life treating you?' Clyde grinned and puffed on his cigar. 'Yup, married life, great institution.'

Isobel stirred her coffee. Married life was a mythic state enjoyed – or endured – by others; arrangements between her and Clyde were considerably more pragmatic. And yet . . . she recalled the flicker of hope in the hay paddock. 'Been married for six, nearly seven years, Cheryl and me, haven't we, dear?' Cheryl nodded. 'Can't beat it, I reckon. And we love each other, goes without saying.'

Isobel twitched with discomfort – one did not speak of love in other people's lounges. 'Overrated, though, isn't it?' she said briskly. 'There are dozens of reasons for getting married and love isn't necessarily the best. I mean, there's . . . there's children and . . .' She faltered, feeling foolish.

'Told you,' Cheryl told her husband. 'Didn't I tell you?'

'You did, dear, you did.'

Cheryl leaned confidentially towards Isobel, exposing an intimidating expanse of thigh. 'He didn't think you'd be a starter but I said, look how she was at the party – the funeral, I mean. I could tell, I can always tell.'

'She always can,' said Cam. 'Got to hand it to her, my wife.'

Cheryl swung her substantial legs onto the couch, nudging Clyde with her bare toes. 'People make such a fuss about sex,' she declared.

'Just a physical act,' supplied Cam. 'Like those hippie people say, make love not war.'

'Not mutually exclusive, though, are they,' said Isobel, impressed by the intellectual turn of the conversation.

'What?' said Cheryl.

'Love and war, not mutually exclusive. In fact they often go together.' She was remembering her mother's tales of wartime romance and heartbreak, overnight engagements and regretful letters to boys serving in India. And, *Of course we love you, you stupid girl, now do as you're told* – eighteen years of love and war. 'More brandy, Cheryl?'

'Thanks, Iz. Like Cam says, we've been married six years. Love each other, goes without saying, but what's it got to do with sex, we say?'

'I don't know,' said Isobel. She wished Clyde would contribute something.

'What we say,' continued Cheryl, 'is you do what you have to to keep your marriage strong. That's what we say.'

Cam clapped his hands on his knees and cheerily surveyed his hosts. 'And if that means spicing things up a bit from time to time, well . . .' He got to his feet and flicked off the main light. 'Put some music on, mate, get us started,' he instructed Clyde.

Clyde did as he was told, as Isobel tried, unsuccessfully, to catch his eye. Cam held out a hand and she jiggled dutifully in front of him on Muriel's carpet. Her head swam with brandy and fatigue, and, before long, with the effort of eluding Cam. He squashed against her – he was startlingly squashy. She fended him off with an impersonal smile. A hand materialised on her breast, and she regarded it with distaste before flicking it off. He made musical pelvic thrusts in her direction, then lunged at her ear and gasped something obscurely intimate. When the Stones finally failed to get any satisfaction, Isobel returned to her chair, feigning breathlessness. At first she thought Cheryl and Clyde must have left the room. In fact, Cheryl had Clyde pinned decisively to the couch. A conscientious arm – his – was holding a cigarette away from the action. Isobel wondered if she ought to take it to prevent an accident, then decided it was none of her business if he wanted to have an accident underneath Cheryl. Cam dropped to his knees in front of her, blocking her view of the other two, and pushed up her skirt. She pushed it down, he pushed it up again with a sporting grin. She peered over his shoulder, but whatever Cheryl was doing to Clyde had obliterated him from view. Was this what couples who were friends did? *I bet you do it, you two.* Cam fumbled with the fly of his Prince of Wales check polyester and wool blend slacks. What emerged was so much more a humorous prop than a sex organ, she had to stifle a giggle. He must have interpreted this as the sound of passion because he began struggling with her pants. Well, why not? she thought. This was the sixties, this was her day. The rules were different, there were no rules now, she was free. Cam grasped her thighs and edged forward, panting with intent.

'No,' she said, leaping up and toppling him to the carpet. 'No. I heard something, the baby.' And she fled.

She would never finally know what made her use the baby as an excuse, what might have happened had she not. Then again, perhaps Dylan really had alerted her with a cry, or a tug at her subconscious – *you're a mother now.* She didn't hear herself cry out either but must have because suddenly they were all clustered around the cot – Cam and Cheryl, Clyde, the blinking little girls – milling about, shouting conflicting orders. Dylan was white in the bottom of the cot, his mouth a sweet mauve bud. In the seconds it took to reach in and seize him, his back arched, his eyes rolled and he bloomed lavender to navy.

He'll die. Because I never expected a baby.

He'll die. I'll leave Clyde and start my real life.

He'll die. And I don't know what next.

She heard a raucous sound that hurt her throat. Cheryl roared, 'Stop it,' and slapped her enthusiastically. Hands swarmed over the small body. Somehow they got him breathing again and she watched transfixed as the glorious navy faded to lavender and back to everyday pale. Someone said it was a fit and ran a cool bath to prevent him having another. Someone else soothed the little girls. And somehow it was decided that Cam and Cheryl would drive Isobel and Dylan over the hill to the hospital. Rushing the swaddled baby out to the car, Isobel noticed Cam's fly was still unzipped. She didn't even see Clyde.

Chapter 21

THEY MADE HER WAIT OUTSIDE THE CURTAINED CUBICLE WHILE they administered a lumbar puncture. She paced the battered lino. Something terrible had happened, something she could not grasp – not to Dylan but to her. The Casualty sister had put a soothing hand on her arm. 'S'pect you'd like to take Baby home with you, dear. We'll just let Doctor take a wee look but I'm sure it'll be good as gold.'

Isobel shook off the hand. 'Don't you have to keep him in?'

The sister eyed her. 'Most mums are keen to get their wee ones back. Chance in a million of it happening again, dear.'

'I thought he was going to die.' *And it would all be my fault. I'm a mother now, so everything will always be my fault.*

A scream pierced the institutional calm. Isobel pictured professional hands, the milky bones and rose-petal skin, a steel needle. She ran.

'Mrs Giltrap? Well, there you are,' reproached the sister, finally locating Isobel in a remote corridor. 'Baby needs you, dear. Where on earth . . .?'

'Toilet,' muttered Isobel, two steps behind as the sister marched her back to Casualty. She fumbled for Dylan. His face was white with shock, but he regarded her knowingly, allowed himself to be held.

'Doctor's eliminated meningitis, dear. He's quite sure it was just a febrile convulsion, a fit. But I've told him how worried you are and he's agreed to admit Baby for a day or two.' She slipped an arm round Isobel's shoulder. She seemed to use Savlon as a personal fragrance. 'An Only, is he? Aaah. You must have thought you were going to lose him. Time to start thinking about another one, isn't it.'

I'm an Only, Isobel thought, and her bones ached with it.

Her heart sank when Adrian opened the door. She felt emptied out, as if she had given birth again, and longed to creep upstairs to the single bed in the spare room. 'You shouldn't have waited up.'

He drew her inside. 'I'll make some tea. I've been so worried.'

She folded into a chair, disoriented by the force of his concern. 'I'm all right. Just tired, I've been up since five, with the hay and everything. He's okay they think.' The hay paddock was a scene from another life.

'Wouldn't they let you bring him home?'

'They said they wanted to keep an eye on him.' She looked away, discouraging further questions.

He was not discouraged, he took her hand. 'It must have broken your heart, leaving him there.'

She hunched over the table, neck and jaw clenched, shoulders like steel. Everyone knew how she felt. Her real feelings lay buried like a murder weapon. She kept seeing the baby in his cot, lips like a blackberry stain, as it hit her over and over again like Jacko's fist that she had made this small life in a stab of blind self-interest, to save her own. It was worse than causing another's death, death at least was the end of it, but the ripples from Dylan's birth would go on and on. There would be no end to her responsibility and her lack of it.

'Jug's boiling,' she said, reclaiming her hand. 'Cheryl was marvellous, and Cam.'

Adrian dumped the teapot on the table and she played her fingers over its fat sides. He said, 'Say what you like about Cheryl and Cam, they're good sorts underneath.' She considered for a moment telling him what else they were but was too drained for humour. He patted her hand. 'Drink up before it gets cold.' She flicked her hand away and drank. She surveyed the familiar jumble of the kitchen, tried to let it soothe her. Exhaustion was descending like a blanket.

'I'll drive you to the hospital tomorrow.'

'No, really . . .' Was there no end to his persistence?

'Listen, Isobel, what I said when Christopher . . . when he died, it's still true.' *Oh God, not this again.* And again, he searched diligently for her hand, was determined to make eye contact. 'You needn't worry, Isobel, I'm not going to take advantage of you. I just want you to know that you can lean on me.'

She didn't want to lean on him, she wanted him to be quiet and leave her alone, why didn't everyone just leave her alone?

'I know you haven't had much . . . much love in your life . . .' How? she wanted to demand, you don't know anything about me, nobody does. She felt his breath on her face but could not summon the strength to pull away, or to avoid his eye. Clyde's eyes were chips of blue glass, Adrian's made her feel like a reluctant guest being drawn into a warm room.

'. . . I know you're suspicious . . . I know you've learned to be independent and look out for yourself . . .'

There's an undertow, she is slipping away with it, something is. She feels how much fight there is in her now it's giving itself up inch by rushing inch. She is losing her footing.

'. . . but it's not the right way to live, I know it isn't. We all need . . .'

His voice is stretching out of shape, curving like space, and she is somewhere out there floating and diving, swimming and soaring, her Isobel edges melting like milk and honey . . .

'I spend all day talking to people who don't trust me, Isobel. But you and I . . .'

You and I, you and I . . . like stones in a pool, rippling out and out to circle the globe until here she is on the far side looking back at Isobel and Adrian as the circles go wider and deeper through you and I and here and there and now and then for ever and ever amen.

'. . . love is all that matters, Isobel. Isobel? You look bushed, let's get you to bed.' He reached for her cup.

She grabbed his hand, clunking the cup against the table. 'What happened? Something happened.'

He shook his head and half rose. 'You're exhausted . . .'

Her head was flooded with light, as if she had stared into the sun, been blinded by the face of God. 'I was looking at you and then . . . I wasn't here or there, I was everywhere and I was you too.' She was breathless, pumping his hand, impatient for the excitement of it to dawn on him. He was tied up like a parcel, yet he had been the cause. 'Adrian, Adrian, listen. People aren't alone at all, are they? We're not separate or single, not ever, we're joined underneath like . . . like continents are. That's what you mean by love, isn't it? That's what love is, knowing that.'

He glimpsed familiar ground. 'That's what I've been trying to tell you – that . . . that I love you, Isobel.'

Love is God. And God – with his vast map and big nicotine-stained finger – had finally found her. She would never be an Only again. She laughed joyfully into Adrian's face. 'And I love you, yes, of course I do.'

She led him upstairs, squeezing his big hand so the warmth of it flowed up her arm and around her heart. Adrian's face was a pale blank. She drew him into the spare room. She felt as radiant as the moonlight falling across the bed, enchanted. Something enormous had happened, something that demanded consummation. Adrian had been the cause of it, it had to be

Adrian. They sat on the bed and she put his hand on her breast. He flinched and pulled away. 'It's all right,' she soothed. 'It's what you've been trying to tell me for years, but I was scared. I thought I was alone, I thought I was *meant* to be alone, that we all were, but now . . .'

He sat on the edge of the bed, shaking his head as if trying to clear it. 'Isobel, this isn't what I meant . . .'

'You love me,' she said, loving the glorious simplicity of it. 'Yes, but . . .'

She pulled her jersey over her head and his eyes widened. She stepped out of her skirt and sat next to him again. His eyes slid away from her thigh but his hand reached out. They kissed briefly before he pulled back in alarm.

'Yes,' she said, 'it's all right. Lie down with me, come on.' She moved towards his mouth, wriggling up against him, trying to unbend him. His arms tightened, and she felt the pressure of him through his trousers. By the time she had unzipped him, though, he was wilting. She had not known erections could be so unreliable – Clyde's was a fencepost. She felt a shimmer of doubt – did she, after all, want him this way, did he want her? Was this what it all meant?

He glanced down blindly. 'Sorry . . .' But the loss seemed to galvanise him into action, his hand found her breast again and he murmured in her ear. 'Remember when we met, remember you were in school uniform? You were lovely, so young, and . . . and like a daughter. I always wanted a daughter.' His hand was moving inside her pants, inside her. She gasped. 'Isobel . . . be . . . my little girl.' He was struggling with his trousers, lifting himself over her. They groaned as he slipped inside. She gripped him tight enough to hurt her arms, tight enough to keep out the doubt. 'My Isobel, my little girl. You love me, don't you, little girl. Tell me you love me.'

'I do, I love you, Adrian.'

'Call me Daddy. Say, I love you, Daddy, say it, say it.'

She held back, but only for a second. Then out it tumbled

like an avalanche, carrying away her doubt, herself and Adrian with it – 'I love you. Daddy . . . Daddy . . . Daddy. . .'

She woke to the thump of feet on the stairs, the aroma of toast, and the knowledge of Jo – Adrian's wife. She imagined her with her usual cup of tea at the back door surveying her garden, oblivious to the domestic chaos behind her. A chaos to which Isobel had now made a shocking contribution. She hid her face in the sheets, sheets Jo had laundered and spread on the bed. Images from the previous day presented themselves like polaroids – Cam's comical sexual equipment, the mauve bud in the bottom of the cot, the gleam of medical tools. And Adrian. Terror and elation surged through her body like foolishly mixed drinks at a party. Her head was two or three times its normal size, the surface of her skin charged. She wanted to shout and wave her arms as if she had scaled a mountain, but she cowered under the covers.

She must pull herself together, it was all her fault – she said this to herself sternly several times, but rather than sobering her up, it had the reverse effect. Ridiculous to think in terms of fault, ridiculous to reduce something so momentous to just another *silly mistake*. Now she knew there was no such thing, ever, as a mistake. Now she knew that everything – every tiny incident and petty setback – was crucial to the splendour she had glimpsed the night before. It was like peering into Andrea Dodds' kaleidoscope, seeing all the glittering fragments click into one glorious design. She leaped joyfully from the bed, heard footsteps on the landing, and leaped back again, heart thumping.

Adrian. His discomfort so contagious she could barely look at him. 'Thanks,' she said, taking the tea. He hesitated, leaned down and kissed her awkwardly on the brow. More from a sense of decorum than anything else, she tightened an arm round his neck and put her lips to his cheek. It lacked the resilience of Clyde's, felt uncertain. She felt a surge of determination – she would show him. He sat on the bed and stared at his shoes.

167

'Look, I just want to say about last night that . . .'

A door slammed and they both jumped violently.

'That's the thing,' muttered Adrian, head in hands. 'Jo. She'll have to know, I can't keep something like this from her.'

Isobel slopped tea on the sheets. Jo would be out in the garden now, hands in the earth. More than likely she knew already, had perceived their guilt seeping into the walls and spreading like a stain. There was an otherworldliness about Jo that it pained Isobel to imagine shattered, yet she had witnessed Jo's anger too, fierce and unreasoned, and always, like her love, directed at the boys. Recalling Jo's anger made her reach for Adrian's hand, slipping it into her nightdress to distract them both. He groaned and lunged across the bed, his tongue falling into her mouth.

'Bye, Dad,' said Martin from the doorway.

Adrian catapulted himself upright. 'Martin,' he managed gruffly. 'Where's Mum?'

Jo's grumpy little Hillman was making heavy weather of the hill. Whenever she could, Isobel pulled onto the shoulder and waved on the exasperated queue behind her. Normally she hated the hill – it was obstinate and ugly, it stuck itself in her way. Today it humoured her, let her climb it the way her father had once let her climb him, gripping his hands, walking all the way up to his chest and flipping over.

She had tiptoed down to the Glossops' kitchen and begun clearing surfaces, depositing cups and cereal bowls in the sink, football boots outside the door, jackets on pegs. The Glossops' mess was her mess. Sweeping toast crumbs into her hand, she wondered if Jo might regard this attitude as an invasion of her territory, yet now Isobel had launched the ultimate offensive on Jo's territory. She had run hot water into the sink, believing she was safe for the moment – Adrian appeared to have left for work. So she was shocked when he followed Jo into the kitchen, shot Isobel an unreadable look and continued on into the lounge, muttering about telephone calls.

'Oh lovely, you've cleaned up,' sighed Jo, sinking into a chair. 'The dahlias have got something, I had to spray.'

'Coffee?' Isobel offered duplicitously, putting on the jug.

There was an angry throbbing behind the Hillman, and in the rear-view mirror the maddened face of a truck driver and his outlandish female passenger. Isobel shrugged and gave a helpless grin. A few more twists of the road and she was able to pull over. Several strands of number eight wire stood between her and the thousand-foot drop. Below, the river twisted like silver ribbon. She smiled down at it. With a furious crash of gears the truck roared by. A familiar stench filled the car and through the slats of the truck, a hundred desperate eyes rolled.

'Coffee'd be lovely,' Jo had sighed. 'Did they leave you any bread?'

Isobel slyly studied her face – removed but amiable. Perhaps Adrian would wait until she had gone home to tell Jo. Perhaps he would change his mind about telling her altogether, perhaps it could be their secret. *I bet you do it, you two.*

'Adrian told me. About . . . you know.' A flush raced up Isobel's neck like a scrub fire. 'I think it might rain later, the garden'll be pleased. But I'd better not be inside too long. I told him not to panic. I told him we'd work it out.'

The flush disappeared, doused by the knowledge that Jo had failed to notice it. Jo's not noticing, Isobel understood, could be both a blessing and a torment.

Jo sighed again. 'It was inevitable really, I knew that. We stopped . . . all that sort of thing ages ago. And men do seem to need it, don't they?' Isobel nodded dumbly. 'He even started going on about divorce,' she said, looking up at Isobel with a wry grin. 'Honestly . . .'

Very carefully Isobel pulled out a chair and sat on it. 'I'm not telling Clyde,' she said, heart banging.

'No,' said Jo dreamily. 'Probably better not.' Another long pause. 'It'll be easier for you – for all of us, really – if he doesn't know, won't it.' She drank more coffee. 'There was a silly girl

Adrian brought home from the office once, I could see he was keen. She giggled nonstop and had awful silver nails. The boys wouldn't stop staring. I think she got engaged or went overseas or something. But you're used to this place, aren't you, and . . .' She petered out. 'I'll have to get going. I don't like the look of those clouds.'

Ahead was another narrow layby, and standing in it, thumb out, the woman from the sheep truck. Isobel pulled over. 'Want a lift?' she shouted through the closed window, although she had never before picked up a hitchhiker. The woman reached for the back door to push in her pack. 'A baby,' she remarked, with as much interest as one might display in a parcel.

'His name's Dylan. He's just come out of hospital.' The woman's indifference made Isobel perversely proud. The woman settled herself in the front seat. Isobel had seen pictures of people like her in the newspaper. 'Where are you going?'

'Wherever you're goin,' said the woman in a north American singsong.

'Home. About twenty miles from the bottom of the hill. Bulls Road.'

The woman – it was impossible to guess her age – leaned back and two dirty feet protruded from under the long faded skirt. 'I'm so happy to get away from that terrible man.'

Isobel persuaded the reluctant Hillman back into the traffic. 'The truck driver?'

'I told him Buddhists regarded trading in meat as one of the most undesirable ways to earn a living and he said if it was still pissing and shitting it wasn't meat, but the sooner the better.'

'My husband . . . we make a living out of meat,' said Isobel frankly. 'We've got a farm. I don't like it when the trucks come but there are good things about being on a farm too. Where are you from?'

'L.A., the armpit of the universe. Tell me about the good things.' The woman was on her knees, rummaging in the pack on the back seat. Dylan slumped in his baby seat like a small drunk, watching closely. The woman sat down with a pouch in her hand and looked expectantly at Isobel.

Isobel shrugged self-consciously. 'It's . . . real. Everything you do matters.' She shrugged again, feeling lame.

'That's what I came to New Zealand to find – reality. Doesn't exist in L.A. Mind if I roll a smoke? Tell me some more about your life.'

'I've fallen in love,' said Isobel, to her own surprise. These words covered only a part of what had happened to her in the last two days, but they were the only ones available – the world had no way of describing experiences that were out of this world. And besides, she had fallen, something had. 'He's married. His wife knows but she doesn't mind. This is her car.'

'Smart woman, you can't own people.' The woman licked a cigarette paper. As the car crested the summit, she nudged Isobel's arm and handed her an untidy roll-your-own. 'Christ knows what people mean when they talk about commitment. I mean' – she spread her hands – 'you commit people to prison and mental hospital. Hey, take a drag.'

Smoke tore at Isobel's throat and lungs like mustard gas and she erupted into violent coughing. She clipped her head on the steering wheel as the car lurched into a tight bend. 'Christ on a crouton,' exclaimed the woman, flinching from the drop. She gasped at the cigarette as if she were drowning and passed it back to Isobel. 'Been here long enough to know that's not a New Zealand accent. Where'd you grow up?'

'England,' croaked Isobel, for once not minding, pleased to establish herself with this new kind of woman as an outsider.

'So where are your family now?'

'Here.' Isobel nodded at the sleeping Dylan. 'Just what I made. I don't think about the rest, it's history.'

'I'll never go back either.' The woman gave Isobel a swift appraisal. 'Great talkin' to you. Great to know someone who's breaking new ground instead of going on in the same old way.'

Isobel had to persuade the woman out of the car at the

bottom of the hill. 'Bulls Road doesn't go anywhere, just farms. You'll get a ride north if you wait here.'

The woman dislodged Dylan's fingers from the straps of her pack. 'Thanks. And good luck, you deserve it.'

And Isobel drove on, believing absolutely that she did. She grinned at Dylan in the mirror and broke into lusty song – *And there's another country I heard of long ago, most dear to them that love her, most great to them that know* . . . She had reached it at last, that other country. There would be no going back.

Chapter 22

CLYDE WAS DOUBLED OVER AT THE BACK DOOR, PULLING OFF HIS boots. He looked so solitary, so self-contained, she was tempted to reverse out again. He turned and grinned – wider than she had ever seen him grin – and ran the few steps to the car in socked feet. 'How's the boy, how's the boy?' he cried, flinging the chortling baby into the air.

Isobel looked at the house and it looked back, Muriel-like. The battered steel bucket by the step, the jumble of gumboots, the muddy spade were startlingly eloquent. She drifted towards the washing line and began unpegging tea-towels she had hung there a century before. Instantly she was captivated by their knubbly whiteness, their narrow stripes of red and blue like lines of latitude and longitude. She fingered them, struggling to recall if they meant time or place and what the difference was. Her head swam. She groped for her bearings.

'Hey,' called Clyde. 'You got a visitor, been here since yesterday. Ted someone.'

She stomped into the kitchen wishing she were still heading

down a country road singing loud hymns. Ted who? she wanted to snap. I don't know any Ted. And if he had not emerged from the lounge to greet her, she might have slipped down the hall and out of the front door. His mouth twitched at the sight of the baby on her hip and he went to hug her. But she stood like a post and he withdrew, one ginger eyebrow raised.

'They must have told you about the baby,' she said, furious at her own embarrassment, as if he had caught her in an act of fraud.

'Looks like his dad.' Isobel set Dylan down, he staggered a few steps then sat and regarded Teddy. Isobel sat too, reminding herself of what she had seen a few nights ago, telling herself Teddy could not spoil it, could not pull her back. 'So,' she asked carelessly, 'what've you been doing?'

'Failed all my A levels, left school, left home . . .'

'I meant . . .'

He squinted at Clyde who had followed them into the lounge. 'What did we do, squire?' He made his voice gruffer, terser.

Clyde was pleased to be asked. 'Checked the ewes over the back. Some of the old bitches had got through to Birchall's. Had a go at some gorse while we were up there' – he nodded at Isobel – 'coming back in a big way. If Blackie calls, tell him we're out of 245T. What else? Killed a hogget. And taught him to sink a strainer. After a fashion.'

Clyde and Teddy grinned. *Teddy's mine.* 'Did you tell him about Dylan going to hospital?' She was a mother now, she would show him.

Clyde nodded and grinned down at the baby who was hauling himself up on Clyde's leg. It was the casual tolerance he displayed towards all young animals, his sort of love, Isobel supposed. 'What about a drink?' she said, turning a brilliant smile on him. He disappeared into the kitchen.

Teddy gestured at Dylan with his cigarette. 'This must have been worse than failing A levels. Did they throw you out?'

'I threw myself out,' she said with knee-jerk defiance.

'I was scared stiff of your ma. Still am. If she walked into the room, I'd jump to attention.'

'Well I . . .' Isobel stopped. She had been going to say *hated your father*, but it sounded intemperate, childish. And surely hate was only a lack of connection, a failure of love? 'Your father made me feel stupid, things went wrong whenever he was around. Your mother never noticed me. I liked that.' *Joined underneath like continents*, even to Uncle Max. And her mother. And Gillian. And Jacko and Muriel and Joan Fisk. Clyde thrust a drink into her hand. She took a huge gulp. 'I think I'm stoned. I gave an American girl a lift and she rolled something.'

Teddy looked less impressed than she would have wished, Clyde more so. 'How do you get used to that sort of thing?' said Teddy, nodding at Dylan who was seeing how big a pool he could dribble on the carpet. Teddy's vowels were a warm hand on her heart, his freckles and curls glowed. Next to him on the couch, Clyde was as dull as a wall.

She grinned. 'Gets worse than that on a farm.'

'I suppose you'll be having dozens more.'

'Let's go for a walk,' she said firmly. 'Clyde'll keep an eye on the baby, won't you, Clyde.'

She and Teddy strolled across the unkempt lawn to the front fence. Even the house's ugly brick veneer was mellow in the evening light. The elation she felt in the car surged through her again. 'I'm in love,' she said.

'Clyde . . .?' He was dubious.

A neighbour gunned his ute down the road and Isobel waved extravagantly. 'A friend, someone who was a friend until a couple of nights ago.'

'Christ, Iz, you only just got married, you've got a nipper. You going to bust it all up?'

She maintained her serene smile. 'Course not, there's no need. His wife says . . .'

'His wife!'

She leaned on the fence, staring back at the house. 'You're so old-fashioned, Teddy. You can't own people. And you can love more than one person at a time.' He stared down the road, but she knew that look and it infuriated her. 'Why shouldn't I be happy, why shouldn't I?'

'Don't ask me, Iz.' In the silence that followed, she realised she had in fact asked him nothing – about himself, why he was in the country, how long he intended staying. Before she had a chance, he muttered, 'Maybe you're lucky, I don't know.'

'It's not luck,' she said hotly.

He turned away from the road. 'It's so empty here.' He seemed to mean much more than rickety fences and sour shelter belts.

'When did you arrive?'

'Flew into Auckland a few days ago, hitched down. Your dad gave me your address, wished me luck. I can tell you what Gillian and Cynthia are up to and . . .'

'What happened? Did you row with your parents?'

He clenched his jaw. 'I'm more or less a permanent disappointment to Dad, he didn't even see me off.'

'So you're going to live here? What have you been doing since you left school?'

'Not much, few useless jobs. Painting.'

'This place needs . . .'

'Not house painting,' he said. 'Oils.'

He never used to paint. She didn't know what to say. 'Girlfriends?' she asked coquettishly, trying to nudge him out of his moroseness.

'Couple.' He shot her an unreadable look. 'Isobel, I want . . .'

'You'll be better off here, much better,' she said decisively. 'Away from' – she flapped a dismissive hand at the entire northern hemisphere – 'all that. The land of milk and honey, remember.'

Clyde's shadow fell across the lawn. Dylan bounced delightedly on his shoulders, holding tight to his ears. 'When's tea?'

She was peeling a potato when the telephone rang. It shot

from her hands and bounced across the floor. Wrong number. She returned to the sink, watched peel curl into muddy water. Adrian and she had promised each other nothing, and it wasn't that she missed him exactly, yet once the telephone had rung the thought of how easy it would be to speak to him niggled. *Call me Daddy. Say, I love you, Daddy* . . . By the time she put the potatoes on to boil, the niggle had become a torment. But it was out of the question. Clyde would not notice one toll call, maybe not six, but in the end . . . She turned to a flaccid row of sausages, stabbed six with a fork. With four to go, she wheeled on the telephone, fingers shaking over the dial. The no-such-number tone protested rudely. She tried to dial again. This time she forgot his number altogether. She put down the receiver, drew a deep breath, redialled and spoke to the operator, who after several seconds said mockingly, 'Engaged, sorry.'

Teddy and Clyde came into the kitchen. 'Snarlers,' said Clyde, fondling her buttock. 'Mighty.' Teddy averted his eyes.

'Turn over,' urged Clyde. She did so, telling herself she owed him a little pleasure. She tried to concentrate as he busied himself behind her, tried to overcome her dismaying sense of detachment. Perhaps it was Teddy in the sunporch. Or Adrian, the knowledge of him – and herself with him – invading her brain cells, oozing from her pores. Clyde fumbled for her breasts and she arched her back, timing her gasps to his thrusts. She pictured her mother dusting, scouring, hoovering, wondered if she had ever regarded sex as just more Domestic Science. Clyde paused strategically. She obliged with a moan, then thought she heard . . . what? A bump, a muffled tap? There it was again. Birchall's dog on the lawn, an escaped ewe? Clyde edged her nearer the headboard and she lunged backwards with a covering groan. 'Aaaargh,' he cried, bouncing against her buttocks. 'Aaaaaaargh. Ugh.'

'Oh. Aaah. Aaaaah,' cried Isobel. And then, 'Aaah,' just in case.

He collapsed beside her, fumbling for cigarettes. She fell back on the pillows, telling Adrian, *you see, I can manage, I can manage everything.*

Clyde leaped to his feet. 'Kill the light,' he ordered. 'Some bastard's out there.' She shot a horrified glance at the gap between Muriel's carelessly drawn curtains, swiped at the over-head switch and missed. She grabbed the sheet and covered herself. Clyde was wobbling on one leg, stabbing the other into trousers. 'I'm going after him,' he said, making for the door. 'Call the police.'

She lay paralysed under the sheet, heard him unlock the hall cupboard. 'Clyde!' she yelled. He reappeared, pushing car-tridges into his shotgun. She had never seen him so decisive – it was as impressive as it was alarming. 'Clyde, don't. You can't.' She struggled upright, desperate for her own ammunition. 'Teddy's in the house, it might have been Teddy.'

'Call the police,' he barked, and disappeared.

She couldn't find the telephone book. Then there was no answer at the local one-man station so she dialled the next town. 'Yes, madam,' said a desultory male voice.

'We've had a . . .' – what the hell did you call them? – 'peeping Tom. My husband's gone looking for him. With a gun.'

The voice snapped alert. It took her name and address, said it would be there in twenty minutes with a dog, and she would do them all a favour, madam, if she'd persuade her husband to put the gun down. Teddy materialised at the back door, pale-chested in jeans. She stared. 'That was the police. They're on their way.'

'What for?'

She pulled her dressing gown tight, aware of her nakedness and the stickiness between her legs. It was hard to meet his eye. 'There was someone outside. Clyde's gone looking.'

'Sit down, Iz. You look awful.' She sank into a chair, watching Teddy fill the jug, rinse cups, bring milk and sugar to the table, while in her mind she peered through the gap in the curtains and saw herself writhing on the bed with Clyde – caught in the act of pretence. *Lies were as undignified as school uniform – lies told the truth about how little freedom you had.* Her skin crawled.

Clyde burst in, panting with excitement. 'No bloody sign. He took off, the bastard.' There was a hunting gleam in his eye.

'The police are coming,' said Isobel. 'They said put the gun away.'

Teddy, pouring tea, said, 'Just some poor sod.'

The sergeant and Clyde were acquainted. They pumped each other's hands and grinned. The dog quivered at the end of a short leash like a massive version of Buster. 'Wouldn't do that if I were you, Mrs Giltrap,' rumbled the sergeant. 'He'll have you.'

Clyde, sergeant and dog disappeared into the dark. Isobel hoped Teddy would go back to bed but he poured more tea and lit up. She could think of absolutely nothing to say and the silence went on and on.

'Well, he's long gone,' said the sergeant from the back door. 'Not much hope of tracking him down. Ground's too hard under the window for any prints.' And Isobel looked down at Teddy's lonely English feet and thanked God.

Chapter 23

THE MEN'S EXHILARATION FLOODED THE KITCHEN. THEY MILLED about, propping shotguns against walls, blowing on their hands, peeling off boots and wet socks. Dylan stared up in wide-eyed admiration. 'Brass monkey weather,' said Clyde, pulling off his Swanndri.

'Feels like snow,' remarked Adrian. He caught Isobel's eye and she wanted to reach out and smooth his hair, but he pulled out a chair next to his wife and patted her hand, and she felt a glow of pride in his ability to do the right thing.

'Snow!' said Clyde, mocking Adrian's urban ignorance. 'Unheard of this time of year.'

Cam dropped heavily into the chair next to Isobel and clapped an icy hand on her knee. He smelled like Bonfire Night, an edgy scent of cold air and gunpowder. Opposite sat Teddy, smoking and sulking. She felt a surge of irritation and went to the other end of the kitchen, stepping around a sleek pile of bodies. 'How many?' she said, returning with a laden tray.

Adrian, Clyde and Cam exchanged grins. 'Let's just say we

got our limit,' decided Cam. They regarded the heap with pride.

'And who's going to pluck them?' demanded Cheryl, all elbows and bust.

'Sweetheart,' oozed Cam. 'You do it so well.' Cheryl, well pleased, gave him a kick.

'Poor things,' murmured Jo into her mug.

'Thousands of them die in the winter when there's nothing to eat,' Isobel told her. 'If you didn't shoot them they'd die of starvation. You're giving the rest a better chance.' She refused to look at Teddy.

Dylan had toddled over to the heap of bodies. His fingers were probing shining feathers and humorous beaks. Isobel took him away – she wasn't sure why – but doggedly he made his way back. She imprisoned him in his highchair and he threw back his head and bellowed. Conversation in the kitchen ceased. He thumped the tray with furious fists, yearned sobbing towards the dead birds. The adults regarded him with something like awe. 'What a child,' said Cheryl, shaking her head. The intensity of Dylan's fury unhinged Isobel and these days she was often tempted to give him his way rather than risk enraging him. One minute his arms would be passionately around her neck, the next he was beyond reason. Adrian leaned towards the maddened toddler. 'What's up, old man? What is it?' Dylan shot him a look of pure contempt and bellowed even louder. Isobel scooped him up and carried him off to his room. His cries unlocked something inside her, made her want to bellow out some long-forgotten misery of her own. She shut the door on him firmly.

Back in the kitchen, Cheryl was inspecting the ducks with a professional eye, pulling out one body after another. Across the floor lay a sorrowful black neck. 'A swan?' said Isobel.

'Fair game,' said Cheryl sturdily.

'Yeah, why not?' Teddy was sarcastic.

She was glad for the knock at the door and opened it quickly, frowning into the dark porch.

'Hi. How you doin'?'

181

Isobel blinked at the American girl. 'Hello,' she said. The girl reached for her pack and stepped with composure into the brightly lit kitchen. Not knowing quite what else to do, Isobel performed hasty introductions, culminating in a slightly sheepish, 'And this is Clyde – my husband.'

'Hi,' said the girl inclusively and put her pack down again. She had exchanged the long faded skirt for a pair of impressively tattered jeans and a poncho that seemed to be constructed from rope.

Adrian shook her hand. 'You're frozen. Would you like some coffee?' He ushered her into his chair.

'How did you find me?' asked Isobel. What she meant was why.

'Thanks,' said the woman, warming her hands on the mug. 'You told me you lived in Bulls Road. I just asked around for an English woman.'

Isobel considered this description, while the men asked the girl why she had come to New Zealand and what she thought of it. 'I was a Fulbright,' she said. 'I defected.' None of them knew what a Fulbright was so they let it pass. She sat straight-backed, apparently unaware that Cheryl was studying her plaits and rather obviously concluding this was an irresponsible way for anyone over twelve to style their hair. Isobel chewed a nail.

'Never been on a farm?' Cam pretended to be aghast. 'Backbone of the bloody country!'

The woman humoured him. 'That's what everyone says, so' – she spread her hands – 'here I am.' She turned to Isobel. 'If that's all right with you guys?'

Isobel twirled before the dressing table mirror – the long skirt flew out from her ankles and the velvet top caressed her arms. The American woman watched, catlike. Her name, she had finally divulged, was Mike but nobody had seemed convinced. 'Short for something, is it?' said Cheryl, self-appointed expert on girls' names. 'Michelle . . .?' She ran out of inspiration. When it became clear the woman was not about to help, Cheryl narrowed her eyes and turned away.

'What about my hair?' said Isobel, from the stool in front of the mirror. Mike's bracelets tinkled exotically as she picked up the brush and ran it through Isobel's hair. Isobel was beguiled and alarmed, men's hands were not half so knowing. 'It was really long once,' she said, half proud, half apologetic.

'All you need now,' Mike said, fumbling in her pack, 'are these.' The beads shone like childish treasure. Isobel put out her hand but Mike stepped forward and placed them ritualistically over Isobel's head. Beneath her musky perfume she smelled dangerously unwashed. 'There you go.'

'Jeez,' grinned Clyde from the doorway. 'You going to roll us one of those joints to go with the fancy dress?'

Isobel prodded Clyde's shoulder and he mumbled, rolled over and temporarily quit grinding his teeth. She lay still, straining to hear what, if anything, was going on in the lounge. Sleeping arrangements had been complicated. Martin was sharing with Dylan, Adrian and Jo were in the sunporch, and Cam and Cheryl had gone rather regretfully home. Teddy had volunteered for a sleeping bag on the couch, and the girl – it was annoyingly difficult to address her as Mike – had said a mattress on Clyde and Isobel's floor would be cool, but had so far failed to come to it. Isobel could feel Adrian's displeasure through the wall. His early courtesy to Mike had faded quickly to intense suspicion and Isobel had cornered him in the kitchen. 'What's wrong?' she had whispered, under cover of filling the jug.

His mouth was set in an expression she had not seen before. 'That girl. And her drugs. And dressing you up like that.' She half expected him to append *young lady* to his reproach. She clattered the jug lid to distract herself.

'Well, I like it,' she hissed unspecifically. They reinstated sociable expressions as Cheryl barged in, and nothing more was said.

Isobel was forced to admit, though, that what Mike called the 'grass' had not been a huge success. Clyde, lungs hardened by years of practice, inhaled deeply from three joints and became, to all intents and purposes, comatose. Mike stared into the fire with her customary straight back and queenly expression. Isobel held the smoke in her mouth before exhaling – she had no intention of disorienting herself again – then stared into the fire like Mike. Cheryl dashed to the bathroom, choking. Adrian, after one sniff, made unbearably bright conversation with Teddy about the art market. Cam decided a professional man should steer clear of illicit substances and promptly got drunk on whisky. And Jo dozed. Before long, Mike had begun giving Teddy her undivided attention.

Isobel lay rigid in the bed. Was that the murmur of voices or the freezer? What could Mike and Teddy find to talk about for so long? But what if the talk had come to an end? She had already been out once, ostensibly to fetch a glass of water, and seen Teddy still slumped in his chair, Mike stretched out before the dying fire. Isobel had briskly thrown on another log, saying in her mother's voice, 'You don't want to get cold.'

'Tell me about London,' Mike had asked Teddy, as Clyde buried his head between Isobel's breasts with a whimper. She half-heartedly stroked his hair, wondering whether Mike was judging this wifely response as cool or otherwise.

Teddy had shaken himself out of a torpor. 'Greater London. Miles of semi-detached houses, neat front gardens. Isobel knows.' Isobel opened her mouth but at that moment Cam turned the music up and conversation became impossible. Mike stood and held out a hand to Teddy, and all those who were still conscious watched as she wove artfully around him, all undulating hips and arms and rapt expression.

The ducks lay denuded in the fridge. Maybe Teddy and Mike were trading observations on the brutality of killing for sport, judging Isobel as heartless a murderer as the others. Clyde mumbled and groped for her and she gave him an unkind shove. How had she ended up in here with him when she belonged out there with Teddy and Mike?

'Isobel? You awake? Get up.' It was Mike at the bedroom door. 'Put something warm on and come with me.'

Embers flickered in the grate. Isobel discerned the unmoving shape of Teddy on the couch but it was impossible to tell if anything had happened. 'Put these on,' Mike said, pushing Clyde's gumboots at her. 'Close your eyes and hold my hand.'

Isobel heard the back door open. She was hit by a wall of freezing air, the sharp smell of winter. 'Trust me,' Mike said, trying to loosen Isobel's grip. They walked a few more paces but before Mike had taken them to the middle of the lawn and said, 'Open your eyes,' Isobel had guessed.

The normally dreary garden was spellbound. Every blade of grass and twig was edged with white, the fence wires were delicate snowy lines. The sky was thick and low, the stars blotted out. Isobel clasped her hands in delight – she had walked into a fairytale.

Mike was on her knees, running her fingers through the grass. 'Should we wake Teddy?'

'No,' said Isobel.

They were shuddering unstoppably when they went back inside. 'The mattress,' said Isobel. She could barely think.

'Too cold,' shivered Mike. 'I'll get in with you.'

She got out of her jeans. Isobel put a hand on the dark hump in the middle of the bed and said, 'Move over,' at a loss as to who should go where. Mike climbed in on one side of Clyde, Isobel on the other. He muttered and flung an arm over Isobel for which she was obscurely grateful. And grateful again when, emerging from a cold dream of Woodland Rise, it was Clyde's fingers she identified inside her. But when he began to thrust clumsily against her thigh, she whispered, 'Clyde . . . Mike.'

'Go ahead,' said Mike. 'I don't mind.' Neither, apparently, did Clyde. Determined not to be old-fashioned, Isobel rolled on her back. After all, how different could it be from that night at the airport with Lurlene and Rats grunting beside them? Yet it was. Mike snuggled against them, murmuring encouragement, and at one point held Isobel's hand. Her muskiness filled Isobel's nose and throat, and Isobel was too distracted to fulfil her own obligations before Clyde was groaning and lunging. She reached for tissues and hoped Adrian was sleeping soundly in the sunporch. She had been unfaithful in some curiously shoddy way she had never envisaged. Yet at the same time she was exultant – as if the three of them had knocked down several more walls of Muriel and Jacko's house.

She was still seesawing between guilt and triumph when the bed began to move rhythmically again. Thought and feeling ceased – she lay a thousand miles away while Mike and Clyde did what they wanted with a minimum of fuss.

Clyde rolled off to the far side and promptly fell asleep. Mike said, 'Wow, I needed that. Tried to get a fuck out of Ted. He gay or what?'

Relief surged through Isobel. 'Actually,' she confided, 'I think he's in love with me.'

Chapter 24

THE WINDOWS OF ADRIAN'S CAR WERE BLINDED WITH RAIN. IT was impossible to believe he was inside until she flung open the door and saw him. She fell into his arms and they kissed for a long time. When the kiss was over, they stared out at the curtains of rain billowing against the windscreen. The summit was obscured, the folds of the hill choked with cloud. Heavy machinery had been chewing at the hillside but lay idle now, and men in sunny parkas squatted in a hut, peering out at the downpour.

'What's happened?' asked Adrian with a tremor of impatience and what she was almost sure was a glance at his watch.

'Nothing. I just couldn't wait until the weekend.' She buried her face in his chest.

'Where does Clyde think you are? Where's Dylan?' He never trusted her to cover her tracks.

She fingered the imprint of his suit button on her cheek. 'Mike's looking after Dylan. Clyde's gone to a stock sale.'

'You really shouldn't . . .'

She glared. 'What do you think she's going to do – get him stoned? It's all right for you, you can walk out whenever you like, pretend you're showing a client some ghastly house, but I . . .'

'I just don't think Mike is . . .'

'What? What don't you think she is? She's my friend and . . .'

'I didn't come all this way for a row.' He looked aggrieved.

'Didn't you? Well, silly me.' She wrenched ineffectually at the door handle and he grabbed her other hand.

'Don't,' he said wearily.

'Don't what? Don't make myself scarce when I'm not wanted? Don't be so in love with you I'm buried alive when you're not there?' She collapsed in a storm of tears.

He folded her in his arms and stroked her hair and neck. 'Izzy, you know this is as difficult for me as it is for you.'

No, it isn't, said a small voice, but she silenced it. With the hill between them, she felt crazed, trapped in the jaws of a monster that bellowed and roared, and left unsatisfied, turned on her, devouring her peace of mind. She wept while Adrian stroked. 'There,' he whispered. 'There's a good girl.'

She drew away, wiping and blowing. 'Last year it was all so simple, but now . . .'

'We still love each other.' His face was furrowed by concern but she was compelled to rouse something more.

'I don't think I can go on.'

His elbow jabbed the horn and they both jumped. A workman looked up then went back to his paper. 'Isobel, no. We can't split up. That's not what you mean, is it? Don't Isobel, please. I love you.'

She fed on his tears. 'I get desperate. I think about next year and the year after and ten years from now.' It wasn't true – it was today and the next day that obsessed her.

He wiped his eyes with the back of his hand. 'We can work something out. We can, Isobel. Have faith.'

She laughed mirthlessly. 'That's not something I'm much good at.'

He squeezed her hand. 'I could . . .'

'Leave Jo?' It was unthinkable, but the monster howled for him to offer it. 'We could live together. We could . . .'

'No. Don't say that, you know I can't.'

She yanked her hand away. 'Why not? People do it all the time. You're just scared of what people will say.' He refused to rise to the bait. 'You don't love Jo. You just . . .'

'Shut up,' he said desperately. 'The workmen.'

'Hah! See! It's like Mike says . . .'

'Fuck Mike,' he growled. 'Mike knows nothing about me.'

'You're just scared of her because she's unconventional.'

'I'm scared of her because that's why you think you like her.'

The monster bayed for blood. 'If you loved me, you'd leave Jo.'

He put his head in his hands. 'I can't stand this, Isobel.'

Neither could she. Something was putting the words in her mouth, and what third-rate words they were. She gritted her teeth against them and for minutes there was only the rain on the roof and other lives whistling by on the wet road. She looked down on the clouds and wished they would smother her. Once, not very long ago, love had been the answer; now she could scarcely remember the question. If this was love, what hope was there?

She rubbed his back. 'I'm sorry, Adrian, I didn't mean it. I do love you, I won't leave you, I know you can't leave Jo, I don't want you to.' *Our Father . . . forgive us our trespasses.* He unbent and crept towards her. 'There's something else,' she said. 'Something I haven't told you.' He waited, trepidation on his face. 'It's sex. It was okay with Clyde for a while. But I can't do it now, it's horrible, I hate it.'

It was a present for him, but he looked dismayed. 'You can't stop having sex with Clyde. It'll . . . make trouble.' He wouldn't look at her. 'You could . . . just pretend.'

'I do.'

She saw him summon up courage. 'You don't with me, do you?'

'No,' she said finally. She wished with all her heart that she did, because then all this would be manageable. *One day when Mummy and Daddy loved each other very much . . .* a neat sanitised lie. Andrea's little book had failed to mention passion and greed and possessiveness and fear. To think she had once believed mopping up with a handkerchief was as messy as it got. *Daddy thinks . . . Daddy wouldn't . . . Daddy says . . .* Had her mother been perpetually in the grip of this monster? Was that why she had had no appetite for motherhood?

Isobel rubbed her hand across the fogged windscreen. 'I saw in the paper about a course at university. Social work, two nights a week.'

'You want to go back to varsity?' This time he definitely checked his watch.

'I want to do something properly, I want to do more than my mother did. I thought I could stay with you and Jo those two nights.'

His face lit up. 'Every week?'

Her own fell. 'Clyde would make a fuss about the money.'

'Use your own.'

She snorted. 'I don't have any, I'm a married woman.'

'Let me pay then. Tell Clyde it cost nothing.' This idea restored his equilibrium; he loved solving problems with money. 'I told you we'd work something out.'

The rain let up. The men clambered back onto their machines, picked up their shovels. And somehow she let Adrian go. His car vanished around a bend, reappeared smaller, and vanished again. It reminded her of watching the ship slip out to sea, but this time nothing snapped, nothing let her go. She watched until his car disappeared for the last time in a glint of watery sunlight, then turned and trudged back to her own.

Chapter 25

LAMBING BEGAN IN A SOUTHERLY GALE. FOR THREE DAYS AND nights, icy wind and rain howled through the paddocks like something with its teeth bared, reeking of the South Pole. Thirty ewes dropped the first night. Three weeks later, lambing was almost over and Isobel, Clyde and Dylan walked across the paddocks in tender sunshine. 'Spring,' Muriel had twittered on the telephone the evening before. 'My mother used to say spring was when life is at its lowest ebb, she used to say she'd die in the spring.'

'And did she?' Isobel inquired with polite savagery.

Jacko permitted Muriel a five-minute call once a fortnight. In between – stamps being apparently free from rationing – she mailed floral cards peppered with underlined warnings and suggestions: for Clyde to quit smoking and remember to get his hair cut, for Isobel not to do too much, but – conversely – to prune the roses, try Dylan on wheatgerm, not forget Aunty Joan's birthday, and say hello to Mrs Birchall. Isobel's mother wrote rarely, her father, in spite of her mother's promises, never.

And not once had they ever telephoned her, nor she them – it was as if they had all tacitly agreed to pretend the telephone had never been invented. Occasionally she woke sweating from a nightmare in which she picked up the receiver, heard her mother's imperious hello and was struck dumb, paralysed – unable to speak or break the connection.

'Look at the lambs, Dylan,' she said. Three or four were jostling for possession of a small mound, flicking up their heels and waggling tails. If Muriel had ever set foot outside the house, their frivolity would have forced her to amend her mother's stupid theories. Spring was a time of hope.

'Better check the old house,' said Clyde. He carried a crook like a character in a nursery rhyme. 'I opened the door so some of the old girls could shelter.'

'I told your mother we'd pulled the roses out,' reported Isobel. 'To make way for the deck.'

He grunted. 'That one with the twins, she's got a prolapse.' He stalked the cagey ewe. She stamped and made useless little runs at him until the crook caught her leg. Wild-eyed, she rolled over while her lambs hovered uncertainly, too young for fear. Dylan's eyes never left his father.

'I'll go over to the old place,' said Isobel. It stood in the next paddock, abandoned years before Jacko bought the farm with the rehab loan and built the new house. In spite of peeling walls, hay-strewn floors and filthy windows, it was startlingly domestic. A shaft of sunlight fell on a painful gap from where the range had been torn. Isobel turned slowly, the sun on her shoulders, enjoying the solitude. She heard a moan. The next room was gloomier and she waited for her eyes to adjust. There was rustling from the corner, a pale bulk. 'Clyde,' she yelled across the paddock. 'You'd better come.'

He dragged the ewe by its back legs into the bright kitchen. 'Is she in labour?' asked Isobel.

'Can't tell. Hold her down, I'll have a look.'

She lowered her knee gently to the woolly neck, in spite of

the general understanding that gentleness was bad for farm animals. Rocks and insults were hurled at dogs, bewildered sheep booted in the face, electrodes jammed into the flanks of cattle beasts and bleeding horns amputated without flinching. Only lambing was conducted with any care. Clyde pushed up his sleeve and greased his fist and arm. She avoided the ewe's glassy stare as he worked his way into her, mapping out an essay due the following Monday. The course had quickly become much more than an excuse for seeing Adrian regularly. She had been exhilarated to discover that social workers turned a cold professional eye on human relationships that others refused to question, that her reading list included titles like *The Death of the Family* and *Sanity, Madness and the Family*. She relished knowing not only that she had stood against the curse of the Midwinters and the Giltraps, but that by being accepted into Adrian and Jo's family, she had, as Mike often pointed out, struck a blow for a new order. These days she pitied her parents for having had to conduct their lives against the stultifying backdrop of the forties and fifties. Some of what had happened to her as a child had not, perhaps, been entirely their fault – it had been the air they breathed. And now the air was fresher, sweeter.

'Jeez,' complained Clyde, 'she's killing my arm. Found a leg, looks like a breach. Can't seem to turn it though.'

'Da,' said Dylan, pointing at the ewe.

'Sheep,' said Isobel.

'Da.' He had no use for words, wanted only to explore and manipulate the world with his hands. 'Don't worry,' Cheryl had said. 'He's bound to talk in the end.' 'Not necessarily,' Isobel had retorted unguardedly. 'His father hasn't.' And Cheryl had shot her a suspicious look.

Slowly Clyde withdrew his arm. 'It's coming,' he breathed. Dylan bent closer. The ewe gave a terrible shudder. 'Jeez,' he said, and they stared, trying to make sense of the dismembered leg. Its tight yellowish curls were like something fresh from the hairdresser.

'It's not your fault,' she said, with more confidence than she felt. 'It must have been dead already.' He sent her a faint grimace of gratitude. 'Have another go.'

Obediently he regreased his arm. The ewe's back-quarters hunched away from him. She wanted to whisper reassurances, to pat the springy wool on the narrow brainless head. It was a punishment to be so close to something that could not discern kindness from cruelty. Clyde, arm deep inside the sheep, was looking up for further instructions. She shook her head. 'You can't pull it out in pieces. And she'll die anyway, of blood poisoning.' He pulled out a squiggle of tail.

'Da,' said Dylan, with composure.

She took the child outside while Clyde cut the animal's throat, but Dylan did not appreciate her efforts to protect him. He went his grandfather's favourite shade of purple and bellowed with outrage. He wound his hands in her hair and tugged. She administered a futile wallop to his well-padded bottom and hauled him shrieking across the paddock. Catching up, Clyde said, 'I'll pick her up later with the tractor,' and shot her that childlike grimace again. He took her other hand, and the three of them walked home, Isobel in the middle, the child and the man on either side.

She was ironing when Uncle Max rang. She rarely ironed, but tonight she wanted to fill the house with the fresh smell of it, drive out the stench of the ewe's rotting innards. Clyde stared at the television screen where a young woman with vowels too perfect to be her birthright smiled brilliantly before a weather map. Isobel frowned at the black and white image. 'It's Jackie,' she said, half expecting a beetroot sandwich to materialise. She pounced when the telephone rang – Adrian.

'Isobel? Isobel Midwinter?'

'No. Well, yes. Turn it down, Clyde.' Black and White Minstrels mouthed grotesquely.

'Max. Max Haines.'

'Uncle Max,' she echoed.

'How are you, Isobel?' He sounded reduced, tentative. Nevertheless she was thankful he was on the end of a telephone, and, to judge from the echo down the line, half a world away.

'Fine,' she said wonderingly. 'Yes, fine.' There was a curious pause during which she sensed he was suffering the kind of confusion he had once evoked in her. 'So how are you?' she ventured boldly, 'after all these years.' Although nothing like as many as it felt, now she came to think of it.

'Er . . . ' Another pause. 'Heard from your family lately?'

She had to think hard. An aerogramme in autumn covered in her mother's fierce script. Gillian engaged to the Cambridge boy. Cynthia in Bristol doing . . . something. Daddy's job. A holiday in August . . . 'Not lately, no. We're not very good correspondents . . . ' How wonderful adulthood was, how splendidly supplied with such euphemisms.

'Oh Christ,' said Uncle Max. She had the distinct impression of him sagging into a chair. 'Oh Jesus Christ. I don't know what to say. You don't know, do you?'

'Apparently not,' she said gaily. 'But you'll have to tell me now.'

'Christ. Are you sitting down? Sit down, pour a whisky.'

'I'm leaning on the ironing board and I've got a cup of tea. That'll have to do.' What a wonderful thing time was. It had passed her out of the hands of Uncle Max, he couldn't touch her now.

'It's your pa. He's dead.'

'Of course he's not.' So it was only she who had changed. He was still given to stupid jokes for which there was no satisfactory response.

'It came through on the telex at work, his firm's part of ours. I thought you must know. It happened in Wales, can't get hold of your mum, must be still down there. Oh Christ.'

'No,' said Isobel firmly, though her legs were giving way and she was slipping to the floor. 'I would have heard. They'd tell me, wouldn't they, I'm family.' Clyde's face was turned towards her, she was looking right through it.

'I'm sorry, Isobel. Get hubby to pour you a whisky. I'm so sorry.'

'I'm sure you're wrong,' she told him firmly. 'We never go to Wales,' and she hung up.

They were on top of a narrow wall. Far below on one side were throngs of strangers, on the other, pallid English waves nagging at a pebbled beach. She held his hand. It was big and warm so that what she really felt was that he was holding her, all of her, in his big warm hand whose fingers were a beautiful golden brown. 'It's a front, Izzy,' he said, miles above her head.

'Where's the back?' she asked, but her voice was small and piping – the first clue that things would go wrong. The people down below heard it and turned their faces up to her. Their mouths opened like holes and terrible laughter came out. Uncle Max and Mummy laughter.

'Down here, Izzy.' He was below her now, holding out his arms from the pebbly beach. 'Jump, I'll catch you.' It was too far, she would never do it on her own. But – her heart leaped – she wasn't on her own. She flung herself from the wall. As her arms and legs flailed, he dissolved.

He called from the water's edge, 'Ducks and drakes, Izzy.' He chose a pebble and they watched it skip over the dreary English water. 'You do it.'

There were millions of pebbles and they were all wrong. She searched with growing dread. The moment she knew she could make him wait no longer was the moment she saw the worst pebble of all. She hurled it in desperation. It splashed and sank. 'A dead duck, Izzy,' he smiled sadly.

But then they were all there, surging over the wall, crowding round and laughing out of their holes of mouths. Laughing and laughing and if she didn't stop them they would kill her. 'Bloody fuck off,' she shouted as loud as she could in her awful child's voice. The laughter faltered. 'Bloody buggering fuck off.'

The mouths slammed shut. 'How dare you,' thundered a disembodied voice. 'Pull yourself together. Speak properly. Say thank you. Think of the Kennedys . . .'

'Ooph,' said Clyde.

'What?' Her pillow was soaked, the bedclothes tangled.

'You thumped me,' he said in meek reproach. 'I'm sad too, you know. I liked your old man much better than mine.'

She wanted to thump him again. She stumbled from the bed. Waiting for tolls to connect her, tears fell as if her body knew something she did not. It rang and rang. She had not expected otherwise. She had absolutely no conviction she was being connected to anywhere her parents called home, no conviction such a place existed. She made an inquiry of directory service then asked tolls for another number. After a series of cosmic silences and odd tones, a prissy Midlands accent announced, 'Whitworth and Co.' Isobel asked for her father as authoritatively as she was able. 'So sorry,' said the voice with real pleasure. 'No one of that name here.'

She went back to bed and lay in the dark while Clyde busily ground his teeth. Whitworth, Whitford, Whiting, Waterford. She returned to the telephone and dialled directory service again. 'A London number,' she said. 'For Waterworth and Co.'

'Waterworth and Co, can I help you?' sang a youngish London voice.

'Could I speak to . . . to David Midwinter, please.' *My father, Daddy.*

'Putting you through,' sang the voice. Far out on the edge of the world, Isobel waited to be let in.

'Are you there?' said the same voice, somewhat less tunefully. 'Look, sorry. I'm afraid he's not available. His secretary says may she ask who's calling.'

'His daughter, from New Zealand.' She braced herself to be caught out in this lie.

'Oh,' said the voice. 'I know all about you. You're married

to a farmer, aren't you, and you've got a little boy. What time of day is it there, is it winter or summer?'

'It's night-time. And it's spring,' said Isobel, charmed by the voice, and astonished to realise her father talked about her, that she wasn't dead to him.

'Putting you through.'

'David Midwinter's office.' Isobel pictured a middle-aged woman with a tweed skirt and immaculate files.

'It's Isobel Midwinter,' she began, her confidence seeping away. 'I'm awfully sorry to bother you but I'm trying to get hold of my father and I don't know . . .'

'Oh my goodness, his daughter,' gasped the woman, and burst into tears.

'What happened?' muttered Clyde as Isobel fell back into bed, but he was asleep before she could find the words. She wanted him to wake up and comfort her. She wanted him to wake up and be Adrian. She wanted to go to sleep and wake up yesterday. *Spring is a time of hope.* But it was autumn over there.

The sun shone. Mummy was unpacking the picnic, Daddy was behind his newspaper. She wished she could see through it, see what he was like on the other side. At last his voice came from behind the paper – 'To thine own self be true, Izzy.' She wanted him to show her where on the page it said it. 'To thine own self be true, and then it must follow as the night the day.'

'It's not fair,' she whimpered.

'Nothing's fair, Izzy. Not even in love and war. It follows as the day the night.'

'It doesn't follow,' she wailed. 'Your day is my night. You're yesterday and it's tomorrow here.'

She strained towards him but his voice was fading. 'Follow thine own self, Izzy. Be true to thine own night and day.'

'Where are you going?' she howled. 'Don't go. I want to see your own self. You can't go, please don't go.'

PART THREE

NEW ZEALAND 1975

Chapter 26

DAYLIGHT HAMMERED ON THE WINDOW, SPLITTING OPEN ISOBEL'S dreams. Adrian rolled over and flung an arm across her, smelling of cigars and clean pyjamas. She wrapped herself around him and his hands moved over her body. There was a rap at the door and Dylan stood over them, shy and defiant. 'It's eight. You said eight. When are we having presents?'

Adrian hauled himself from the bed, ruffling Dylan's hair. 'Now, mate. Last one downstairs is a rotten egg.' They thundered off.

Isobel burrowed down into the bed, reluctant to begin the day. For as long as she could remember – since her mother had ceased managing the occasion, in fact – Christmas had been more enjoyable in anticipation than in reality. It wasn't Adrian's fault; he was good at Christmas, enjoyed providing the setting for her rituals, a properly decorated tree and the conspiracies of present-giving. He was good with Dylan too, generous and affectionate – possibly more generous and affectionate than with his own son – but firm. And he loved her, there was no doubt of it. So this was what ten years of love came down to – a shopping list of Adrian's virtues. *Not arguing, are you. It's Christmas.* She stretched diagonally across the bed and yawned, wishing he would come back – only in bed were things uncomplicated. Sun spilled across the bedspread like melted butter. Perhaps it would be a proper antipodean Christmas for once, the kind promised northern immigrants but rarely delivered – hot and endlessly blue. *Merry Christmas and a Happy New Year to you all, with love from Mum.* As usual, her mother had absolutely no idea who *you all* was. As usual, the card depicted robins and muffled carol singers in a blizzard. Isobel clasped her hands behind her head and warbled, *'In the bleak midwinter, frosty wind made moan. Earth stood hard as iron, water like a stone. Snow had fallen snow on snow, sno-ow o-on sno-ow. In the bleak midwinter, lo-ong ago.'*

'Isobel?' It was Martin, or the portion of him he allowed to show around the doorpost.

'Happy Christmas,' she called, more heartily than she felt. At the end of his first year at university, Martin was a taller, more diffident version of the small boy to whom she had read Dr Seuss. Not quick but dogged, and an observer, so that even when he averted his eyes she could feel him watching. Only with his mother did he relax. With Isobel and his father he maintained a wary formality. 'He's a good boy,' Adrian would say with a tinge of sorrow, the mischievous spectre of Christopher hovering at his shoulder. Isobel was aware of Martin's affection for her as well as his resentment. Reason told her his reserve sprang from the loss of his brother, but increasingly she suspected she was to blame, for having stolen from him a conventional family life.

'Dad says are you getting up? We're opening the presents.' He disappeared without waiting for a reply.

Maybe, she thought, pulling on Adrian's old dressing gown, it was social work that spoiled her Christmases – picturing all the desperate people in bedsits and farmhouses and villas up and down the country coming face to face with their unfestive lives, resorting to bottles, pills, exhaust fumes and firearms. Knowing those who failed to solve their problems this way – the resentful survivors – would be waiting when she returned to work, tucked into beds with hospital corners, waiting for her to tell them there were better ways, waiting until next Christmas, or the one after, to prove she was wrong. Maybe that's what it was, she thought, slowly descending the stairs, not believing it for a second.

In the lounge Dylan was practising moves with his new cricket bat. From beneath a macrocarpa branch hacked from the back of the farm – Isobel had long ago given up expecting a proper tree – Jo smiled, 'Happy Christmas, Isobel,' and held out a gift.

By mid-morning, the sky had clouded over and a vicious little breeze had sprung up. Out on the lawn Adrian was cheerfully bowling balls at Dylan's bat. Isobel, sipping Bristol Cream at the kitchen window, glanced from them to Adrian's present, and back again, vacillating between pleasure and irritation. What place had the expensive pigskin briefcase he had presented with such pride at the bedside of teenage overdose victims, frail old ladies in dire need of resthome places, aging alcoholics pretending they wanted to dry out. Surely, after ten years, there was something deliberate about Adrian's failure to grasp the nature of her work? Behind her, at the kitchen table, Martin worked his way through a fat biochemistry textbook and a plate of mince pies. Each time he turned a page, he glanced up at his mother and Isobel.

'Mother prefers chestnut stuffing,' worried Jo, committing obscenities on the turkey, 'but I couldn't get chestnuts. It's ordinary old thyme and parsley, I hope she won't be disappointed.'

'When will she be here?' inquired Isobel. The Bristol Cream tasted like cough mixture with an undertone of jet fuel.

'Oh dear, soon,' said Jo, crashing the meat tin into the oven. She straightened up and shot Isobel a grateful look. 'I couldn't manage all this without you, you know.' They both knew she meant far more than a stuffed turkey.

Dylan burst in on a blast of fresh air. 'When's Dad coming? Will Dad be here soon?'

'Yes,' said Isobel, 'soon,' and she drained the crystal glass.

Within minutes she was doubled up over the toilet. When she emerged pale and shaken, Dylan wagged his finger and grinned. 'Told you not to eat chocolate fish for breakfast,' he said, in a bad imitation of her own voice. 'Hey, it's Dad.'

Isobel took three thoughtful steps backwards and fled upstairs. She would lie down, just for a little while – she had vomited, after all. The pillow beside hers held the imprint of Adrian's head and their combined scent lingered in the sheets. She lay perfectly still, drifting on the edge of consciousness. Doors banged and jovial greetings rolled up the stairs. It was a temporary reprieve only, within minutes Clyde would come searching, would stand by the bed waiting, hoping, expecting. He might sit beside her, stroke her hair, even kiss her, pretending to them both to be giving rather than taking and taking. Her stomach heaved. She lunged at the open window and threw up into the camellia bush below. The first malicious spots of rain hit her head.

'Isobel, you okay?'

She pulled her head back into the room. 'Mike? Mike. What are you doing here?' Her dismay was hard to disguise. Adrian liked Mike no better than he ever had. Her presence was one more string to pull, one more potential tangle.

Mike shrugged and inspected herself in the mirror. 'Clyde invited me. What's up? Don't you want me here?'

'Course I do,' smiled Isobel. She lowered herself gingerly to the bed. 'It's just that Clyde should have mentioned it to Jo.' She didn't believe Mike – Clyde could never have managed anything as decisive as an invitation.

'Jo's cool,' said Mike.

'Well,' said Isobel, repelling another wave of nausea, 'we'd better go downstairs and be sociable then.'

'To be honest,' said Mike, as Isobel followed her downstairs, 'I invited myself. You're always saying what great Christmases you have here, so I asked Clyde if I could come along.'

Isobel paused on the bend in the stairs. It was difficult – discomforting even – to picture Clyde and Mike communicating directly without her as an intermediary. 'You rang him?'

'Nope.' Mike waited several steps below. 'Saw him, last night.'

'Saw him?' echoed Isobel, still unmoving. 'I didn't know.'

Mike carried on downstairs. 'Why would you? You were here, with Dylan and everyone. Clyde was lonesome, I guess. He gave me a call and came over.'

'Lonely? Clyde?'

'You all right, Isobel? Dylan said you'd been throwing up,' Mike inquired carelessly from the bottom of the stairs.

'Mike,' said Isobel – it came out choked, possibly incomprehensible. 'Did Clyde spend the night with you?'

'Yeah,' breezed Mike. 'We do from time to time.' And she disappeared through the lounge door.

Marooned on the stairs, Isobel's knees folded. She fingered the carpet – parts of it were threadbare, and she wondered crazily how much her own feet had, over the last ten years, contributed to its condition. The question tormented her then vanished. Something was happening in her head, something disruptive and deafening. Crucial chunks of her life were being rearranged by incompetent workmen who could barely lift them, who banged them into corners and got them stuck in doorways, cursed and shouted at each other. The racket and pain doubled her over, made her groan softly. Clyde and Mike. Mike and Clyde. The workmen gave it a final hard shove. *They'll have to go . . . spoiling Christmas for the girls . . . not fair . . . not fair . . .*

She practically tumbled downstairs, and crashed through the lounge door. Faces turned like beacons flashing smiles and greetings. She scanned them, jaw clenched. Mike stood by the window. She was wearing an embroidered white muslin blouse designed to endow its wearer with an aura of innocence and simplicity. It was the blouse that did it. Isobel strode across the room and delivered a resounding slap. It hurt her hand. Mike staggered. There was a collective gasp. As Mike straightened up, hand to her cheek, Isobel hissed, 'You bitch. You fucking betraying bitch. We treated you like one of the family.'

There was a respectful silence. Then Adrian's mother exploded with a 'Well!'

Isobel's fury was like the top of a hill on a clear day and she did not want to come down.

Dylan said, 'Mum said fuck.'

Adrian's father said, 'Sit down, Mother. Loosen your top button.'

Mike said, 'Christ on a crouton.'

Jo said, 'Oh dear.'

Adrian said, 'Isobel, are you drunk?'

Martin said, 'The oven timer's going off.'

Isobel said, 'Say something, Clyde. For Christ's sake, say something.'

Sleep was impossible. The house seemed alternately stunned and electrified. Clyde dedicatedly ground his teeth and Isobel squinted at the luminous hands of her watch. Three ten. Three eleven. Three twelve. The dark was a prison, she wanted to rattle its bars. She slithered from the bed and out of the room, taking great gasps of air on the landing as if she had narrowly escaped suffocation. She thought Adrian might be in one of the bunks in Martin's room but she turned resolutely for the stairs. The seventh stair sighed, the third creaked. She prayed she would not wake Jo; Jo, least of all, deserved to be disturbed. Hand on the banister, trying to keep as much weight as possible off each stair, she winced at jabs of memory.

'If she stays, I go.'

'I can't throw her out of the house, Isobel. Not on Christmas Day.'

'Why not? You've never liked her. You've said for ten years this was my home.'

Adrian looked as if he would expire from confusion. 'Please, Isobel, be reasonable.'

'Reasonable!' she screeched.

It must have been sheer anxiety about what Isobel might say next in front of this audience of friends and relatives that made Adrian finally turn to Mike and say, 'I think it probably would be best . . . in the circumstances . . .'

'Okay with me. Clyde, would you drive me to the station?'

'No,' said Isobel, 'he will not.'

She reached the bottom of the stairs and flicked on the lounge light. What she saw brought back the day so palpably, she flicked it off again and groped her way across the room.

Christmas Day had continued like a parody of itself. There had been seven of them at dinner, although God knows what time they had eaten it. Adrian's father manfully donned an orange paper hat. Dylan blew on a plastic whistle, which no one had the heart to forbid. Martin had withdrawn to a friend's house, where he had decided to also spend the night, and Adrian's mother harped particularly on this theme. 'Driving out your only son on Christmas Day. Poor Martin, you should ring him up, Adrian. You can't let him be on his own today. Of all days.'

'He's not on his own, Mother,' said Adrian, making a dreadful hash of the turkey.

'But without his family, poor boy. And all for someone else's troubles.' This with a meaningful look at Isobel.

'Peas, Mother?' inquired Jo. 'Dad, give her some peas. Isobel, you've hardly got anything. Give her more turkey, Adrian.'

'I want more turkey,' said Dylan.

'Say please,' growled Clyde. He never growled.

'Who wants the wishbone?' said Adrian. There was a dismal silence and he abandoned it on the edge of the platter.

Reaching now for the kitchen door, Isobel was suddenly fiercely hungry. She had eaten virtually nothing all day and thrown up three times. Light rushed out, blinding her. 'Hello,' said Jo, through a full mouth. She was ripping pieces of flesh from a carcass.

Isobel blinked. 'Sorry,' she mumbled, groping for a chair. She meant sorry for disturbing Jo's solitude. Then, sorry for driving her son from the house, for once more horrifying her mother-in-law to the point of medical emergency, for wrecking her Christmas, for letting her husband make love to her ten years ago and several times a week ever since. Sorry, sorry, sorry. Jo only wanted a quiet life, it wasn't much to ask. Isobel had let her down and the idea of it tore at her. She imagined it was how people felt about letting down their mothers.

'I couldn't sleep,' said Jo.

'I'm not surprised,' said Isobel abjectly.

'I ate so much. It sort of lies on your stomach, doesn't it? Is that why you couldn't sleep?'

Sometimes – and this was one of them – Isobel wondered if Jo were the same species as herself. 'I'm too wound up.'

'What a shame.' Jo dug deep in search of stuffing. 'There's some bread if you want. You could make a sandwich.'

'Can I butter some for you? Or put the kettle on? Or anything?'

Jo giggled. 'A midnight feast.'

They ate in silence. Isobel thought of several things to say but none of them, in the face of Jo's equanimity, seemed appropriate.

'Pity about Clyde,' said Jo, wiping her fingers on a paper napkin decorated with holly berries. 'Pity he had to find out, I mean, about you and Adrian.'

Isobel cringed. From Jo, it was close to a reproach. 'I thought he knew already, I thought Mike must have told him.'

'Yes,' considered Jo. 'Although if he had, he probably would've made a fuss by now, wouldn't he. Men do. Jealousy and things.'

Isobel chewed. Among the hideous morass of feelings in which she had wallowed all day, she had, to her shame and bewilderment, identified *jealousy and things*. As if she loved Clyde. As if he wasn't owed some love. *I love you, Isobel. Good.*

'I suppose Mike never mentioned it because sex isn't a big deal to her. She thinks it's like eating.'

'Strange,' wondered Jo, licking her lips. 'Eating's so much nicer. Anyway, Clyde's got Mike, and you'll make it up with Adrian in the morning, and everything'll be back to normal, won't it.'

Isobel kept silent. She lacked the courage to tell Jo how easy it had been to insist Clyde never see Mike again, how eager he was to please. But Jo had lost interest in the topic. 'Shall we pull the wishbone?'

Their fingers twined around the greasy bone. It broke cleanly in Jo's favour.

Chapter 27

CLYDE SPREAD THE PLANS ACROSS THE KITCHEN TABLE WITH much important rustling. 'Two thousand square feet,' he announced, and waited for Isobel's approval.

She squirted dishwashing liquid into the sink and flooded it with hot water. *Star Trek* theme music boomed from the lounge and she tried not to picture Dylan sprawled across the carpet, assuming membership of the class that did not have to concern itself with household chores. She plunged a fistful of cutlery into the water and poked at it with the brush. She was a coward, she ought to insist. It was far easier to be stern with a recalcitrant client than it was with Dylan.

'There's a double sink,' said Clyde. 'With an under-sink heater. You'll never run out.'

'Take evasive action,' ordered Captain Kirk. 'Do not return their fire. I repeat, do not return their fire.'

'Lovely,' she murmured, reaching for a stack of greasy plates. Captain Kirk snapped another order and drowned out Clyde saying something about heating costs. Isobel scratched at a baking tray and stared through the window as soupy water ran out with a slurp. In the garden, Dylan's pet lamb Ditto was nibbling forbidden foliage but she lacked the energy to go outside and stop it. Light drained from the sky. She got out Ajax to scour the bench. It was in a kitchen ten years earlier that she had been given the key to the universe. How had she lost it? Where had it gone? She wrung out the dishcloth and draped it over the taps.

In a final effort to snare her attention, Clyde was smearing dishes with a tea-towel and scattering them along the bench. Mentally she snarled at him to put them straight in the cupboard if he wanted to be useful. But he didn't want to be useful, he wanted to be loved.

'Thanks,' she said. Speedily he abandoned the tea-towel and reached for her. 'The plans,' she said, slipping through.

At the top of each sheet in blue pencil it said *Residence for Mr and Mrs Clyde Giltrap*. In the bottom left-hand corner stood two tiny stick figures and a third tinier one, gazing in awe at what they had constructed. 'I'm not that little,' Dylan had grumbled. I am, thought Isobel.

'Want a drink?' asked Clyde, determined to make it an occasion.

She shuddered involuntarily. 'No, thanks.'

He leaned over the plans with an arm around her. It was terribly heavy. 'Our bedroom opens onto a deck, and the en suite goes off here.'

Already she was wording a letter to her mother – *The new house is going ahead and we expect to move in by the end of the year. It'll be lovely to have more room, and we're so looking forward . . . so looking forward . . .*

The telephone rang and they both froze. She prayed it would be Adrian, prayed it would not. Clyde would turn to stone. She would be compelled to devote the rest of the evening to soothing him, even, finally, allowing him to make love to her. Yet on several such occasions something else had happened, something that both elated and disturbed her – Clyde had talked. About himself, about the time he broke a window and hid from Jacko in one of the sheds, crammed his small body into a filthy corner behind machinery reeking of dung and engine grease and stayed there from three in the afternoon until nine at night, when Muriel came to tell him the coast was clear, that Jacko had gone out. He had spoken of it in a flat voice, devoid of self-pity. Another time – as punishment for some long-forgotten misdemeanour – he had been forced to sit for several hours on a high stool. He had been forbidden meals, locked in his bedroom, berated, belittled and beaten – with Jacko's fist and boot, with whatever came to hand – canes, rulers, electric cable. Dozens of items had been hurled at him in the course of his childhood, including, once, a fencepost. Clyde had watched it arc in slow motion through the clear air and land soundlessly on his small foot. A neighbour had driven him and Muriel to Casualty.

'Didn't anyone complain? Didn't your mother threaten to leave him if he didn't stop? Didn't you ever tell anyone?'

Clyde had shrugged. Years after his parents left the farm, Isobel had found in the back of a cupboard a photograph of a charming curly-headed child in dungarees, pulling a cart. 'Me,' Clyde had said. And Isobel had yearned to reach in and rescue him while there was still time. She had wept into Clyde's greying hair, clasping him to her with an intensity that felt so much like love it shocked her.

'Miss Jackman, next door to Aunty Joan,' said Clyde now, hanging up the telephone. 'The old girl's had a stroke.' Isobel tried to picture Joan Fisk felled.

Dylan emerged bleary-eyed from deep space, heading for her arms. She was still angry about the dishes. 'Bed,' she said.

'Going anyway,' he said coldly, veering away.

'The quack's given her the once over,' continued Clyde. 'She doesn't need to go into hospital, just bed rest, Miss Jackman said.'

'How's she going to manage?' asked Isobel.

'Miss Jackman said she'll have to stay with us.'

Joan Fisk tottered into the house with Clyde at her elbow, a white veiny hand clamped to a shiny handbag as if it held the remnants of her dignity. Her lipstick was smeared. She halted when she saw Isobel. 'Shorry. Won't be a nuishansh. Mish Jackmash idea sheesh shingle she shinksh . . .' The lurid mouth made all the wrong shapes. She looked proud and stricken.

Isobel stepped forward. 'Let's get you into bed. It's all made up in the sunporch.' It was her mother speaking – brisk and capable, no time for silly nonsense. Guiding Joan through the lounge, feeling the frail body against hers, some of Isobel's fury dissipated. As Clyde had driven over the hill to collect his aunt, Isobel had attacked the sunporch carpet with the vacuum cleaner, cracked sheets across the bed, thumped pillows into cases with a burning resentment. Joan Fisk had been against her from the start. Joan Fisk had bullied and manipulated, even, Isobel remembered with a hiss of venom, sent an anonymous letter to someone little older than a child, a lonely bewildered child. She had reached for the top sheet to wipe away a tear – the first she had ever shed for that distant Isobel. And, she had raged, pulling down the blinds and banging a box of tissues onto the bedside table, now she was to be forced to care for the wicked old woman.

Gently Isobel parted the handbag from the white hand. Still clawed, it wobbled towards cardigan buttons. Isobel understood that it was scared to death and a sense of decency made her look away. But when she looked back, the old lady was no further advanced. Isobel longed to call for Clyde, she was his aunt. 'Shall I . . .?' she said, reaching tentatively. And Joan Fisk stood while Isobel unfastened layers of old lady clothing and dead-looking underwear. She sat her on the bed to remove her stockings. Next to the soft bruised skin, the tan nylon felt coarse and indestructible.

Several times next morning Isobel peered around the sun-porch door expecting to find Joan asleep. Or dead. She was scared of not knowing the difference. But each time, Joan's eyes were waiting, the loose mouth fumbling for declarations of apology and independence. They had given her an old chamber pot Clyde had found in a shed, and once Isobel backed away hurriedly from the sight of rumpled haunches.

She wanted Adrian. It would have been her night to stay at his house if she had not taken time off work to look after Joan. She sat on the end of Joan's bed, sipping coffee, wondering why, exactly, she wanted him. Increasingly she had to bite back a compulsion to be scathing. Too often when he telephoned, she froze – something froze. She felt driven to punish him, yet she had no idea what his crime was.

'Shush shoo yun fee,' said Joan. Coffee dribbled down her chin, and the hand holding the cup shook wildly.

Isobel took the cup. 'Try not to worry,' she said calmly. 'It only happened last night. You'll be back to normal in a week or so.' She scarcely believed it herself, the wreckage of Joan Fisk seemed so absolute. Yet, her professional self told her, she had seen many stroke victims recover from much worse. She opened a window and crisp autumn air filled the little room. 'Clyde's putting the rams out today,' she said cheerily, but it triggered a wave of depression. A decade of putting the rams out, of seeing lambs torn from ewes, the skins of the dead tied to orphans to fool bereaved mothers. Ten years of a kitchen littered with mis-mothered scraps of life that were stiff and cold by morning. Ten years of torture by docking, ten years of trucking bewildered survivors off to the abattoir in time for Christmas. What had once been exhilarating was now a deadly cycle.

'Door,' said Joan, with startling clarity.

Cam stood hands in pockets, grinning, and Isobel was surprisingly pleased to see him. He pecked her cheek. 'Where's the old man?'

'Up the back. I'll make you coffee, then you can come and entertain Clyde's aunt.'

For half an hour, Cam perched plumply on the end of Joan's bed, cracking feeble jokes and telling stories of how his womenfolk got the better of him. Joan seemed more bemused than entertained by this man who refused to treat her as a lady. But at least, thought Isobel, it was a distraction. For whom and from what, she was unsure.

'Well,' he said, rising stiffly. 'Better hit the road and make a buck.' He leaned over Joan Fisk and squeezed her hand. 'Keep your powder dry, Joan, never know when you might get a shot away.'

'Thanks for coming, Cam,' said Isobel when they reached the kitchen.

'Anything for you, Izzy,' he said, scooping her up.

She wriggled free. 'Anything?'

He sank to one knee, hand across his heart. 'Name it.'

She turned to the table. 'Will you take a note to Adrian for me? You'll pass his place, won't you?'

He got to his feet. 'Why don't you phone?' It was sombre, not like Cam.

She tried a wry grin. 'The old lady's lying just through there and I don't want her to hear. I just thought . . .'

'No, I won't.' Her mouth dropped open. He inspected his polished toes, then said, 'It's bloody disgusting. Everyone tries to ignore it. But I won't carry notes between you, I won't condone it.'

'Hah,' cried Isobel, as all the breath rushed out of her. She pulled out a chair and sat in it. After a moment, Cam did the same. The air was heavy with things about to be said and Isobel wished she had the strength to make a run for it.

'At first everybody thought it'd pass, that you'd both get over it. We all felt' – 'We all?' mouthed Isobel – 'we all felt sorry for Clyde and Jo. But now – well, Jo's as bad as the two of you and it makes us sick.'

'What a self-righteous load of horseshit!' She sounded like Mike. 'And how do you know Clyde hasn't been having an affair all this time?'

'Poor bugger's got to go somewhere for consolation. Anyway, he's given her up, hasn't he. You saw to that. You . . .'

Isobel was furious. 'Clyde offered to give her up. It didn't mean anything, he just . . .'

'Exactly,' said Cam. 'It didn't mean anything. But you and Adrian, that means something, doesn't it.'

'Yes. Yes, it does. We love each other.' It impressed her, even now.

'And if he'd asked you to run off with him any time in the last ten years, you would've, wouldn't you?'

'Yes,' cried Isobel, eyes filling with triumphant tears. 'Yes, gladly.' Gladly?

'You'd break up two families, hurt children, deceive people . . .'

'But we didn't . . . he didn't . . . he never . . .' She sagged onto the table. Next to the Adrian she had fallen in love with she saw Adrian now – a comfortable middle-aged estate agent. And next to him, not, after all, an enlightened young woman of her times, but a shabby number two wife. She hung her head, waiting for Cam to offer some gesture of comfort, but he went on simply sitting there. She screwed up the paper on which she had been intending to write to Adrian. Only then did Cam relent. 'I suppose, if it's important . . .'

'No,' she said, blowing her nose with gusto. 'Don't worry, it's not at all important. Just that I think I might be pregnant, that's all.'

Chapter 28

SHE WAS NOT PREGNANT, OF COURSE. BUT HAVING BLURTED IT out to Cam, she was obliged to at least mention it to Adrian. He patted her knee. 'I don't suppose you are, you're much too well organised.'

'It's only that I've put on a bit of weight and can't seem to drink alcohol anymore,' she repeated gaily to the gynaecologist's receptionist. And even as Mr Singh peered over his bifocals a week later, and said solemnly as he dried his hands, 'Congratulations, Mrs Giltrap,' she did not believe it.

She smiled. She would charm him out of his diagnosis. 'I'm not pregnant. I can't be.' If she was, she wanted to add, it was only because she had made this expensive appointment and given him the opportunity of saying so.

He smiled too. 'Indeed you are, Mrs Giltrap, getting on for four months, I'd say. I'll work out some rough dates for you.' He bent over a scribble pad.

Now she frowned. 'But I'm religious about my pills. I've never missed one. I can't have another baby.' In spite of her conviction, she registered a visceral shock at that word.

He offered a slip of paper. 'There. Sometime in August, I'd say. Can't be more accurate as we don't know exactly when you conceived. It would help if you'd missed a period or two.'

'That's just it – I haven't, so I can't be, can I . . .'

He pushed his glasses onto his shiny brown forehead and folded his arms. 'Now you know better than that, Mrs Giltrap. Not genuine menstruation on the oral contraceptive, is it. I'm afraid you have, through no fault of your own it seems, become another happy statistic.'

Isobel rose. 'But I'm not happy. I don't want it. I can't have it.' He was ushering her out with soothing noises. As she reappeared, Adrian rose from a seat in the waiting room. 'He says I'm pregnant,' Isobel burst out. She meant it as an indictment of Mr Singh's professional competence but three or four women shot her sympathetic looks over their magazines, and a toddler astride a rocking horse paused mid-gallop and stared. Isobel stared back, and so long and hard that his mother gathered him into her arms.

By the time Adrian got her outside, she was wailing. The long lonely sounds bewildered her. She had made them – they had made themselves – when her father died. They swallowed all the space inside her then fled through her mouth. She sank onto the step and howled into a bed of canna lilies, 'I can't be. I've been so careful. I can't be.'

Adrian fidgeted with embarrassment. She wanted to punch his estate agent's belly, rampage through the papery brown leaves, bang together the heads of the stupid cowlike women pretending not to stare out of the window, shake Singh until he saw sense. She got to her feet and Adrian took her hand.

'Come on,' he urged. 'We'll work something out. We always do, don't we. It's not the end of the world.'

The road to the prison was punctuated with grim warnings to unauthorised visitors. She tried imagining the state of mind of the hundreds of convicted men who had been driven down it on their way to life sentences. She passed a vast unfriendly vegetable garden and dozens of men in blue squinted up from the rows as she drove by. She looked away, ashamed of her freedom. But then her hand found her abdomen – her own unauthorised visitor, her own life sentence. The road curved back into the hills, a stone's throw from her parents' old house. She remembered Clyde leading her determinedly up into the pine trees behind the house – *other girls do* – and craned through the side window as if their ghosts might linger. The car hit the gravel shoulder. She wrenched the wheel. The car lurched, threatened to roll, recovered. Heart pounding, she thought, so I don't want to die, then. That's something.

A building like a maternity hospital came into view. She parked under a barrage of even sterner warnings and took a minute to arrange her professional demeanour before leaving the car. The guard at the main office was unctuous but obstructive. She could see him thinking *do-gooder*. The client – or rather the client's husband – was pale and sullen as an undernourished child. Twice she explained how sick his son was and why his wife needed to move to Auckland for the right medical care. He picked at his pimples. 'Bitch,' he said wearily.

Isobel explained for the third time, adding – somewhat inaccurately – that his wife had asked her to explain it to him because she cared about him.

'Fuck her,' he said.

'I know you must feel angry,' she began. 'I know it must seem like she's abandoning you, but . . .'

'And fuck you too,' concluded the man.

Isobel looked out of the window. It was, by ordinary stand-ards, a beautiful day, yet the sky was tarnished and the visitors room smelled of captivity. 'Right,' she said standing up. 'Fuck me too.' The guard smirked as he led the man away. She retraced her steps down the ugly corridor. A party of men in blue shambled into the building as she was signing out and she avoided their ravenous eyes.

'Gidday, Isobel.'

She saw a sloppy uniform, a prison haircut. He waited while she stared. 'What on earth are you doing here? In this?' She plucked humorously at his coarse jersey.

'I'm an inmate,' said Rats.

The chaplain unlocked the chapel and said he'd give them half an hour. 'Good bloke,' said Rats. 'Some of the screws are all right too. You get by.'

Isobel sat in a pew. The chapel was dim between shafts of dusty sunlight. She felt outside time and space, and understood why prison turned many men into churchgoers. Rats stood in the aisle, hands in pockets. Beneath his jersey he harboured a paunch, his hairline was receding and he had an uncharacteristic air of sobriety. But he was still Rats.

'I can't believe it,' she said, trying, nevertheless, to moderate her incredulity. It seemed insensitive to exclaim as if they had met on the street after all these years.

'Neither did the judge,' he said.

'What did you do? I mean, did you do anything?'

'Nobody asks that in here, the place is full of innocent men. I borrowed money from clients without their knowledge, to keep my wife in the manner to which she was accustomed.'

'Your wife?'

'Married six or seven years ago. Didn't we ask you and Gil? Maybe not, you'd left the valley by then. Big do, all the trimmings.' He stared at a stained glass Christ struggling with a cross. 'She filed for divorce the week I was arrested, then left for England. Penny. You remember Penny Lambert?'

'You married Penny!' It was laughably inevitable. 'And you were arrested?'

'They don't knock on the bloody door and ask you nicely to come to prison.' An echo of his old uncouthness. It jolted her, made her realise how long it had been since she had heard it from Clyde. 'They tell you your rights and they put you in the dock and they sentence you to four years without a fucking blink. I' – he said, with a grandiose gesture – 'am an example. That's what the judge said – old Geange, went to school with my father – "We must make an example of you."'

Had he been a client, Isobel would have withheld judgment, focused on his anger, his remorse, his coping skills. As his friend – was she his friend? – she wanted to rail against the system. But then he had, apparently, committed a crime.

'Relax,' he urged, patrolling the aisle. 'I did some fucking stupid things and got caught. End of story. Tell me about you and Gil.'

Briefly she surveyed the respectable outlines of her life and discarded them. 'I'm pregnant.' She expected him to say, bloody old Gil, at least congratulate her. But he waited. 'I'm pregnant and I don't know whose it is.'

He whistled. 'Gil know?' She shook her head. 'Abortion?'

'Only if I go to Australia. I'm four months.'

'Penny and I never got as far as kids. She wanted a nice house, then a nicer house, then a holiday house, then more overseas holidays.'

'What about you, what did you want?' asked Isobel, with a hint of scepticism.

'Yeah, I wanted it all too. Everyone else seemed to have it, why not me?'

'We're building a new place, Clyde and I,' she said morosely. 'The foundations are down. Two thousand square feet, a family room, decks, en suites . . . Clyde thinks it will make me happy.' She pictured the holes in the paddock dug by the builder's mate, the lengths of string stretched between pegs. It filled her with as much dread as the clenched fist in her belly. 'I can't have a baby, it'll wreck everything. Dylan's going to boarding school next year, and I've got my job, I'm a social worker at the hospital. Everything's mapped out.'

Rats propped his blue drill bottom against the end of a pew.

'I had everything mapped out. Another couple of years and I reckoned I'd've paid it all back and no harm done. They'd been poking around so long, the police, asking questions, looking at files, I'd got used to it, used to laugh about it. No one really believed I'd done anything wrong. Was leaving the office one night and this police car pulled up and four cops leaped out and arrested me, just like that.' He stared up at the pitched ceiling, then looked at her. 'And you know what? It was a bloody relief. I tried telling people but Penny took it as a personal insult and the probation officer thought it meant I was ready to pay my debt to society. But . . .'

'It meant you could stop keeping one jump ahead.'

'Yeah. And I still feel it. Every morning I wake up in that fucking narrow bed in that dingy slot, and I think, no more bullshit, Ratner. Now everybody knows what you are. And it's a bloody relief. I've taken up woodwork,' he said a few minutes later. 'There's a great workshop here and I always liked it at school. I told the old man once I wanted to be a carpenter. He cracked up, laughed at me. "Ratners are lawyers, son." Some of the blokes here sleep their lags away. Every chance they get, they're out to it. Some are on the make – drugs, porn, you name it, trying to get to the top of the shit heap, or licking the screws' arses. By the time I get out, I'm going to be a shit-hot carpenter. Hey, I could make you and Gil some furniture for your new place.'

She lacked the heart to tell him Gil was dead, that she had slowly but surely crushed the life out of him. They sat for several minutes in silence. 'Oh,' she said, straightening up, a hand on her stomach. 'Oh God.'

Rats looked alarmed. 'Jesus . . .'

'No,' she said, 'it's just . . . I remember that fluttery feeling, oh my God.'

Rats looked eager. He crossed the aisle. 'Can I . . .?' She shrugged, more from awkwardness than indifference. When the chaplain peeped in with much murmured apology, they were side by side in the pew, Rats' hand on her belly. The chaplain beamed, clearly misconstruing Rats' role. 'You'll be right,' said Rats, following the chaplain to the door. 'You're like me – a bloody survivor. Tell Gil to come and see me. We can sit in the visitors room and hold hands.' He and the chaplain headed off across the dismal courtyard.

'Rats!' she called after him. 'Penny's parents. How did they take it – you, all this?'

'How d'you think? End of the bloody world. Their poor little girl.'

'Good,' she shouted, in response to some ancient and surprising loyalty. 'Bloody good show,' and Rats disappeared around the corner of a concrete block building, guffawing.

She called Blackstone, Glossop and Steel from a telephone box in a desolate suburban street. She kept thinking of escaped prisoners, wondering how many were tempted to call home from this very box, or whether they headed – sensibly – for the hills and went bush. Freedom versus family – it always came down to that. Her trembling fingers misdialled twice, and she was shouting at the receptionist before she remembered to press button A.

'Isobel.' She could almost hear him thinking, *what now?*

'Adrian, I have to see you.'

'I'm . . . er . . . in a meeting.'

'No you're not, or you wouldn't have said my name.'

'I'm due in one, with some new clients. Can it wait until tomorrow?'

She almost growled with exasperation, picturing the clients – *nice young couple, first home; older couple, kids off their hands; young executive on the way up* – fairytale families from the happy world of real estate. She had once wrecked an entire afternoon and evening trying to convince Adrian that these were her clients too, that beneath the neat suburban façade lay conflict, rage, disappointment, loss. He refused to be convinced, declared that her work was warping her view of human nature – 'People aren't all miserable, all at loggerheads, Isobel. Thousands of families love each other and are happy together.' *Like you were before me,* she longed to retort, yet how could she, with Jo at the other end of the couch, gazing dreamily into the fire. She had stopped arguing then – for Jo's sake – yet her scorn had smouldered for days, was never, now, entirely extinguished.

She transferred the grubby receiver to the other hand and drew a breath from its stale mouth. 'I'll come to the office if you like.'

'No,' he said hastily. 'Give me ten minutes.'

She sat at a sandblasted pine table in the Black Cat coffee lounge, which had once been the Comet milkbar. Jackie the weather girl had finally captured her St Pat's boy, now an All Black, and had appeared triumphantly in full bridal regalia on the cover of *Woman's Weekly*. Jackie, Isobel thought gloomily, still had aptitude. She burned her mouth on a cup of fierce tea and ate a doughnut, continuing to bite and chew in the hope that sooner or later the faintly oniony stodge might disclose a proper doughnut flavour. Why was it nobody in the southern hemisphere could ever make a proper doughnut? And why, when her life was teetering on the brink of the unimaginable, did it matter?

Adrian greeted her with minimal warmth and pulled out a chair. Immediately she saw it had been a mistake to make him come. She held her hand across the table. He glanced around the empty coffee lounge then yielded his own. They were six doors up from his office. 'I should have waited,' she said. 'This is all wrong.'

'It was difficult to get away. Tim was expecting me to go with him to meet some people. But I'm here now so what's up?'

'You know what's up. I'm pregnant.' He started and glanced around again. She withdrew her hand and fingered the swirls on the table top. The words blocked her mind, they were mountainous. 'What if I had the baby?'

He sagged as if she had punched him, then just as quickly rallied. 'You know that's not possible, not in our situation.' This time he took her hand, and smiled as if at some distant prospect. 'If things were different, if there weren't other people to consider . . . I've often thought about what it would have been like to have a baby with you, Izzy. A girl, I always wanted a little girl. She would have been so sweet, wouldn't she.'

'Possibly.' She felt horribly unreal. 'Or possibly it would be a boy who wasn't sweet at all, a boy you couldn't do anything with. But whatever it is, it's on its way.'

'And that's the other thing,' he went on. 'We'd never know for sure who the father was.'

'But we're a family, just like a family, you've always said. Why would it matter?'

'Look, I know when you're pregnant you feel lots of funny things. Jo always did. But of course it matters, you know that as well as I do, Izzy.'

'Don't keep calling me that.'

'What? Izzy?' He retained the hand and projected his most winning smile. 'I always call you Izzy, you know I do?'

'And don't keep telling me what I know and feel.' She felt a shriek in her throat and blocked her mouth with her hands. But she had to try again. 'It moved this afternoon.'

A woman in a pink nylon smock clattered cups and saucers. Adrian was fumbling for his wallet. 'Good thing you made me come because it's time I gave you this.' He opened his cheque-book and pulled out a pen. 'How much did they say, those women you got in touch with? There's the ticket, then accommodation in Sydney. And the . . . er, operation. And I'll add a bit extra, shall I? You can cheer yourself up at the shops. Fifteen hundred? Let's make it two thousand, it's only money. There.'

He looked extremely pleased. She took the cheque, put it between them on the table and stared at it. 'What if I had the baby?'

Pure panic passed across his face. 'Izzy . . . Isobel . . .'

'What if I did?' Five o'clock traffic was clogging the main street outside the gingham-curtained window. 'What if I did?'

'You can't,' he said. She was fleetingly sorry for him. It was his world too she was turning upside-down.

'But you see, I think I could. I suddenly saw I might be able to, that it mightn't be impossible.'

He shook his head. 'No.'

'Why not? Why won't you even think about it? Why shouldn't I?' He was a kind man, and he loved her, she was his girl. It was her fault he was saying all the wrong things. She could have wept with frustration.

'You listen to me,' he said with such startling coldness she reared back. 'If you have this baby, how do you think Jo will feel? How do you think she'll explain it to people?'

Her flesh crawled. Jo would never be embarrassed by a baby. 'Have you told her I'm pregnant? If she said it was all right, if she didn't mind, what then? Why shouldn't I have the baby then?'

''Scuse me,' said the woman in pink nylon. 'We're closing.'

Adrian stood. He leaned across the table, his knuckles white, and spoke into Isobel's face, 'If you go ahead with this, it'll be on the understanding that you won't get any support from me. I won't be able to help you.'

Isobel dropped her eyes. 'Adrian,' she breathed, deeply ashamed for him.

He and the woman waited for Isobel to get to her feet, then the three of them walked in single file to the door. It felt like a very long way. Isobel stood on the pavement while passersby flowed around her. 'I mean it,' he repeated as if she did not understand English. 'I won't be able to help you, not if you have the baby.' Behind them, the woman bolted the door of the Black Cat.

Isobel heard herself say, 'Fine. Then I'll manage without you.'

He turned abruptly in the direction of his office. Once he

was out of sight, she was disoriented, confused about where to go and what to do next. Then with relief, she pictured her kitchen – Dylan home from school, Joan fumbling with potatoes, Clyde taking off his boots at the door. She didn't need Adrian, she had a place.

She was halfway to her car when she turned back. She had to thump long and hard on the door of the Black Cat before the woman grumpily reappeared, cardigan over her smock.

Isobel squeezed past. 'Sorry. I left something.' Noughts were strung across the cheque like beads. She slipped them into her pocket.

Chapter 29

But home was not as she had pictured it. Only Joan was there, wedged into an armchair with a book whose cover showed a creamy-bosomed woman swooning in the arms of a man built like a wall. Isobel slumped on the couch. The builders had begun framing up the new house and its skeleton threw long shadows across the paddock. 'Dylan's playing with that boy down the road,' said Joan. Her speech was restored although she still walked hesitantly. 'I haven't seen Clyde since lunch. You're exhausted. When are you going to tell him?'

'What?' Isobel ached with the need to call Adrian. Need gnawed at her bones.

'That you're expecting. You ought to stop work, all those people who can't sort out their own problems.'

'How did you . . .?'

'The stroke didn't affect my hearing,' said Joan sharply. 'I heard you telling that friend of yours.' She referred to Cam in the disparaging way she had once referred to Adrian. 'Anyway, I can tell by the look of you. I can always tell.'

Isobel was disinclined to argue.

'Tell him tonight,' Joan was saying. 'He'll be pleased, they always are.'

'I didn't want another one,' murmured Isobel. Already it felt like history, that not wanting.

'I know, dear,' said Joan, almost kindly, making Isobel flinch. 'I'll make you a cup of tea, then we can think about a meal.' She geared herself up for the struggle out of the chair, but Isobel automatically got to her feet. The old lady's arms and legs flailed then she was upright, seizing determined breaths. 'Let me,' she gasped. 'For goodness sake, just for once let someone else do something.'

Close to unaccountable tears, Isobel did as she was told. But it took all her willpower to stay seated as Joan wavered back across the carpet, tea tray rattling perilously. 'Lovely,' she murmured, although the tea was too weak and she had gulped it down before Joan was settled in her chair again. 'I'll go and put the meat in the oven.'

'No,' said Joan. 'I want to say something.' Isobel badly needed to be alone, to replay her exchange with Adrian, to piece together what they had each said, work out if she had actually claimed that she could manage without him. Joan said, 'You've been good to me. Very good, considering.' Isobel stopped thinking of Adrian, and considered. 'I won't forget what you've done.' Joan paused again so they could both remember cups held to a tremulous lip, toilet accidents mopped up, bedraggled limbs lowered into baths. 'Good as a daughter. And I want to explain something. Why I sent that letter . . .'

'Letter?' echoed Isobel, vividly picturing the inept typing, the vicious formality.

'Don't play the fool, you know the one.'

'You don't have to . . .'

'I don't expect you to forgive me, I don't want to be forgiven. I had my reasons, I want you to know what they were. My husband,

Noel' – she uttered his name with difficulty – 'didn't die, he left me, ran off with a female from work and expected me to set him free. There was a divorcee down the road when I was little, she went to the letterbox in her dressing gown and curlers. Mother was always polite but she never had her in for afternoon tea. I wouldn't divorce him. Ever.' Her face contorted. 'He did die in the end, and he left her comfortable. I wasn't left comfortable. She was pretty and she gave him children and she knew how to please him. So he stayed with her and left her comfortable.'

'Clyde has cousins?' wondered Isobel, but Joan did not hear.

'You were so young and wrong-headed,' Joan said fiercely. 'You had no idea – of men, their . . . their appetites, and their pride. How they can leave you with nothing.'

Isobel fingered the cheque in her pocket. 'Divorce isn't like that now. There's social welfare, there's going to be a matrimonial property act.'

Joan ignored her. 'Clyde was a dear little boy. But he wasn't a little boy when he met you, he was a man and I knew what he was like. I've watched poor Muriel with Jacko for thirty-five years. She learned. She's managed . . .'

'Managed!' cried Isobel. 'I'd rather die than put up with . . .'

'Rubbish.' Joan was scornful. 'You think you can make everything fair by passing laws. I didn't want what happened to me to happen to you. I wanted to warn you. But once you'd got him, I wanted you to hold him. You've got to hold them.'

'I have,' said Isobel, lowering her head, giving up the fight.

Joan eyed her narrowly. 'You could have done worse. He's not got a temper like his father. Doesn't drink hard. And lots wouldn't put up with their wives working, especially farming men. Just don't go getting any ideas, you're going to have a baby, don't spoil it now.'

Adrian rang and relief flooded every cell of her body. 'Feeling better?' he inquired pleasantly. 'Izzy? Are you there? I said . . .?'

'I heard you. I'm fine.'

'That's good,' he enthused. 'It's only hormones, you know. I talked to Jo and she said . . .'

'Adrian, I can't talk.' The words threatened to choke her.

'Don't be silly, Izzy.' She could hear him smiling.

'I'm going to hang up.'

'Listen, Izzy. I'll drive over if you like, we need to see each other.'

She could feel his arms around her, smell his skin. It would be the end, the end of the end. 'I don't want to see you. Or talk to you. I'm hanging up.'

It was like cutting her own throat so she could breath, and he forced her to do it again and again. She pleaded sickness and stayed away from work, abandoning clients whose need, in the face of her own, seemed negligible. Under Joan's approving eye, she kneaded bread, dug the garden, cleaned out kitchen cupboards. As if Domestic Science would save her life. Day and night fell apart. People moved around her like ghosts. She lived from one breath to the next. *Don't go, please don't go.*

She wondered if she should call Jo, to explain. But Jo called her. 'Adrian's very upset. I thought you ought to know.'

'I do know,' whispered Isobel, in anguish. 'But there's nothing I can do.'

'That's silly,' said Jo. 'Come and see him, make it up.'

'I can't. He said things, terrible things.' She could barely remember what. 'He's a coward, I don't like him.'

'That's a bit naughty,' said Jo. 'He loves you.'

'I love you,' said Adrian. 'Nobody will ever love you like I do. You know that, don't you, Isobel?'

She did. She knew it so thoroughly that she locked the bathroom door and sobbed until she vomited. She wondered if she would sob until she lost the baby and what she would do then. She sobbed until her face swelled to a weeping blob and she could barely see. Joan tapped on the door then went away. Dylan called 'Mum?' in a scared voice. Finally they fetched Clyde. He put his shoulder to the door and was suddenly beside her, surprised and embarrassed. He had been crutching ewes and he stank. He stood, filthy arms at his side, and waited to be told what to do. She wiped her eyes and blew her nose, studying him. She did not hate him, that was a start.

'Shut the door,' she said, and Joan and Dylan's pale faces disappeared. 'Sit down.' He lowered himself to the edge of the bath. 'I'm going to have a baby.' His face lit up in slow motion. 'In August.'

'Lambing time,' he grinned. 'He can have that little back room in the new place . . .'

'It's a she,' she said quickly. 'I'm sure it's a girl.'

'Mum'll be over the moon. And Aunty Joan.'

It might have made all the difference had he been able to put his arms around her, had he not been plastered with shit and reeking of the woolshed. As it was, he remained sitting on the bath, she on the lid of the toilet. 'It might not be yours,' she said.

He left the bathroom as abruptly as he had entered it. She caught up with him in the night paddock. 'But it might,' she panted. 'Clyde, it might be your baby.' He kept walking. 'Clyde, stop. Listen to me.'

He stopped, but his stoniness appalled her. He was entitled to rage, even take a swing at her. She had robbed him blind. 'I'm sorry,' she said, facing him. 'It's terrible, what I've done all these years. I'm sorry. But' – she reached for his hands, ignoring the filth – 'it's over, all that. We can start again, I want to, with you. We'll make it our baby, we'll be a proper family. Please, Clyde.'

His fists were rocks in her hand. His face never even twitched. 'Clyde.' She was pleading. 'Please, Clyde. I want the baby. And I want to be with you.'

When she had run out of words, he took back his hands and headed for the house. She stared after him until Joan came tottering across the grass. 'What is it, Isobel?' she wheezed. 'What have you done?'

Isobel whirled on her. 'What you said to do – told him about the baby. And he's not pleased at all, he doesn't want it. I should never have listened to you.' She relished the punishing dishonesty, the old woman's bewilderment.

She heard the car reversing wildly down the drive and broke into a run. Dylan was at the gate, eyes wide with excitement. 'Dad's gone,' he yelled. 'He got his twenty-two from the cupboard and he's gone. What bastard is he going to shoot, Mum?'

'Martin, it's Isobel. Is . . .?' She dithered uselessly between Dad and Adrian.

'No one's here. Only me.'

'I need to speak to Adrian. Or Mum.' She shook with impatience. She could not remember what day of the week it was or where she might expect anybody to be.

'Mum's gone to see Granny or shopping or something. Dad's probably at work.' He was maddeningly vague.

'He's not, I tried. I've got to find him, Martin. I've been ringing your place for ages.'

'I just got in.' His voice had that faraway quality she found so appealing in Jo. It made her want to shake Martin till his teeth rattled. 'Hang on,' he said. 'There's a car.'

He went away for so long she began yelling his name into the mouthpiece. 'Just Clyde,' he said eventually. 'Looking for Dad too. I told him you were on the phone but he didn't want to talk to you.'

Isobel groaned. 'Tell him he's got to. Tell him . . .'

'I told him Dad sometimes goes to De Brett's on Saturdays. He went there.'

Isobel marched up and down the kitchen while Joan made tea and Dylan pretended to watch television. 'I'm calling the police,' Isobel decided.

Joan was horrified. 'You can't drag the police into it.'

Isobel was contemptuous. 'He's got a gun. Are you more

233

worried about what people think than whether he'll kill some-one?'

'Gone off with a gun, Mrs Giltrap?' said the sergeant who had come to the house the night of the peeping Tom.

'A twenty-two,' supplied Dylan from the door.

Isobel's brain was cluttered with images of Rats and Clyde sharing a cell, of chatting to them both in the visitors room on Saturday afternoons, the baby in her arms. The more immediate consequences of a firearm being aimed and fired at Adrian were unthinkable. She pictured Clyde presenting her with Adrian's foot, for luck.

'What's it all about, then, Mrs Giltrap? Had a bit of a tiff, have we? Shouldn't worry, he'll be back, Gil wouldn't do anything stupid. If I were you . . .'

'Listen,' snarled Isobel, 'I'm pregnant and I told him it might be someone else's. He said he's going to kill him.'

Joan whinnied and fell back in her chair. There was a sharp intake of breath at the end of the telephone. 'Bloody hell. Poor old Gil.'

'Now look . . .' said Isobel.

The sergeant recovered his professional demeanour. 'Best thing you can do, Mrs Giltrap, is stay put. I take it you've tried to warn your . . . the er . . . other party? Tell me where you think they are and I'll see what we can do.'

'Thank you,' breathed Isobel.

'No worries,' boomed the sergeant. 'Odds are they'll be knocking back a few jars by the time we get there.'

Isobel bit back a sharp response and hung up.

'I want to go home,' said Joan in a wobbly voice.

'You can't, Clyde took the car.' Isobel was glad. Even Joan's presence was some kind of anchor.

They all heard the car swoosh down the drive. 'Clyde,' breathed Isobel. 'Thank God,' and flung open the door on a startled Teddy.

'Why have I got to stay with Aunty Joan? Why?' demanded Dylan, from the back of Teddy's beaten-up Holden.

'Because your mother says so,' quavered Joan, beside him. He didn't deign to reply. The battle, as always, was between him and Isobel.

Queasy from the car's drunken gait over the hill, Isobel turned and honoured Dylan with a reasonable look. 'It's better for you there, Dylan. You can watch TV and . . . and keep Aunty Joan company.' It was lame and they both knew it.

'I want to come with you and Teddy. Why can't I? He's my father.'

'Sit back, Dylan, and do as you're told.'

'I'm not staying, you can't make me.'

The Holden rolled into Joan's street, and Isobel clutched the door handle to prevent herself falling against Teddy. 'Dylan, please don't argue, not today. I've got a lot to think about. Anyway, we're going to a pub, you can't go into a pub.'

'I can wait in the car. I want to wait in the car.'

'No,' she said, as the Holden sailed to a halt. 'Get out with Aunty Joan.'

The old woman unfolded gingerly from the back seat. Teddy got her case from the boot and took her arm down the path. Dylan stayed put, staring fixedly ahead. 'Get out,' she ordered. 'Now.' He did not budge. 'If you don't get out by the time I've counted to five . . . One, two, three . . .'

Every fibre of Dylan's body declared refusal. With a cry of outrage, she launched herself through the door, scarcely registering a sharp crack on the head from the door arch. Her hands locked on his neck. He fell back across the seat and she toppled after him. His feet and fists pummelled her. She shook throttled sounds from his throat.

Then something was hauling her off. 'Stop it,' ordered Teddy. She heard the shock in his voice. 'Isobel, for fuck's sake, stop it. You'll kill him.' She saw a shaken child emerge from under her, saw him read her helplessness as Teddy pinned her

arms, and saw the small fist draw back and take aim. She collapsed weeping on the grass verge, cradling her throbbing
breast. It felt not merely hurt but damaged, irreparably.

'Get out of the car, Dylan,' ordered Teddy. The boy did as
he was told.

A barrier of tobacco smoke and stale beer hit Isobel and Teddy
at the pub door. And the noise – a male roar they seemed to
have to wade through. They split up to search the vast crammed
interior. The sea of faces made Isobel giddy. On all sides beery
mouths opened and closed like trapdoors, gulping down booze,
emitting leers and barks. Meaty hands slopped jugs, hard backs
turned against her. Man's country – she wondered how she had
ever come to call it home. At first her eyes ran past Adrian and
Clyde – more mouths, more glasses. Clyde was inclined towards
Adrian, his grin tellingly lopsided. Adrian's arm was round
Clyde's shoulder. Before them were many empty jugs, a couple
half full. She pushed forward, craning for a glimpse of the
twenty-two, but already her anxiety was absurd, replaced by
irritation and disgust.

She stood before them, oddly shy of breaking in. They
seemed to be exchanging spasmodic observations on rural
property values. 'Isobel!' Adrian half rose and fell back. Clyde
was completely drunk, Adrian pretending not to be. She didn't
know which repelled her most.

She sat. 'Beer?' inquired Clyde with a goofy grin, as if he had
been expecting her.

'Probably rather have something from the top shelf,' Adrian
informed him. 'Top shelf sort of girl.'

'Right, mate. Right.' They regarded each other lovingly.
Clyde lumbered to his feet, exploring his pockets for cash.
'Drink for my wife,' and he stumbled off towards the bar. If he
were clever, thought Isobel, he'd get the twenty-two now.

'Are you all right?' she asked Adrian. Against her will, her
body soaked up the reassurance of his.

He fell across the table at her. 'Izzy, wonderful to see you, so glad you came.'

'Why? Has he already threatened you?' He frowned stupidly and she wanted to douse him with cold water. She spoke slowly and carefully in a way Dylan would never have tolerated. 'I told Clyde about the baby. I said it might be yours. He took his twenty-two. He said he was going to kill you.'

'Izzy,' he crooned, 'little Izzy.'

'I mean it, Adrian. He's got it in the car. That's why I came.'

'You don't have to pretend, I know you came to see me. Can't keep away from each other, can we?' Clyde was back with her drink and Adrian offered him a sloppy look. 'Mates, Clyde and me, aren't we, mate?'

Clyde – or possibly the ghost of Gil – handed her a drink with a clumsy bow.

She grimaced. 'What is it?'

'A fallen angel, you like fallen angels.' He fell into his seat and Adrian replaced the arm round his shoulder.

'Not going to fall out over a woman, are we, mate?' he said.

'Wonderful woman,' crowed Clyde. 'My wife.'

'A fallen angel,' said Adrian. And for half a minute they were helpless with the humour of it.

She fished the straw, the cherry and the orange slice from the glass and filled her mouth with sweet pink froth. It tasted of numb sex behind the railway station, Big Ben booming before the BBC news, and *What have you been up to, young lady?* She drained the glass, watching the two men watch her, thinking, what have I been up to?

'I'm going home,' she said coldly, knowing they would stare after her with stupid crestfallen expressions. She forced her way through the crush, more aggressively this time, and did not look back.

Teddy was outside, leaning against a wall, smoking. 'All in one piece, I take it?'

She ignored his sardonic tone – he had been kind enough

to drive her over the hill, after all – and they set off towards the Holden. The sweetness of the fallen angel clung to her mouth. 'I can't believe one of those two idiots is the father of this baby.'

'Can't you?'

Suddenly she was enraged. She grabbed his arm and yanked him to a halt. A black dog went berserk in a nearby car. 'What the hell's that supposed to mean?'

He regarded her coolly. 'It means when the hell are you going to stop pissing around and . . .'

'Pissing around! Anyone'd think this was all my fault.' An overdressed young woman skirted them cautiously.

He started walking again, not bothering to turn his head as he said, 'Time you grew up, Iz, and made a proper life for you and the nipper.' He unlocked the Holden and got in. 'Both nippers.'

She slammed the door, eyes brimming with furious tears. 'You've no right to talk to me like that.'

'Course I bloody have. Here, stop snivelling.' He passed her a grubby handkerchief and she blew into it vengefully. Neither of them spoke as he navigated the back streets.

'Left here,' she reminded him sulkily. 'We have to get Dylan.'

'Poor little bugger,' murmured Teddy.

Her hand found her bruised breast and she was on the attack again. 'You single people always make the best parents, don't you. When you finally get the courage to put your theories into practice you'll find out you can't *be* a parent without inflicting some damage.'

He pulled up in front of Joan Fisk's house. 'A blessing it'll never happen then, isn't it.' He met her eye, then when she gazed at him blankly, 'Surely even you must have noticed by now?'

'Noticed?'

'That I'm gay. Queer. Bent as a two-bob watch.' He was savage.

Her mouth fell open. '*Even* me? What do you mean, *even* me?'

He gave her a horrified look then seized her shoulders and shook her once, hard. 'Fuck you, Isobel. Fuck you. I just told you the most important thing about me and . . .'

'Gay? But . . . no . . . I thought . . .'

'Thought what? That I was in love with Isobel Irene Midwinter? Like those other poor suckers.'

'You spied on us,' she accused wildly. 'On Clyde and me, I know you did . . .' Did she? Surely she had been wrong, surely Teddy would never . . .

He crumpled. 'I felt . . . excluded. I thought you had everything and I had nothing.'

There was a long painful silence. Eventually she touched his arm. 'I'm sorry, Teddy. I didn't realise. I should have.'

'Waiting for me to find a nice girl and settle down, were you? I've tried to tell you over the years but . . .' He shook his head.

'You *should* have told me. I wish you had, I feel so stupid. You should have made me listen.'

'*Made* Isobel Midwinter do anything? Do me a favour.'

'Do you . . . you know, have someone?' She tried to conjure a picture of a man Teddy could love.

'Not the real thing, not yet. So we're quits, aren't we.'

She opened her mouth to protest – but it was only a reflex action and she closed it again. Dylan's face flickered in Joan's window. He was waiting for Isobel to come in and hold out her arms before he would allow her to forgive him. She loved Dylan but he gave her unbearable heartache. She did not love his father but ought to try. She loved Adrian but had to stop. And Jo . . . and the new baby . . . Once, for an instant, love had presented itself as an exquisitely simple answer. Every day since it had been drummed home to her that it was neither simple nor exquisite, that love – maternal, sexual, familial – was only more questions. So why try? Why not be Joan Fisk and live alone in a bitterly neat house?

'Don't start again,' said Teddy. 'I've run out of hand-kerchiefs.'

Between sobs, she spluttered. 'I'm sorry, Teddy . . . I haven't been . . . a proper friend . . . I'm not a nice person . . .'

'Nice?' He grinned. 'No, but what's that got to do with it? Come on, cheer up. Clyde hasn't killed Adrian, and Dylan's waiting for you, and I'm still here.'

She studied him, wiping and sniffing. 'You are, aren't you.'

He shook his head, slithered across the Holden's long seat and took her in his freckled arms. She let him hold her. The weeping stopped but she did not pull away. She let out a big breath she had been holding all of her twenty-eight years. *Milk and honey* . . . 'There's something I want to say.' She hesitated – it might sound stupid, he might laugh. 'I know I'm not much good at it but . . . I do love you, Teddy.'

'Yeah, I know,' he said matter of factly. 'And I love you too. Now what are you grinning like an idiot for?'

'Don't know. Must be the fallen angel.'

Chapter 30

THEY HOPPED FROM ONE FLOOR JOIST TO ANOTHER THROUGH the airy structure of the new house. 'Great ceilings,' said Teddy, tilting his face to the sky.

'This is my room,' said Dylan, tugging him into it. 'Dad says I'll be able to lie in bed and shoot ducks off the pond.'

'And this is the baby's room,' Isobel forced herself to say.

'What do we have to have a baby for?' Dylan scowled. 'Why does it have to be next to me? What if it's a girl?'

'Have to keep your door shut, then,' said Teddy. 'In case it's catching.' Dylan refused to laugh. He leaped on his bike and pedalled away with Ditto bleating full tilt after him. Teddy and Isobel sat on the step and stared out at the empty paddocks.

'What's Auckland like?' she asked.

'Come and see, bring Dylan, my house is huge. The garden's lush, rotting grapefruit over the front lawn, bougainvillea and banana passionfruit all over the back. And there are thunderstorms, like Home.'

'Don't call it that!'

Someone was crossing the paddock. Male, but not Adrian. He had rung five times since she had seen him in De Brett's. Each time she had stood quaking as Teddy told him she would not come to the telephone. Clyde had stayed away four days, she had no idea where, and she prayed Adrian would not call again, not now Clyde was finally home.

'It's me,' said Martin.

'Martin, how nice.' She could not keep the query out of her voice. Martin had not visited since he was old enough to refuse to accompany his parents. He stood unsmiling, arms stiff at his sides, shot Teddy a look of childish suspicion and said, 'I want to talk to you, Isobel.'

'I'll go inside and get packed up,' Teddy told Isobel. 'I'm leaving after lunch.'

'Why?' she implored, but he was already striding away. Don't go, she wanted to call after him. Don't leave me here with the rest of my life.

'I've got to talk to you,' Martin repeated aggressively. He seemed unable to get any further.

'Come and see the house,' said Isobel, hovering between amusement and irritation. 'This is the lounge. There's going to be a raised fireplace on that side, and over here . . .'

'You've got to see Dad,' said Martin, teetering on a floor joist in the middle of the room. 'He cries. I can hear him at night, it's horrible. He's crying about you.'

Isobel faced him. 'It's not my fault, Martin.'

'Yes, it is,' he cried. 'You're the one who's trying to end it.'

'I have ended it.'

'You can't, it's not fair.'

She took a deep breath. 'Martin, you don't understand . . .'

'It's not fair on Mum. She has to be with him when he's crying and going on and on about you. What about her?'

'Martin, I can't stay with your father just to keep your mother happy.'

'You did all those years. If it was all right then, why isn't it now?'

'This is ridiculous. There are things you can't possibly understand, things that go on between two people.' As if anything was ever just between two.

She stood in the bedroom wondering how long it would be before it looked like somewhere she would lie next to Clyde every night until one of them died. Martin came up behind her and pinned her arms. 'I don't care,' he said in a torn voice. 'I don't care about you and Dad, I just care about Mum. Why should she suffer because of you?'

She shook him off. 'Did she send you? Did she tell you to try and make me come back?' They glared at each other, breathing heavily. 'Listen, Martin, Mum made decisions a long time ago about her life. All I know is I don't love . . . I don't want to love Adrian anymore and nothing you can say will make me. If I stayed with him just because I was having his child, it would be all wrong. Anyway, he doesn't want it.'

Martin fell back. 'I didn't know. Mum never said . . .'

'I wasn't going to tell you. I didn't mean to.'

'It must be related to me.' He was staring frankly at her stomach then suddenly he was on the floor looking up at her. 'It wasn't my fault Chris died, it wasn't.' He put his face in his hands.

She bent to put an arm around his shaking shoulders. 'Of course it wasn't. Why . . .?'

'It's always felt like it was, like I have to make up for it, and I'm never going to be able to. Chris was the good-looking one, the funny one, the clever one. I'm just Martin. The living one.'

She held him while he cried like a baby. He was a baby, the age she had been when she married Clyde and gave birth to Dylan. She rocked and rocked him, thinking, poor Isobel, poor stupid little Isobel. At last he rubbed his face with the backs of his hands. 'Sorry . . .'

'It's all right, Martin.'

'Sometimes I hate Dad for what he's done with you. Yet Mum wanted him to. You're right, I don't understand anything.'

'You will, one day,' she lied. He waited for more. 'I think it's brave of you to come here and say all this. Not many men' – she choked back *boys* in the nick of time – 'could do that.'

'I've never understood about you either, what I'm meant to think.'

'Think?'

Abruptly he planted his mouth on hers. It tasted of tears. Adrian's son, came the thought like a temptation before she reared back. 'See,' he said, not at all discomposed. 'Are you like a mother or a sister or what?'

'I'm sorry, Martin. It's a mess and it's my fault. I'm sorry.'

'Don't cry,' he begged, panic-stricken. 'I'll go. I'll tell Mum you can't come back to Dad because you love Clyde, shall I? That might stop her being angry.'

'Jo's angry?' At last she was alone on the far side of the gulf. She had lost them both. 'Yes,' she said, 'tell her I love Clyde.'

She cut a buttercrunch lettuce from the garden, determined to make an effort for Teddy's last lunch. She plucked Russian Red tomatoes from the vine, pulled spring onions. Next season's salads would come from the new garden. It took years to establish a proper garden, a lifetime. She would start tomorrow, when Teddy had gone. It would be her consolation, a reason to look forward, a defence against looking back. She was walking back to the house with her arms full of vegetables when he bawled across the paddock, 'Isobel, it's Clyde. You'd better come.'

She ran, scattering tomatoes, as Teddy loped ahead between Jacko's sheds. He stood to one side of the woolshed door to let her peer inside. 'You scared me. What is it?' He pushed her forward and she squinted into the gloom. Dylan was bent over a sheep. It lay placidly on its back like a stuffed toy, brainless trusting Ditto. Clyde loomed over both of them.

'What's going on?' she asked, as her heart subsided. Clyde's face was still hangover grey, he looked as if he would never re-cover.

'Not carrying this bloody thing through the winter. Short enough of feed as it is.' He spoke as if spitting out stones.

Dylan looked up at Isobel in mute anguish. Behind him on a ledge was the killing knife. 'Clyde, for God's sake, you can't. Not Ditto, she's Dylan's.'

He sucked on his cigarette. 'I'm not going to. He is.'

Ditto waved her silly hooves. 'Clyde, please. Don't make him.' He handed Dylan the knife. 'No,' she shouted, and grabbed.

Dylan's small hand got there first. 'Let go, Mum! I want to.'

She spoke urgently into his face. 'Dylan, you love Ditto. You can't kill her . . . you mustn't . . .'

'Yes, I can, I can. Dad wants me to.' He sobbed, his nose and eyes ran and his small shoulders heaved.

'You mustn't. She loves you, look, she trusts you.'

He looked blindly at the knife. 'I want to kill her, I want to.'

She shot a last desperate appeal at Clyde but he showed no sign of relenting, no sign of anything. His eyes were slits, his mouth a bloodless line. She had forgotten Teddy was there until he stepped forward and swept Dylan up. The knife clattered to the boards and Ditto rolled over and trotted perkily off. 'Put me down!' bellowed Dylan, pummeling and kicking. 'Put me down, you're not my father!' Teddy shouldered the weeping boy out of the shed.

Isobel shook Clyde's arm, trying to bring him to his senses. The danger was past but she would have to start all over again, from the very beginning. 'Clyde, it's me you're angry with, me and your father and mother, not Dylan. I can't let you take it out on Dylan. You mustn't. Don't you see that?'

For a second, as a million dust motes spun in a shaft of sun-light and a hen peck-pecked its way across the boards, she believed he must see, that she could make him see. She searched his face for a trace of the laughing child in dungarees, but he was gone, too far gone. The woolshed reeked of fear. Clyde was a lost life.

'I'm sorry, Clyde, sorry for everything,' she said. 'But I can't stay with you. I'm going with Teddy and I'm taking Dylan. Today.' Then she turned away so she would not have to see him shrug.

PART FOUR

ENGLAND 1985

Chapter 31

'More meat, Isobel?' inquired Gillian's husband from the head of the table. A fawn slice of lamb quivered on the carving fork, its frill of fat glistening.

'Isobel doesn't eat meat,' said Holly. 'Specially lamb. But I do.'

'Oh dear, I had no idea,' said Isobel's mother, as if she were fully acquainted with every other aspect of her daughter's life. 'Whatever will you eat, darling?'

'This is fine,' murmured Isobel.

'I eat lots of meat,' enthused Holly.

'Yes, darling, but little girls must wait for older people to be served first.' Holly made a face and her grandmother giggled. 'Little monkey. Mint sauce anyone?' Then, in a tone of genuine scientific inquiry, 'She always calls you Isobel, does she?'

'Not always,' said Isobel, swallowing a mouthful of sacrificed lamb.

'Oh well,' sighed her mother bravely, 'it's the modern way, I suppose, but I've always thought it rather a pity. You only have one mother, don't you?' There was an ambiguous silence from the three sisters.

'I've got three fathers,' said Holly, sprinkling mint sauce. Isobel bent over a brussels sprout as Holly chattered on. 'There's Teddy that we live with and Dylan's father and my other father.'

'Other father, darling?' repeated Isobel's mother. She was attempting to cover bewilderment and suspicion with a sporting smile, but the little finger crooked over her knife suffered a distinct tremor.

'We only have one,' said Piers in disappointed BBC tones. He looked sadly at Jeffrey.

Isobel mentally rehearsed her speech about Holly's paternity to the brussels sprout. *But you always led us to believe* . . . it protested. She cut it in four. *The modern way, I suppose,* sighed the last piece just before she swallowed it.

'More meat anyone? Jeffrey dear, would you mind . . .? Lovely, isn't it. My little man down the road looks after me. He knows I don't like that frozen stuff from New Zealand, terribly overrated, I always think. Like that singer, you know the one. Quite overrated.'

'Prince Charles wouldn't agree,' said Isobel as mildly as she could.

'Can't afford meat at our place,' said Cynthia. 'Wherever it comes from. Not with everyone on the dole.'

'You must take the leftovers home, darling,' said her mother.

'I was on the benefit for a few years,' said Isobel, stabbing a carrot. 'After Holly was born.'

'Benefit, darling? Jeffrey dear, do have some more. It'll only be wasted.'

'No, it won't,' said Cynthia.

'Domestic purposes benefit,' said Isobel. 'For single parents.'

'Dear old Letty down the road, her granddaughter's just split up from her husband and she's had to go on social security.

Such a shame. I met her once, nice young woman too.'

'They tried to stop it a couple of times,' continued Isobel, sawing a potato. 'They tried to say Teddy and I were cohabiting.'

'Teddy,' said Cynthia, 'fancy you ending up with him.'

'I haven't, that was the point.' Isobel forged on, taking comfort from the mention of Teddy's name, its evocation of real life. 'He's making a name for himself in Auckland now, doing murals in restaurants and on the outside of buildings. I've got some photographs.'

Her mother shook her head, put an absurdly small piece of lamb in her mouth and repositioned her cutlery on her plate. 'It broke poor old Max's heart, that business. Thank God Iris didn't live to see it.'

'Teddy emigrating, why?'

Her mother swivelled her eyes meaningfully at Holly and back to Isobel. 'No darling, that . . . other business.'

Isobel chewed and swallowed fury.

'Well, there's no doubt in my mind that some girls do try it on,' announced Jeffrey to no one in particular. 'I see a lot of that sort of thing in my line. And I see no reason why we should all foot the bill.' Cynthia pushed back her chair and left the table. 'Too many young women seem to think they only have to get pregnant by the first ne'er-do-well they fall under . . .'

'Jeffrey,' murmured Gillian. 'You do realise that Isobel . . .?'

'. . . and the state owes them a living. I am not of that school of thought.'

'Christ,' exploded Cynthia from the armchair.

'Jeffrey, dear,' said Gillian. 'No, Piers, sit still. Yes, I know Aunty Cynthia left the table . . .'

'And I,' said Isobel's mother with considerable energy, 'am not of the school of thought that believes children should be punished for their parents' sins nor women for the misfortune of getting pregnant.'

There was brief but intense silence. 'Sin, Irene?' echoed

Jeffrey sonorously. 'I didn't mean for us to stumble into the realm of metaphysics.'

Isobel considered emptying the gravy boat into his lap. Her mother seemed not to hear. 'Why should women have to beg for a pittance when they're bringing up the next generation? Men will never understand what it's like, how it goes on day and night for years, and even when they leave home . . .'

'Good lord,' cried Jeffrey. 'It must be catching, this women's lib stuff. I'd better get you home, Gill.'

'No need to worry about her,' said Cynthia distinctly, from behind *The Observer.*

'I read Betty Friday when we were in New Zealand. I used to say, Isobel's got to have a career. All the girls do. Oh yes, I had to fight to get you all to university.'

'Friedan,' said Isobel, fiercely scraping plates. 'I'll get dessert, shall I?'

'You mean pudding,' said Holly. 'What did you say dessert for?'

Her mother leaped up as if reprimanded. Gillian released a deep sigh, and Piers delivered a swift ungentlemanly punch to Katrina's arm. Katrina let out a piercing scream. 'Leave the room,' thundered Jeffrey.

'Hit him back,' said Holly. 'Like this. You make a fist then you aim past the bit you want to hit so you hit it really hard. Don't you do self-defence?'

'Good lord,' cried Jeffrey.

'I practised on Teddy,' Holly informed Katrina. 'You could practise on him.' Katrina looked as if she didn't think so.

'How marvellous,' said Isobel's mother, returning with bowls, 'that they teach girls how to look after themselves now. Many's the time I'd've liked to have given someone a good whack.'

'You don't say,' said Cynthia. Gillian stood abruptly, almost yanking the cloth from the table. She went to the far side of the room and took the other armchair. Her children looked shocked.

'Well, I'm sure we don't spend all that hard-earned dosh on

Katrina's school fees so she can go round beating up men,' declared Jeffrey expansively.

'Katrina and Piers go to a nice little private school,' said Isobel's mother, distributing pear halves. 'The state schools here aren't like New Zealand, the children have knives and sell drugs.'

'Compulsory subjects, actually,' said Cynthia. '"A knowledge of blade skills is essential to the lucrative drug deal. Discuss, with illustrations from your own experience."'

'You may mock, Cynthia . . .' said Jeffrey.

'I do, Jeffrey, old son.'

'Oh dear,' said Isobel's mother. 'Now, what would we all like to do this afternoon?'

A walk was the only feasible option and they milled about the hall trying on old jackets and battered footwear which Isobel's mother handed out from the cupboard under the stairs. 'I was scared of the cupboard under the stairs,' Isobel told Holly. 'In the old house.'

Holly hooted. 'What a wimp.'

'Not at all. Your mother was a brave little thing,' said Isobel's mother. 'Here, try this, darling.' It was Isobel's father's old anorak, too big and not warm enough.

'I've got pictures of our house in Auckland,' said Isobel without much hope.

'Lovely, darling. You're going to keep that one on, are you?' She passed a hand over her face as if to hide a spasm of pain. 'Oh dear, poor Daddy.'

They trooped along a lifeless street of brick semi-detacheds to a park gate. The air bit Isobel's cheeks and hands and burned her throat. After a pearly Auckland spring, it was fierce and uncompromising. 'We might see some deer, poppet,' her mother called to Holly.

'Seen deer,' shouted Holly, swinging on Cynthia's gloved hand. 'Clyde's got them.'

'So her father doesn't mind not being called Daddy either?' It was impossible to tell if she remembered that the person she was referring to with such formality was the unsuitable boy with whom she used to flirt.

The wintry expanse of parkland was muffled in fog. Holly swarmed up a gnarled oak with Cynthia close behind. Piers struggled on the lower branches while Katrina held Gillian's hand, looking wistful. Piers addressed Holly through the branches, curiosity overcoming his lordliness. 'Have you lived on a farm?'

'No,' admitted Holly. 'But stayed on one. With Clyde and Dylan. And when they dock the lambs, they get these little orange rubber bands and they hold it on its back all wriggly and then . . .'

'That's nice,' said Isobel's mother. 'They're going to be friends after all. A shame about Dylan, isn't it, that he didn't come too.'

'He's nearly twenty,' said Isobel, not looking at her. 'He has his own life.'

'Yes,' sighed her mother. 'I know they *think* they do. You were always very . . . independent. But they're still children, really, aren't they?'

'Careful, Holly!' called Isobel for no obvious reason.

'Of course, that was the thing about homosexuals, I always thought – they avoid responsibility.' Isobel strode on, thinking, I *was* a brave little thing.

'Crap,' said Cynthia. 'Complete and utter crap.'

'Cynthia, please. Not in front of the children.'

'Then don't you in front of the children.'

'I was only saying that these people dodge their responsibilities by not having normal relationships which lead to children.'

'Fuckin' hell,' said Cynthia.

'Aunty Cynthia said a rude word,' observed Piers.

'Fuck isn't rude,' said Holly. 'It's a real word. It means . . .'

'Well,' said Isobel's mother. 'Time to turn back, I think, don't you? What we all need is a nice cup of tea.'

Holly tugged Isobel down the hall to where Gillian, Jeffrey, Cynthia and the children were waiting to leave. 'Please,' she begged. 'Please, please, please.'

'Yeah, go on,' said Cynthia. 'I'll take her sightseeing – Buckingham Palace, Tower of London, museums and everything.'

Isobel was on the brink of tears. 'Are you sure? You won't get much peace.'

'Yes she will,' said Holly. 'Don't hug me so tight.'

'Come along then,' urged Jeffrey.

'What you say,' said Holly, 'is rattle your dags.'

'What's a dag?' inquired Piers avidly.

Isobel's mother waved from the gate until the car lights disappeared. It was four fifteen and almost dark. Isobel felt as if she had been hurled onto the planet farthest from the sun. Her mother excluded the last glimpse of the outside world behind a fold of flowery curtain, then turned to Isobel with a determined smile. 'Well, now darling, just the two of us.'

Chapter 32

Isobel emerged from the small station — like something from Toytown — and gazed up and down the street. Everything was so shockingly familiar and solid, it made her giddy — she had expected the place to seem ghostly, not to feel like a ghost herself. Her mother had affected amusement at her outlandish intentions — 'What on earth do you want to go back there for, darling?'

'Just to see,' she had answered lightly. But what she saw, as her mother bent over the sink and she herself waited with a spotless tea-towel, was that old uncanny ability to diminish. Fear and insecurity, she told herself in professional tones, that was all it had ever been — even as she stood there and was diminished by it. Her mother launched a ferocious attack on a bench harbouring armies of life-threatening bacteria. 'It's all changed, you know. A waste of time, going back. I wouldn't dream of it.'

So why on earth do you think I'm here? Isobel wanted to demand. Instead she said, 'I'll go tomorrow,' and watched her mother's face cloud.

A Greenline bus thundered past nearly sweeping her from the pavement. A tiny girl in skin-tight jeans was approaching with two toddlers and an intimidating pram. Isobel peered into the pale face looking for . . . who? Rita? Ridiculous, Rita was her age, might even be a grandmother by now.

'Whatchoo starin' at?'

'Sorry?'

'You 'eard,' said the girl, administering a shove to a toddler. 'Miss Lah-di-dah.'

Isobel opened her mouth to retaliate with an affronted *I beg your pardon* – exactly as her mother would have done – and shut it again. A one-four-two rumbled to a halt. The conductor was as shoe-polish black as one of her mother's blue-rinse neighbours had warned her 'everybody' was now, 'up that way.'

'Nearest stop to Manor School, please.'

'Fifty-five pee, love.' She fumbled until he took pity and extracted the right coins from her palm. She took a seat, longing for an impenetrable accent or a colourful ethnic costume – anything that might be an alibi, might allow her to be something other than a third-rate English person. The bus overtook the girl with the pram and Isobel averted her eyes. She had stared, she realised now, not in the hope of recognising the young woman, but in the hope – and fear – of being recognised herself. As if the skinny girl might suddenly proclaim, 'Isobel Midwinter! After all these years, what on earth are you doing here?' and reduce Isobel to a stammering wreck.

'Okay, love,' bawled the bus driver.

It took Isobel a full five minutes to cross the murderous road. She peered through the rusty railings. The school's red brick buildings had stood smug and stolid for a hundred and fifty years and would stand for a hundred and fifty more. The yard reeked of . . . Friday . . . egg pie topped with steam-rollered tomato. She considered dashing inside and rescuing as many children as possible.

'Summing out of Dickens, innit?' The man on the other side

of the railings was wrinkled like an old potato and wearing a potato-coloured storeman's coat. He had a broom, and a cigarette butt stuck to his top lip.

'I used to go to school here.'

He frowned through a thin ribbon of smoke. 'Don't remember you, darlin'.'

'The nineteen fifties,' she said, enjoying an illicit glow from the endearment.

'Didn't get here till the sixties meself,' waggled the butt. He leaned closer. 'What's that accent you got there?'

She grinned sheepishly. 'I've lived in New Zealand for twenty years.'

'Aaah, Noo Zealand.' Behind the smoke his wrinkles took on a faraway expression. 'Had a nephew went there. Real man's country, he says. Keeps writing, saying to visit, but the old girl won't budge. All green and empty, Ritchie says, long golden beaches and no bugger on 'em. Got his own business – 'ardware. Own house and boat too. Rotty-rua, or somewhere, know it, do you? Land of opportunity, he says.' He surveyed the grimy yard and inhaled from the quivering dog end. 'Bugger-all opportunity here. Boilin' mud in his own back yard, Richie says. You got boilin' mud in your yard, darlin'? And trout! Rivers full of 'em. Even the Queen Mum's had a go, bless her soul.' He ripped the butt from his lip without flinching and flung it away. 'What anyone'd stay here for, I dunno. Get home, darlin', fast as you can, that's my advice.'

She walked on to the village, past whitewashed cottages festooned with bare wisteria vines, a muddy pond and little green that was home to several bored ducks, St Oswald's and the Pig and Whistle. Its picturesqueness took her by surprise, not only that such places actually existed but that she had grown up in one. She pushed open the gate into the churchyard, feeling, in spite of her jeans, as if she had strayed into a Jane Austen novel. She shoved at the hefty porch door, tiptoed through the chilly gloom and sat down in a pew near the front, staring at the altar. She recalled arranging harvest festival produce under the bossily inartistic supervision of Mrs Runciman-Brown, pictured piles of shiny apples, pears and potatoes, huge plaited loaves of a sort never seen in the baker's, and great sheaves of flowers. Every year since, little girls like her had been doing exactly the same. She heard footsteps and froze, imagined being sprung by pompous Reverend Pottinger, and feared he might bless her or invite her to join him in a prayer. She leaped to her feet and scurried out. She had absolutely no idea what she would pray for.

The air outside was fresh and lively after the church, and she sat on the bench amongst the gravestones. She had sat here with Dan – bored, bickering, necking, two kids in an overgrown churchyard. *I love you, Isobel. I love you too, Dan.* Even as the words left her mouth, they had shocked and bewildered her. Nothing over the three months they had been secretly going out – that curious time when her parents' eyes were so firmly fixed on the other side of the world that Isobel and her activities were invisible to them – nothing had shifted him closer to her idea of a proper boyfriend. He lacked romance, for a start, probably because she had once seen him in his pyjamas. Real boyfriends came out of a clear blue sky, without a history, as Clyde had done. Dan was frequently prickly and sulky, too, a lot like the old Danny. And she . . . well, she was just as bad. They argued, viciously sometimes, refusing to speak for hours on end, until the least offended party cracked a joke whose utter feebleness reduced them to helpless laughter, or said something so cutting about someone else they were left breathless with pleasure. Of course she didn't love him, she was only fifteen; the words just spilled out when you kissed too much. And soon she would be in the antipodes so what was the point of love?

Penny Lambert came forward to greet her with both hands outstretched and Isobel had no idea what she was expected to do with them. 'Isobel. You look brilliant.' In fact, she had never felt more dull. It was partly the grubby tube, partly this sparkling café. But mostly it was Penny who was so glossy Isobel felt the need of dark glasses. 'Do sit,' urged Penny, 'and tell me everything.'

So Isobel sat, with the conviction that Penny had forgotten who she was. She ran her eyes over the menu and wished she had not come. When Rats had insisted on passing on Penny's telephone number, Isobel had acquiesced with no intention of ever dialling it. 'Weybridge,' her mother had remarked. 'Very nice. I looked there but everything was out of my price range.' She spoke without rancour or even particular interest. She seemed to have forgotten Penny was the daughter of the woman who had once been her best friend, and the man who had stabbed her beloved husband in the back.

A waiter inclined petulantly. 'Just Evian for me,' said Penny with a dismissive little wave.

Determined not to be intimidated – this was the Museum of Mankind, after all – Isobel said, 'Tea, please.'

'Earl Grey, madam?' She nodded, although she would have preferred the kind the Manor School caretaker brewed up in his smoky den.

'They have super little homemade biscuits here. Do try them,' said Penny.

'Fine,' said Isobel, and the waiter sauntered off.

'Well,' they said together.

The telephone had rung long enough in Weybridge for Isobel to consider hanging up an honourable option. But then an answerphone had cut in saying it was Penny Hardcastle and terribly sorry but this was her day at the gallery and if she wasn't too absolutely knackered when she came home, she'd call you back, ciao. Isobel had been tempted to sneer aloud at Penny and Weybridge and days at the gallery; something other than charity had held her back. At home with her mother – preparing and eating yet another overplanned meal, watching creatures stalk and devour one another on nature pro-grammes, deferring to one another at the bathroom door –

she was continually resentful that her mother had no idea who she was, continually on guard lest one ill-judged remark might surrender her life back into her mother's hands. Penny had felt like a lifeline.

Holly had called. 'It's me, it's neat here, can I stay longer? Cyn's flatmate's got a dog and I take it for walks and I saw a man in the park with no trousers on. We went to the Geological Museum and there's a stupid earthquake room and all the English people were scared. Can I stay longer?'

When it looked as if Penny would never call back, Isobel wracked her brains for anything that might, in spite of the horizonless grey cold, get her mother and herself beyond the confines of the house. The sunny interior of the supermarket beckoned like an Auckland summer's day. She walked miles of careful streets and across the park in pretence of exercise. And she evinced such a burning interest in tourist spots that her mother promised to drive them out on the first good day. Gazing into the lifeless garden, Isobel could not imagine such a day ever dawning.

'So have you come back here to live?' inquired Penny, sipping wintry water.

A dozen answers sprang to mind. 'I don't know,' said Isobel finally.

Penny flicked a shining strand of hair. 'It's not like it was, you know, things have got very tough. Julian, my husband, has taken a frightful hammering in the last couple of years.' She sighed. 'There's even some question of selling the place in Provence. That's why I'm doing three days a week in this place up the road. Well, half-days really. Frankly, we need the money.'

'Things are hard at home, too,' said Isobel. 'I was made redundant. But then someone left me enough money for a trip back.'

A quiver of pleasure rippled the groomed features. 'An inheritance, how brilliant. I pray for one. Though not from someone dear, of course. Julian, maybe.'

'It was an old aunt of Clyde's. She had a stroke when Clyde and I were still together, and I looked after her. We never liked one another so it was a surprise, the money. And it made me realise . . . people do die, even those you've wanted dead. I thought I should come back and see my mother.'

Penny had stopped listening. 'I haven't been back to New Zealand since Dad's funeral. It killed him, you know, that frightful business with Simon. It's a brilliant place, but I couldn't live there now.' She sighed, broke off a tiny crumb of biscuit and slipped it between gleaming lips. Isobel watched in wonder – Penny's parents had shelled out thousands of dollars to ensure that she was unfit to live in her native land. Not a lot different, though, now she came to think of it, to what her own parents had done for her.

'You went home for your father's funeral?'

'I hadn't met Julian then so Mum paid, then she died over here on a visit last year. How many children do you have?'

'Two.'

'Brilliant.'

'Dylan's nearly twenty, he's Clyde's. I took him when I left but he only stayed with me a couple of years.' Penny maintained a vague impersonal smile. Isobel topped up her cup, forgetting to use the silver strainer. 'He never stopped saying he wanted to be with Clyde, never let me forget I'd taken him away. In the end I let him go. But I still don't know if I kept him too long or let him go too easily. He used to visit in the holidays and Holly went to the farm once or twice, but in the end . . .' – the familiar lump filled her chest and throat – 'I don't know where he is now, he doesn't keep in touch, I haven't seen him for two years.'

She withdrew a length of her mother's pink perfumed toilet tissue from a pocket, blew her nose and flicked away a tear. The waiter deftly removed Penny's glass as if Isobel might contaminate it. 'Holly is someone else's, she's nearly ten. I don't know why I'm telling you all this.' She did – it was because Penny had absolutely no interest in it.

Penny sighed. 'Julian had this total thing about children for a while but I held out, I mean, the way things were going, our standard of living would have been too totally ghastly. And now it's too late, thank God. So much easier to be poor at home, isn't it? Costs a bomb to live within cooee of London. It was fine when Julian's business was really raking it in, but now . . .' She parted her hair to fiddle with a large gold earring. 'We went skiing last month, but God, it's not the same when you have to watch every last penny, and Julian's such a stickler.'

Isobel nibbled a sugary almond biscuit. 'Rats is doing well,' she ventured. 'He's got a carpentry business in Auckland, renovations mostly, doing up villas. He drops in now and then.'

'We're having our place remodelled, such a bore. Men in big boots tramping all over the place, grunting. One of the advantages of coming out to work, actually. That, and the potential for getting laid. What about you? New husband, lovers?'

Isobel shrugged. 'The odd fling, nothing major.'

Penny shuddered. 'Good lord, one doesn't want anything major, does one? Little affairs will do nicely. I have a chap at the gallery, the owner, actually. Keeps up one's self-esteem. More tea?'

Isobel shook her head and checked her watch. 'I'm meeting my sisters at Covent Garden.'

'A little swimming one and a bigger scared one, wasn't there?'

'The scared one is married with two children in Kent. The swimming one is on the dole in Tooting.'

'Tooting. Heavens.' Isobel might as well have said Soweto.

Slipping on her pale expensive coat, just as she had in the caff twenty years before, Penny said, 'You know, I never liked you much when we were young. Can't remember why now.' Then in the same neutral tone, 'You must come out to Weybridge, meet Julian and everything. I'll call you, shall I? When the builders have gone.'

Chapter 33

HAMPTON COURT REARED UP UNNATURALLY AT THE END OF AN undistinguished high street. 'Wonderful,' enthused Isobel, mostly for the benefit of her mother, who was clutching the wheel white-faced from the stress of heavy traffic and uncertainty over the route.

'Whoo,' she exhaled, hauling on the handbrake, and Isobel felt a pang of guilt for bullying an old lady into chauffeuring her across London. On the other hand, she had not once offered to let Isobel drive.

'We must try the maze,' she burbled.

'Not what it used to be,' said her mother, checking the car doors a second time. 'Letty took her grandchildren and they kept crawling through the gaps in the yew.' They made their way through a vast deserted carpark. Her mother's gloved hands were pushed into pockets and she wore furlined boots, a bulky three-quarter coat and a fake fur hat. She looked like an embattled old teddy bear. Isobel thrust an awkward arm through her mother's. The small body tensed beneath its muffled layers.

'Two adults? Four pounds,' mumbled a man in a shiny serge uniform, although Isobel had fully expected him to say *one adult and a child*. She withdrew her arm and let go the breath she had been holding.

'One adult and an old-age pensioner, thank you,' said her mother crisply.

'Sorry, madam. Had me fooled.' She disguised her pleasure with a raised eyebrow and a search for notes.

They followed a curving path through woodland where watery sun played on uncut grass. 'It's wonderful here in spring,' she said. 'Thousands of daffodils, a real picture. Do you think you'll still be here then, darling?'

'I don't know.' Isobel, caught off-guard, almost stumbled.

'Oh dear, I've tried not to ask. I don't want to pressure you.'

Isobel pushed her hands deeper into her jacket pockets and kept her head down. Voices filled her head like bickering children. The loudest shouted furiously, what makes you think you can pressure me?

'There can't be much to keep you in New Zealand now,' continued her mother with complete confidence.

'Only my life,' said Isobel with a forced smile. The formal garden behind the palace was as surreal as the redbrick façade. A few tourists wandered its symmetrical paths. 'And my work.'

'Your work, darling? I thought you'd been made redundant.'

'Yes, but . . .'

'I'm afraid social workers aren't very highly regarded here at all. People think . . .'

'I love my work,' said Isobel through gritted teeth. 'I believe in it. It helps people, helps break patterns that get passed from one generation to the next.' She was wasting her breath – hadn't her mother considered it her primary responsibility to ensure that just those patterns were passed on? 'Anyway, there are my friends. And Teddy and our garden.' She wanted to block her mother's path and shout, look at me, look at the life I've made without you!

Her mother sighed and arranged her expression into that of someone older and wiser. 'I know you must be fond of him, darling, but I'd hate to see you get hurt.'

'Hurt?'

'They don't form lasting relationships. It's well known.'

'They?'

'Homosexuals, darling. They're very promiscuous.' *You silly girl.*

Isobel planted a foot on the steps of a statue and glared down the canal. 'Teddy's no more promiscuous than I am,' she said, then wished that she hadn't. 'Anyway, he and I don't have a sexual relationship.' She even hated telling her mother things she already knew.

Her mother also pretended to be looking at the sinister water. 'But any day he could find someone . . .'

'In a toilet, you mean?'

'. . . I mean, there's no real security with him, is there?'

Isobel managed a sardonic laugh. 'There's no real security anywhere, the world's an insecure place.'

Her mother resumed the walk. 'Well, I can't speak for you, of course, but I was always very secure with Daddy.'

The last word. The closed bedroom door. In her most innocent tone, Isobel said, 'Why were you always so angry then?'

'Angry, darling?'

Isobel fingered the needles of a yew. 'Angry, nearly all the time. Tense, anyway.'

'I'd like to sit down a minute, darling. I feel rather breathless.' They found an iron bench whose freezing bars struck through Isobel's jeans. Her mother patted her chest and made little 'whoo' noises.

'What were you always so scared of?' continued Isobel. 'Why did you never touch us, except for photos?'

'Oh dear,' said her mother. 'I had one of these turns in the summer. Letty had to get me to a doctor.'

'Why did you say the other day that homosexuals were

avoiding the responsibility of children? Were we a character test for you, a sort of moral warrant of fitness?'

'Excuse?'

'Is that why you were never really interested in *us*? Why we were just . . . projects to be managed?'

'Excuse, please?'

A Japanese tourist was pushing something into Isobel's hand and backing away. For a wild moment, she wondered if it was a bomb, saw a dozen palace chimneys hang in the air for a split second before collapsing. The man clamped an arm around a woman in bright clothing and they grinned determinedly. 'Er, what do I . . .?' Her mother was on her feet, trying to look through the viewfinder at the same time as Isobel. Isobel gave her a small but definite shove.

'Press, press,' instructed the man through grinning teeth. Isobel pressed. There was no explosion, not even a controlled demolition. He retrieved the camera, bowing profusely.

'Well, I could do with a nice cup of tea,' said Isobel's mother, as though they had come through an ordeal.

They drank the tea accompanied by dry scones in a conservatory where tourists warmed their hands around cups and gazed bleakly through the glass. The sun had given up again, leaving behind yet another short dark day.

'Are you all right, darling?' Her mother's hand touched her arm and Isobel fought not to pull it away. Afterwards, she could feel the finger-marks.

'Fine.' She studied a pamphlet. 'We haven't seen the knot garden or the grapevine, and there's still the maze.'

'You go, darling, I've seen it all before. I'm quite happy here.'

Isobel inspected the intricate pattern of tiny hedges that formed the knot garden, and walked each of its tiny paths like a ritualistic child. A man with three cameras took her photograph and walked off quickly as if he had stolen something. She gazed at the Great Vine. It was truly great, and utterly bare. Its gnarled roots and lower trunk were housed in the temperate zone of a glasshouse, its branches ranged in the open air – the best of both worlds. She fingered the grooved bark, pondering centuries of English tradition, English brutality. There was a decisive click, and the man with three cameras gave her a sly smile. She regarded him coldly and stalked off.

If she did decide to come back for good – for better or worse – it would not be for what the pamphlet referred to as *our glorious heritage*. It would be for the tinkle of the ice-cream van in the next street, the scent of coal smoke, the label on Marks and Spencer underwear. Bits of inglorious heritage trapped in her crevices like pebbles after the tide has gone out.

The man was following her. She quickened her pace, as if serial killers sought their victims at stately homes. Probably only a lonely tourist wanting conversation. Still, her heart thumped beyond reason until she was back in the conservatory with its comforting clink of crockery, bewildered to find she had run back to her mother.

She insisted her mother accompany her to the maze. 'It'll be fun,' she said, and her mother looked touchingly pleased. The official at the turnstile was phlegmatic. 'We used to go looking for people at closing time. Not anymore, they seem to get out, not found any bodies yet.'

Isobel struck out confidently and her mother followed. From somewhere on their right came a conversation in puzzled German, then from their left. The hedges were disappointingly scrappy, little more than mental barriers. Should it prove necessary, they could, like Letty's grandchildren, simply force their way through – a thought that was both a comfort and a disappointment.

'We've been here before,' said her mother sometime later.

'No, we haven't. How can you tell?'

'We have, darling.'

'Einlich heraus!' someone shouted triumphantly a long way

off. Then there was only the pad of their feet on the dirt path. The next junction looked familiar even to Isobel. She hesitated, searching for some principle by which to proceed. She dimly remembered having heard there was one. She turned to her mother – her mother was good at rules, and rules were better than nothing in the absence of a map.

'Let's go back, darling.'

Isobel produced a hollow laugh. 'How?' It crossed her mind that her mother might branch out confidently in another direction, leaving Isobel to fend for herself. She lengthened her stride, refusing to look back, willing her mother to follow. The hedges were thicker now, and she wondered if it were a sign of progress. Her toes and fingers were numb with cold and her legs ached. She strode on, picturing her mother's strained mouth and faltering step. *Think of fairies in a bluebell wood.*

'I don't know why I never touched you.'

'What?' Isobel was contemplating another meaningless choice of direction.

'I don't know why I never wanted to cuddle you girls, I can't understand it.' Isobel strode off again, paying attention to the length of her stride and the swing of her arms. 'I see you with Holly, the fun you have. I never had fun with you, did I? Every-thing seemed so hard. Yet millions of people have it harder. I wanted children, we both did. When I was pregnant with you, Daddy and I were so romantic.'

Suddenly they were there, at the centre – and it was nothing, only a small dusty rectangle with a bench at each end. Isobel sat, her mother stood, staring ahead. Isobel could not remem-ber another occasion when she had not known exactly what her mother would say next. 'I did my best, I did what I thought was important. You were clean and fed, I kept the house nicely. We went out on Sunday afternoons and always had a summer holiday. Daddy wasn't a bad man, he loved you kids.'

Isobel's heart was thumping more violently than when she was being pursued by the serial killer. 'I should have been at his funeral, you said everybody was there, but I wasn't.' Her mother was frowning, shaking her head. 'Max told me he was dead, Uncle Max of all people. I spent eighteen hours trying to find out if it was true. None of you got in touch with me.'

Her mother sagged but Isobel made no room for her on the bench. It seemed to force her to speak. 'We'd just walked up Snowden, Daddy was so pleased with himself. It happened on the way down. He collapsed and never got up again. Gillian and Jeffrey came to Wales. Jeffrey made all the arrangements and I sat in the hotel room. Nobody seemed to think about you. I remember worrying I had nothing to wear to the funeral. When we got home I made Gillian take me out and we searched everywhere for a dark suit. As if it mattered.' The voice cracked.

Isobel battled on. 'The worse part was how long it took me to get angry that none of you thought of me, to stop expecting not to count. Now he'll never be really gone for me, just like he was never really here.'

Her mother lowered her face into her hands and cried noisily. It was so uninhibited, so guileless, that for a moment Isobel seemed to be witnessing a natural phenomenon like a storm or a waterfall. Then a voice in her head said, you've made an old lady cry. She got up, took her mother's arm and led her to the seat. The hand that did so felt detached and charitable. After a few minutes, the sobs abated. 'I had no money of my own,' gulped her mother, dabbing her eyes and honking into more pink toilet tissue. 'And Daddy could be so mean. You girls never realised, I didn't want you to know.'

'We should have known. We should have known all about him but you always got between us, you were like his . . . his lieutenant, his field marshal.'

'He was so handsome the day we met, so tall, and all in white from playing cricket. Four months later he joined up and he looked different in khaki. By the time he was demobbed, when he came back from France, he wasn't the same man. I thought we should call it off, but the wedding was all arranged. And anyway' – her voice quivered – 'we thought I was pregnant.'

'Me?' ventured Isobel.

'No, darling, you weren't born for another couple of years. It was a miscarriage, the first of many. Daddy – well, he wouldn't use condoms.' Isobel groaned, an involuntary sound as if her mother were just another woman telling a woman's story. 'The last time I was nearly forty-five, it was just before we left England. I drank gin and had a hot bath and Daddy was so angry he left the house . . .'

'Christ,' said Isobel. As if her father were just another man.

'I miscarried that night, on my own. Daddy went off to Max's and they polished off a bottle of Scotch. He didn't come home until after work the next day.'

Twilight was falling, Isobel could almost hear it. 'I want to visit his grave,' she said at last.

Her mother dabbed her eyes. 'There isn't one, darling, he was cremated.'

'There must be a plaque, his name on a wall?'

Her mother shook her head. 'You can look at his name in a book, one day a year.'

A party of children burst into the centre of the maze, yelling in North Country accents and tearing round and round the small space. 'We ought to move, darling. We'll catch our deaths sitting here.' The voice had recovered authority, the back had straightened.

Isobel set off and once more her mother followed. She made two left-hand turns and one right, then spoke clearly, without looking back. 'Clyde is not Holly's father. Her real father lives in Wellington, he's married with grandchildren and Holly has never met him.' Her mother did not reply.

As she headed the car towards home and the palace receded in the rear vision mirror, her mother said brightly and with a distinct measure of pride, 'Your Great-aunt Dora was a lady-in-waiting to Queen Victoria, you know, darling.'

Chapter 34

Isobel stood under the elm and stared across Woodland Rise at number fourteen. Its neighbour's windows and doors had been treated to a glossy coat of paint, and its small front garden was neatly hedged and groomed behind the closed gate. Number fourteen slumped beside it, sills peeling, hedge neglected, curtains carelessly drawn across upstairs windows although it was gone three in the afternoon. The macrocarpa was as shabby and dismal as she remembered it. The walk from the station had overheated her and she unbuttoned her jacket. The severe cold had retreated – inexplicably, her mother said, for the time of year. The air was soft, still, holding its breath. The house – the whole street – seemed deserted, and she wondered if women like her mother still washed, cleaned and baked all day behind its closed doors. As if in answer, a woman emerged from number nine with a shopping basket and a wheezing Labrador. She and Isobel assessed each other politely and exchanged nods. In spite of basket and brogues, she was, Isobel saw with surprise, younger than herself by several years.

As the woman disappeared towards the village, Isobel leaned against the elm, shuddering a little, as if her own semi-detached, her own Jeffrey, existed in some narrowly avoided parallel universe.

The two-tone bell at Rita's front door summoned a woman in fluffy mules with a yapping dog underarm. 'Hello, dear?'

'Sorry to bother you. I was just . . . I used to live in this street and I knew the people who lived here – the Coops – and I was wondering . . .'

'Ooh no, dear. Shush, Montgomery, naughty boy. Let me see. No, Monty, shush. We – that's my late husband, Derek and I – bought the place, let me see – no, Monty, quiet – he died twelve years ago next March, it was, and we bought the place in . . .'

'Do you know what happened to the Coops?'

'Montgomery, quiet! We bought it from . . . let me see, big woman, short chap, three grown-up children . . .'

'Rita and Judy and Dennis.'

'Hmnn, yes, hang on, Coot, did you say?'

'Coop.'

'That's right. We used to get their mail but I didn't forward it because I mean if people can't be bothered . . .'

'Where did they go? Do you know what happened to them?'

'Would you like to come in and have a look round, dear? We've done ever such a lot to the place. I mean, between you, me and the gatepost, it was pretty run down and . . .'

'The Coops, do you know what happened to them?'

Disappointment flickered across the woman's dumpy features as she realised Isobel was not to be enticed indoors. 'I believe they went off to the south of Spain, dear, where everybody goes when they've made their pile.'

'A pile? The Coops?'

'The pools, dear. They won big on the pools. Are you sure you won't . . .?'

Woman and dog watched regretfully as Isobel skipped back

down the path. She wanted to cheer loudly enough to be heard in Torremolinos, for the Coops who believed in luck. She ran down the road to number fourteen, up its short path, and rapped boldly on the door. Nothing. She knocked twice more then poked her fingers through the brass flap marked Letters and peered inside. There was a hallstand she had never seen before, a small dusty table holding a telephone, and someone else's carpet. She backed away, wondering if a neighbourhood watch scheme was in operation and if even now responsible fingers were dialling the police to inform them of her interest in number fourteen. The telephone rang, a piercing old-fashioned ring that made her start guiltily. She did not want anyone to emerge from the house now, did not want to have to confront its new owners. It rang ten times then the house was silent again. She made her way down the side, and discovered the memory of the snapping gate latch still in her fingers.

The barrenness of the winter garden came as a shock, as if she had expected a magical flowering of peonies and Russell lupins, Michaelmas daisies and lily of the valley. Even the grass was despondent, and the beds, after the lush volcanic loam of her own and Teddy's garden, was rocky and infertile, given to stony gaps. She set off down the nearest path. The crooked apple tree was so familiar she almost said hello, and longed to sink her teeth into one of its huge rare apples. She peered through the fence at the allotments – the nearest held the same regiments of brussels sprouts, the same mouldering compost heap. By contrast, number fourteen's vegetable bed was a weedy mess, its raspberry patch a shambles of dead cane. She pictured, somewhere below, the perfectly preserved shell of William the Tortoise, recalling his leathery neck and beady eyes. He had never been her idea of a pet. All he did was patrol the boundaries of the back garden, clunking his shell against the palings, and vanish every winter – that was his entire behavioural repertoire. Once, when no one was watching, she had held open the gate, hoping he might make a bolt for freedom, but he had only stretched his horrible neck and hissed ungratefully. So she had not been at all sorry when they told her he had died, only sorry that the funeral was such a fiasco – her mother had no idea how to talk to God properly, and her father lit up and peered over the fence at Mr Dodds' cabbages. Isobel had insisted on at least one verse of *I Vow to Thee My Country*, but Gillian kept snivelling and Cynthia chimed in with random excerpts from *I'm a Pink Toothbrush* . . .

Isobel took several deep breaths – the past was a swamp, it would pull you under. A movement at the top of the garden made her freeze like a naughty child and she briefly considered hiding. Then she pulled herself together and stepped forward. 'Hello?' she called, with a good deal more confidence that she felt.

The man halted on the edge of the lawn, hands on hips, looking at her. 'Hello, Isobel,' he said.

She couldn't speak. He motioned her into the house. In the dingy kitchen, he pulled out a chair and she dropped into it. He kept slipping in and out of focus. With his back turned, filling the kettle at the sink, he was an unknown Englishman on whose property she had trespassed. Facing her, asking if she preferred coffee or tea and what about milk, he was Danny. Danny pretending to be grown up.

He sat on the other side of the table and pushed across a chipped mug. She said. 'Why aren't you surprised?'

'I knew you'd come back.'

'How could you, I didn't.' She gulped poorly brewed tea flavoured with sour milk.

'Who's going first?' he said, draining his cup as if there were no time to lose.

'You. Only let's go in the sitting room.' As if it were still her house, as if it had ever been hers.

He surveyed the big shabby room with a frown then got to his knees to crumple newspaper in the grate. 'I'm an engineer,' he said, arranging aromatic firelighters. 'I got a degree at Loughborough and I've worked for the same small aircraft company ever since. I bought this place about eight years ago from the people who bought it from your parents. They put the central heating in and did up the kitchen, but it still looked like your old place.'

'You were only here once. You were what – ten, eleven?'

He arranged lumps of coal on chilly flames. 'Maybe if I'd come here more often, I wouldn't have had to buy it.' He sighed as if he had already given the matter too much thought. 'It wasn't a particularly good buy. It needs major work on the roof, the guttering's rotting . . .'

Isobel said, 'I walked round the village. There are Fiats outside the terrace houses and townhouses almost in the churchyard. I stood over the road by the tree . . . I don't know why I came back.'

'Why didn't we ever write to each other?'

'We were kids.'

The fire crackled. The room's furnishings were prissy, its surfaces cluttered with china shepherdesses and minstrels. In one corner stood a glass-fronted cabinet and out of it stared a couple of dozen captive dolls in various national costumes. 'Snooty as ever,' he remarked. 'What about a drink?'

'White wine'd be lovely.'

'Stone the crows, this is Hertfordshire in mid-winter, not California. It's Scotch, with or without water.'

She was unnerved by his disappearance into the kitchen. Superficially the room meant nothing to her, yet it was the shape of her childhood. She kept sliding from the past to the present and back again. When he returned with two glasses, she was examining a brown doll with a grass skirt, woven headband and plastic smile. 'Maori,' she told him. 'She looks the way I feel in England.' She replaced it next to the Scottish doll and left the cabinet door ajar.

'Cheers,' he said. 'Now tell me about you.' He listened as he always had, intently, eyes on her face. The meagre light faded and firelight flickered on the walls. It was almost dark when she finished and the fire was embers.

'I have to call my mother,' she said. He left her to find the phone.

'Darling, where are you? I was worried.'

Irritation rose like heartburn. 'Irene, I'm almost forty, for God's sake.'

'Yes, of course. Silly me. How was the Tate?'

'The Tate? Oh, fine. Listen, I won't be home for a while, I've met someone and . . . and I'm spending the evening with them.'

The line hummed with maternal curiosity. Isobel waited it out. 'Well,' said her mother manfully. 'Right. Have a nice evening, darling, and I'll see you later.'

'Still lying to your mother?' said Dan, handing her another Scotch.

He had resurrected the fire and turned on a lamp with a swathed peach shade. 'Tell me about your wife,' she said.

'Home economics teacher . . .' He cut himself off by gulping Scotch.

'Children?'

'Not everyone's as fecund as you. We can't, she can't.'

Her eyes flicked to the doll cabinet and back to him. 'It's not . . .? My God, it's Andrea Dodds, isn't it? But I introduced you.' She tried to cover up the unaccountable pang this caused with a grin.

'You don't have a monopoly on mistakes.'

'Mistakes! I don't view my life as a series of mistakes.'

'No, you just assume other people's are.' His aggression dropped away. 'I thought Andrea was what I wanted, what I needed. I thought she'd make me a home.'

'In my home!'

He regarded her dispassionately. 'We always used to bicker, didn't we.'

She remembered what else they had done and it made her

277

acutely uncomfortable, as if teenage Isobel and Dan were on the carpet in front of them, necking to the point of suffocation. 'I want to go upstairs,' she said. 'I mean, just to look.'

'Shall I come?'

'No.'

The bathroom was damp and cold, and mould grew between the tiles. She enjoyed a moment's disdain for a race that had no use for showers. She glanced more from duty than curiosity into her own room, then slipped down the landing and pushed open the door to her parents' bedroom. *What do you want, Isobel?* It was still intimidatingly huge, but the queen-sized bed was unmade, the broderie anglais duvet less than fresh. There were men's socks, shirts and underpants scattered across the floor and she sensed the curtains had not been drawn for days.

Dan put his hands on her shoulders from behind and when she turned, he kissed her. Or she kissed him. But only briefly, and when she opened her eyes, the bed loomed and she pulled away. 'Not like it would be the first time,' he said slyly. 'And this is more comfortable than gravestones.'

'A girl never forgets her first, you mean?' she mocked.

'You really didn't know I was here, did you. So what were you looking for? Skeletons in the family cupboard?'

She pulled a face. 'There is a body in the raspberry patch. My father killed the tortoise when he was digging. My mother said it died of old age, but I knew she was lying. I dug it up and saw the holes in its shell. She said I was a wicked girl, that Daddy wouldn't hurt a fly.'

'I wish I could remember that much of my parents,' he said morosely.

She looked at him and took a breath. 'I did miss you, it scared me how much, I thought I was going mad. But you got all muddled up with missing Rita and England, and the old life. Every time I thought of you I heard my mother say, don't be ridiculous, pull yourself together, you're only children.'

'I thought you rebelled against your mother, I thought you

didn't believe a word she said.'

'Only the small things, as it turned out. I swallowed the big things whole. Most people do, don't they. Anyway, why did you buy this place?'

'I thought I could buy what you had.'

'What was that?'

He picked up a small bottle from the dressing table and absentmindedly examined it. 'A mother and father, a home, a dog, proper Christmases, holidays at the seaside . . . '

She couldn't resist a snort of derision. 'I've seen inside hundreds of families in my work and none of them has what they think everyone else has got.'

He was annoyed. 'I know that now.'

She took the bottle from him – it contained something pink and creamy. 'Andrea's not coming home, is she?'

'She left a month ago and went to her mother's in Carshalton. This afternoon I had a strange feeling she was here so I rang, and came home early. I've been wanting us to separate for ages but didn't have the courage to say so. I was going to say it this afternoon.'

'Would children have helped?'

'We had a couple from the Caledonian a few times but we didn't do much better than you lot. Having our own wouldn't have made me love Andrea, only made me more guilty. And that's what I wanted – love. Probably too much to expect at our age.'

'God, you English make resignation into an art form!'

He backed towards the bedroom door, refusing to laugh. 'You will stay, won't you?'

There was a moment when she wondered exactly what he meant, then she said, 'For dinner, yes, that'd be nice. If you actually have anything edible in the house.'

Chapter 35

DAN DROVE HER BACK TO HER MOTHER'S. HE PULLED UP AT AN intersection and Isobel stared into a lighted front room. The bay window was filled with rangy pot plants and a smug ginger cat blinked on the windowsill. A woman came into the room, put something on the table and turned towards the window. She tickled the cat's head then drew the curtains. Isobel tried to read her face, to discern if she were happy, if she had a child, a job, a lover. For thirty seconds Isobel lived in that room, walked to the tube each morning and drove to her mother's on Sundays. Then the car moved on.

Lights were burning in every room of her mother's house. 'She's waiting up,' sighed Isobel. Since she had no key she would have to be let in like a teenager. Dan cut the motor and lights, and showed every sign of getting out of the car. She looked at him first in amusement then astonishment. 'Don't be daft. You can't come in.'

'Why not?'

She grabbed his arm. 'Hang on, we're going to talk about

this. You can't just go waltzing in there.'

'Why not?'

'Stop saying that, you know perfectly well why not.'

'You're not the only one with ghosts. I want to see her, that's all.' He put a hand on her shoulder. 'It's all right, Isobel. I know what she's like. You don't have to worry about me.'

'I'm not worried about you,' she snapped. It was true, it was her mother who needed protection, who always had.

'I'm coming in and you can't stop me.'

They stomped up the path side by side. It was Dan who raised his hand to the knocker, but it wasn't Isobel's mother who opened the door. 'Holly!' cried Isobel. The little girl was enveloped in one of her grandmother's quilted dressing gowns. It hung down over her hands and trailed along the floor. She even smelled like her grandmother.

'You're squashing,' she said, wriggling madly. 'You're late.'

'When did you come back?'

'Cynthia brought me, we went on the tube, she said people jump under the trains, she said . . .'

'Hello,' said Dan, edging past. 'I'm Dan.'

'Hello. Granny's got a man too.'

Isobel grimaced. 'Some boring old fart of a neighbour, I suppose. Shouldn't you be in bed? What's got into Granny?'

'Darling,' cried Isobel's mother from the couch. Her appearance made Isobel blink – full makeup, sprayed hair, high heels and vivid dress. 'You remember Max, don't you?' she said, as if it were a cocktail party.

Isobel nodded dumbly. Beneath basset hound folds of flesh, Uncle Max looked sheepish. He levered himself up, held out both arms as if he were going to embrace her, then withdrew them and sat down again. Isobel felt Dan ease into the room behind her. She took a deep breath and said, 'And you remember Dan, don't you? Danny McBride?'

Her mother sent him her best smile and extended a hand from the couch. 'So you're the friend Isobel spent the evening with. How nice. Do sit down, Dan. Can I get you both a drink?'

'Yes, please,' said Isobel, profoundly relieved that her mother had no memory of Dan. Irene picked her way across to the drinks cabinet, hips swinging under the synthetic fabric. Max watched them wistfully.

Holly said, 'I think I ought to have a drink too.'

'Yes, poppet, of course you should.' Her grandmother poured ginger ale into a tumbler.

'Our little chaperone, isn't she, Max.' She perched on the edge of the couch and smiled coquettishly at Max. He didn't look, even to Isobel, like someone with whom a chaperone was necessary. 'Darling, you haven't introduced Max to your friend.'

Dan shook the gnarled hand. 'Actually we've met.'

'Don't think so, old chap.'

'Years ago,' said Dan. 'I was a kid.'

No light dawned on Max's enfeebled face. Isobel's mother leaned forward and touched his knee. 'You remember Max – the little boys from the orphanage? They spent a Christmas with us. We'd have liked to have had them back again but what with one thing and another . . . How's the little one? Andrew, wasn't it?'

'Andy's in Glasgow. He did his time as a plumber. He's got four kids and a grandchild on the way.'

'And what about you?' She looked with approval on the dark suit and tie which marked him out as more than a tradesman. Isobel wanted to slam off to her bedroom.

'I'm an engineer. Separated from my wife. We don't have children.'

Her satisfaction was visible. 'Max began as an engineer, didn't you, Max. He started his own company and retired at fifty-five.'

Max grinned at the attention. 'Thinking of looking for a place around here,' he said, admiring Isobel's mother's knees. 'Nice area.'

Isobel's mother got to her feet. 'Let me get you another, Dan.'

'No thanks, Mrs Midwinter . . .'

'Oh, Irene, please,' she tinkled.

'Thanks, Irene, I'm driving so I'd better not. Anyway' – he looked at his watch – 'work in the morning.'

'Do come again, Dan. Perhaps you'd like to join us on Christmas Day, since you're on your own. That would be nice, wouldn't it, Isobel. I'll get her to give you a ring.'

Isobel hustled him from the room. At the front door, he said, 'Thanks for today. It's helped me decide – it's over with Andrea and we'll put the bloody place on the market. That is unless . . .'

She was aghast. 'It's your house, your life. I'll . . . I'll give you a ring.' She shut the door quickly and shooed Holly up to bed.

'I don't understand about families,' said Holly, from under the covers.

'Join the club,' said Isobel, sitting next to her.

'I don't understand other things too, like really liking someone and liking being at their place but wanting to go home.'

'What happened? Did you get homesick at Cynthia's?'

Holly sniffled. 'We went to Brixton market and there was a man with balloons and Cynthia bought one each and we let them go. Mine was red and it went up for miles but it made me feel funny and I told Cynthia I wanted to come back.' She grabbed a tissue from a flowery box and snorted fruitily.

Isobel put her arms round her. 'Better now?'

'Yes,' said Holly uncertainly.

Isobel switched off the lamp. Car lights swung across the ceiling and a motor echoed down the bricked canyon of the street. She tried to remember how cars sounded in wooden New Zealand streets.

'Why doesn't Uncle Max like Teddy?'

Isobel sighed. 'You know why, Holly.'

'But it's stupid, it's like hating someone who likes dogs better than cats.'

Isobel smiled in the dark. 'It seems stupid to us because we love Teddy . . .'

'Uncle Max must have loved him once.'

'Some parents are better at it than others, I suppose.'

'You're all right,' decided Holly. 'Most of the time. Was Granny?' A bit later, she said, 'Aren't you going to answer?'

'Granny did her best,' said Isobel slowly. 'She did some things well, things Dan's parents didn't do. But' – her throat was constricted, reluctant to let go of the words – 'I suppose the truth is she wasn't good enough at it for me. I didn't feel . . . loved.'

Holly found her hand. 'She loves me,' she said smugly. 'Do you think my real father would love me?'

'Holly, it's not that he doesn't love you, he doesn't know you. It's nothing to do with you really . . .'

'Yes it is,' said Holly sharply.

'What I mean is he was very angry with me a long time ago and I was angry with him. And because you had Teddy and sometimes Dylan and Clyde, I thought . . .'

'But they're not my real father.'

'Do you think about him a lot?'

'Since we came here I do. Because Granny didn't know me and she loves me, and so does Cynthia and her flatmates, so if I met my real father, he might too.'

'I'm sure he would.'

'But if we stay here, I won't ever see him. The balloon just floated away and got lost,' she said dreamily.

'I know, Holly,' said Isobel, stroking her hair. 'I know. But . . . we'll just have to wait and see.' Holly was already asleep.

Downstairs her mother was briskly erasing all sign of their guests. Isobel began washing glasses. 'Max's quietened down a bit,' she ventured.

'Poor old thing,' murmured her mother. 'Not the same

without Iris.' She passed back a glass that had failed her standard of cleanliness. 'You know, I really think Daddy would have been lost without me too.'

'I expect so,' said Isobel. 'Men aren't much good at managing alone.'

'Since poor Daddy died, I've learned to do so much – arranged mortgages, insurance claims, made my own will. Daddy used to do everything.' She scoured the draining board as Isobel dried her hands. 'Max asked me to marry him tonight.'

'Christ.' *Language, Isobel.* 'What did you say?'

Her mother folded the tea-towel precisely and hung it up. 'No, of course.'

'No?' echoed Isobel.

Her mother put on the kettle for a hotwater bottle. 'I've no intention of saddling myself with an old man. Max would expect to be waited on hand and foot, and in a few years he could be bedridden like Letty's evil-tempered old so-and-so. No, thank you very much, I don't need that.'

Isobel gaped. Surely her mother wanted a husband, surely Max was the logical choice?

'Before I forget, darling,' her mother went on, bustling to the sideboard. 'There's something I want you to have. Cynthia's got Daddy's walking stick and I gave Gillian his watch, so I thought you might like this.'

'The photo,' said Isobel. 'I've been wondering what happened to it.'

Her mother turned, frowning. 'Photo, darling?'

'Your wedding photo, the one that used to hang on the stairs, I'd really like to have it.'

Her mother ran a hand along the shiny surface of the sideboard as if testing for dust. 'Oh, that. Actually, I'm afraid I . . . got rid of it.'

'Got rid of it?'

'After . . . afterwards, I couldn't . . . he was so handsome and I couldn't bear . . . I burned it, I think, or put it in the dustbin.'

She pulled open a sideboard drawer.

Isobel stared open-mouthed. 'But it . . . it was a piece of history, that photo. Family history. You can't just . . .' She was bewildered by how much she cared.

Her mother seemed not to be listening, she was taking something from a drawer. When she turned back to Isobel, she was holding a bronze cross on a red, white and blue ribbon. 'A medal?' wondered Isobel. 'What did he do? Something brave? Did he kill Germans?'

Her mother's hand flew to her mouth. 'What a dreadful idea. Daddy wouldn't hurt a fly.'

'He was a soldier, it was war,' said Isobel, rather less tartly than she once might have.

Her mother smiled wistfully. 'Oh no, Daddy wasn't a hero, I'm afraid, darling. He said they gave one of these to everybody who served in France. It was routine, just an acknowledgement of duty done.'

Isobel pretended to inspect the medal on her mother's palm. *Say thank you, Isobel.* 'A shame there's no such thing for women,' she said. 'For wives and mothers, I mean.'

'Who would award it?' said her mother sharply. 'Certainly not the men.'

Say thank you, Isobel. She took a deep breath. 'Other women. Daughters.'

The world momentarily stopped turning.

'Well,' said her mother finally, 'there you are, darling. It's not much, I know, but it is something, isn't it?'

Isobel unclenched her hand, took the medal, and at last met her mother's eye. 'Yes,' she said, 'it is something. Thank you.'